MEMENTO MORI
THE FATHOMLESS SHADOWS

Praise for Brian Hauser's *Memento Mori: The Fathomless Shadows*

"...an engrossing, baffling horror debut that veers hard into the weird [...]. Fans of the uncanny (and especially of Robert W. Chambers's *The King in Yellow*, to which this work alludes) will find much to love and laud."

—*Publishers Weekly*

"I want to tell you about Brian Hauser's *Memento Mori*. I want to tell you about the fanzine that reopened the door, and the memoir, and the lost films. I want to tell you about the medium being the message. How that message is transmitted, and how it can be trans-formed through translation into different—new media. How the message is corrupt and corrupting, infected and infectious. I want to tell you about Tina Mori, and C.C. Waite and the disappear-ance of Billie Jacobs. I want to tell you these things and how they all spiraled together into a coherent wave of madness. But I can't. Brian Hauser won't let me. It's not my place. I have seen—but you must see—must read—for yourself. Come and see. Say that you will. Please. Will you come?"

—Pete Rawlik, Editor of *The Chromatic Court*

"Brian Hauser's *Memento Mori* is a mysterious deep dive into the dark waters connecting underground film, music and weird fiction. A fascinating blend of found footage, lost writings, and incanta-tions, Memento Mori leaves its imprint on your psyche."

—John Palisano, Bram Stoker Award-Winning author of *Ghost Heart*, President of The Horror Writers Association

MEMENTO MORI
THE FATHOMLESS SHADOWS

BRIAN HAUSER

WORD HORDE
PETALUMA, CA

First Edition

ISBN: 978-1-939905-48-2

A Word Horde Book
www.wordhorde.com

*For Ken and John and Wes
and what they found in the North Country*

INTRODUCTION

Several years ago, I was deep into a research project on horror fan-zines when I came across a copy of issue #3 of Billie Jacobs's *Final Grrrl* in the garage archive of a private collector in New Paltz. It stuck out, to say the least. In a small zine sub-sub-culture dominated by male fans, *Final Grrrl* pulses with a fierce feminist punk excitement that radiates through its fan musings like veins of lightning. It was not unusual, as some might think, to find a female fan of horror films, but it was the first time I had found a horror zine entirely authored by a woman. I should say a young woman. Billie Jacobs was barely fourteen when she mailed out issue #3. She was a first-year high school student in Rochester, who was reveling in her love of horror movies by sharing that enthusiasm with a far-flung community of zine readers and creators. I wanted to read more of her work, but that was the only issue in the garage.

Even though the issue was almost twenty years old, I gambled that someone at Billie's old address would know how to get in touch with her. I often found that going to the source was the best way to track down back issues of zines. Even if authors didn't have any copies left, they could usually point you in the direction of people with good collections. But when I searched for Billie and the mailing address that she listed in the back of the zine, I soon discovered a sad story. Billie had gone missing in the spring of

1996, just a couple of years after she published issue #3. I read the few, brief articles about her disappearance, but since the authorities never found her, there was no follow-up. I set that avenue of research aside and kept an eye out for more issues in other collections and outlets. I was able to buy issues #1 and #4 from online outlets, but #2 and any others remained elusive. Zines often do not follow a regular publication schedule, so there was no telling if there was a #5 or a #6 or more.

What I did see from the issues I had was a young voice growing in confidence and intelligence as she matured and honed her expertise in horror films. Billie was no prodigy, but she was a bright young woman who found a passion for art and a refuge from the slings and arrows of adolescence in an imagined community of horror fans and Riot Grrrls. Knowing that she was gone, I felt a growing obligation to collect her work, preserve it, and possibly find a way to present it to a broader audience.

I found fewer and fewer leads on the remaining issues of *Final Grrrl*, and eventually I decided to contact the Jacobs family. I had never before had to make such a delicate approach in my research, and I hesitated for some time. However, the pressure to publish will motivate the most timid among us. Billie's parents split a few years after her disappearance, but her mother kept the Sears craftsman bungalow the family shared. Like many devastated parents before her and since, she has been unable to touch Billie's room beyond occasionally dusting it. Over the course of several months, she and I progressed from telephone conversations to an invitation to the house. I shared the copies of *Final Grrrl* with her that I had collected, and I learned more about what Billie's parents thought of her obsession with horror films. Though both her father and mother prohibited going to rock shows and parties where there might be adults and drugs and drinking, as long-time Kodak employees they were more sanguine about movies, especially when it came to Billie watching VHS tapes at home. They did not actively encourage her hobby, but they did not discourage it either, and her part-time job at her uncle's copy shop seemed to provide her with the spending money she needed for it.

On my second visit to the Jacobs home, her mother offered to let me look through Billie's room. In her closet, behind a battered pair of combat boots, I found what I was looking for: a white cardboard file box. I lifted the lid and saw an unruly stack of zines. I hauled the box out, registering as I did that one of the floorboards it sat on was loose before I set the box on the floor in the middle of the room. I imagined that this was where Billie spread out her zine-making supplies many nights as she drew, cut, and pasted her pages. In the box, I found a small treasure trove of horror and Riot Grrrl zines, some of which I had seen (*Chainsaw, Girl Germs, Bikini Kill*), while others were new to me. I found an issue #2 of *Final Grrrl* to round out what I had, and I also found two or three (it was difficult to tell at first) master pages from issue #5, but there was not a complete issue in the box. I laid the materials out on the floor and took photos of every page as quickly as I could with my phone. I did not want to overstay my welcome, and the guilt from my selfishness was beginning to loom over me. I packed the box back up as neatly as I could and returned it to the closet. As I did, I recalled that the floorboard had been loose, and I froze. I could not ignore the hunch I had that this was Billie's hiding place. I had to gingerly work the plank back and forth before I figured out how it came away, but I was rewarded with a thick manila envelope hidden between the floor joists.

Inside the envelope was a complete issue #5, a dog-eared copy of C.C. Waite's *Memento Mori*, and a letter written on a stack of yellowing motel stationery, all bound with a disintegrating rubber band that crumbled at the first touch. The envelope itself was addressed to Billie at her home address with a return address from Dr.

C.C. Waite in Columbus, OH. The postmark was March 1996, the same month that Billie disappeared.

This discovery was something else entirely. Though my mind was reeling in a dozen directions, one of the most obvious was a certainty the police had never seen this envelope or its contents. By the time I opened it and looked through the contents well enough to get a sense of them and realize they were very likely evidence, my fingerprints were already all over the documents. After an initial surge of panic, I calmed down enough to think about what I ought to do. I decided the only thing to do would be to tell Ms. Jacobs and to urge her to share this material with the police. I knew that I held the pieces of a mystery in my hands, but for a moment I was also clear on who I was. I was a horror film scholar in the house of a grieving mother, and I was already taking advantage of her. First, though, I laid out issue #5 and photographed it and then did the same for the typewritten letter. The book was too long, but I was confident that a photo of the publisher's information page would lead me to another copy.

Ms. Jacobs did turn the documents over to the local police, who re-opened their investigation into Billie's disappearance. The fact that Waite had been in contact with Billie from Ohio, and so close to her disappearance, prompted the local PD to transfer the case to the FBI. Despite her renewed faith in answers, Ms. Jacobs was destined to be disappointed. After a year of hearing nothing, the FBI agent in charge of the case informed Ms. Jacobs that the new leads resulted in no clearer information about what happened to Billie, though they had a new theory. It turned out that C.C. Waite had disappeared at roughly the same time. She had taken a medical leave from her teaching job at a small liberal arts college in central Ohio in the winter of 1996, and after she failed to show up for a number of social engagements with friends and colleagues, a welfare visit revealed that her house was empty. Given this information, and the content of some of the materials in the envelope, the FBI thinks it is plausible that C.C. Waite and possibly Tina Mori lured Billie Jacobs away from home. New information led investigators to contact Interpol but to no avail. Waite, Mori, and Jacobs all remain missing to this day.

Ms. Jacobs approached me about publishing these materials, since I let her know that I took images of them for my research. Having read through them at greater length, I was reluctant, even though the original publisher of *Memento Mori* was all too eager to see a new printing of Waite's memoir. At first, I thought I was still feeling guilty about reopening these wounds of hers, but later I had to face the fact that there is something else in these documents that both fascinates and repels me. There is a nameless fear pressed into these pages, something that threatens to unleash itself with each reading. But like seeing a caged predator, there is something that draws you to the bars to look in awe. It is only my faith that the bars are solid that allows me to invite you to stand by my side while we both look upon the madness within. That madness is in my dreams now, where I cannot look away.

B.R.H.

Paris, 2018

FINAL GRRRL #5
By Billie Jacobs

Probably none of you were wondering when you would get to see another issue of *Final Grrrl*. Here you go anyway! I know you've barely recovered from issue #4, but I had enough stuff ready to go. So, hang on to your butts.

I told you before about why I wanted to start a zine and why I chose to do *Final Grrrl*: 'cause I love ALL THINGS HORROR. But I don't think I've told you what got me into horror in the first place. Maybe you don't care, but shut up, 'cause it's STORY TIME!

When I was really little, I had this tiny rocking chair. It was blue with rose-mulling flowers painted on it. It was in our living room, and I sat in it whenever my parents were watching TV. I didn't like feeling so small when I sat on the regular furniture. Instead, I sat in my chair when mom was watching *Chicago Hope* or whatever.

One night, my parents were done watching TV and told me it was time for bed, but I didn't want to go to sleep yet. I wanted to stay up watching TV. They turned off the TV and the lights and said that I could stay down there in the dark if I really wanted to. They said goodnight and went upstairs. I know now what they were trying to do, but that night I felt abandoned.

I remember feeling my face burn up and the tears start to come. That made me angry. I didn't like feeling that way. I wanted to watch more TV. I got out of my chair and went over to the coffee table and wrapped my hands around our banged up remote.

When you turned our TV off, it reset the channel, so I needed to try to find something good to watch. I had no idea what was on which channel, but I'd seen my dad channel surf enough to think that was a good way to find something.

I got the TV on and kept pointing the remote at it with both hands as I pushed the channel button and tried to think seriously about whether I wanted to watch each channel. I was getting really bored with this when I found something weird.

A dark-haired lady with black clothes was sitting at a table with a man with crazy hair. She looked like some kind of goth-punk assassin. He looked like Neil Gaiman's Sandman. Actually, she could have been Death, but she looked more Asian. This was in 1985, though, before *The Sandman*.

I couldn't follow what they were talking about. I'm not sure I cared. I felt very grown up for watching TV on my own. But I wanted to be able to tell my parents about what I saw after they went to bed. I watched some more and tried to figure out what was going on. They were talking about movies, but not any movie I had ever seen. The lady was calm. The man was angry, the way my mom was sometimes angry when talking about other moms in our neighborhood.

Crazy Hair Man was getting angrier, waving his hands around and talking into the camera when the woman's right arm suddenly shot out in a smooth arc toward the man. It almost looked like she brushed something off his shoulder. She didn't say anything.

Blood sprayed across the table. One, two, three spurts. The man fell back away from the lady and then slumped forward. His fingers grabbed at the table, but slipped and streaked the blood.

The image on the TV flickered as the lady stood up. Color bars flashed across the screen for a moment, along with that ugly tone. I was worried this might wake up my parents and make them angry, so I scooted across the living room toward the TV.

But when I got inches from the TV set, the tone stopped and the image switched to something completely different. A man (I think) in pale yellow robes, tattered but not dirty. A glittering gold symbol stitched into the forehead of the mask that hung down over his face. There was a strange sky behind him. I remember it as a negative image, because the stars were black and the sky gray. But now I don't know.

I don't remember screaming, but my mom says I was. I believe her. She and my dad came running down the stairs to see what was wrong. She says I screamed forever. My dad says it was half an hour. Nonstop. All I remember is the figure in yellow.

Well, I also remember how the blood made me feel. Hot and prickly and trembling. Every spurt was a secret.

I didn't understand anything that I saw, but all of it stuck somewhere in my head. When I ran into new things later on, some of them tickled this memory. I realized later that this was the first time I ever saw Tina Mori. That I had actually seen her. That I was one of the people who watched her kill Jeremiah Swayne on his own public access show. I read about this stunt when I was older. At the time, I was convinced it was real, but I wasn't old enough to understand.

From that night on, I was obsessed with the dark, the strange, the bloody. I looked forward to Halloween more than the other girls. I never wanted to go trick or treating as something pretty. I loved fairy tales, but only the old-fashioned ones without happy endings.

Later, after I became friends with Jen and Craig, I saw scary movies and read scary stories. Every shiver and shock carried me back to that first night in the dark, watching Tina Mori slit Jeremiah Swayne's throat with a celluloid straight razor.

Two years ago, when I first started working at the copy shop*,

Matty showed me a course packet he was running for a college class, and it had a section from the book *Men, Women, and Chainsaws* by Carol Clover. I got that book from the library and did my best to read it all the way through. I realized that there were people who took scary movies seriously.

I wasn't crazy! Or, well...you know. I've been a serious horror fan ever since!

*See *Final Grrrl* #1 for how working at the copy shop also led to me finding Riot Grrrl and real music and starting this zine!

THE BACK ROOM: This is where I talk to you about stuff we would never keep out in the front room for public view. This is the stuff you find when you go through the door in the back of the shop that says KEEP OUT!

My uncle, the one who owns the copy shop where I work, is a collector. He collects magazines and posters and playbills and other papers things. He calls them EPHEMERA. Okay. Whatever. Usually, he buys all these things on his own. Sometimes it's an estate sale or he just gets a tip that some hoarder died and he wants a chance to look through the poor dude's stuff. That's when he has me come with him. He could get someone bigger and stronger than me, but he knows I don't care about this stuff and won't try to move in on any of his deals, and I won't tell anybody, 'cause WHO CARES?! So, I'm his girl when it comes time to haul shit out of some dead guy's house.

So, at our big Thanksgiving meal, my uncle casually mentioned as he's putting on his coat that he needed me for an estate sale that weekend. He said he would pay me twice what he usually does if I don't say anything about it before or after. No argument from me! (You won't tell him, right?) I told my parents that Saturday that I was working an extra shift at the shop. I got into his Volvo station wagon, the one that wheezes and has headlights that look like they have glaucoma, and he drove us to a part of the city I've never been in before that has a lot of junkyards and warehouses and trailer parks. It's one of these trailer parks where we're going. We bounced and swayed down the dirt drive all the way to the back of the park where there was a faded and rusting blue trailer, the last one. The two concrete pads leading to it were empty, with brown weeds growing through cracks, making the blue trailer seem even more lonely. There were already two cars outside the trailer. That made my uncle curse a blue streak as we skidded to a stop in the dirt.

When we got inside the trailer, my head spun. The smell was horrible. The worst BO you can imagine. Worse than that even, 'cause you could also smell mold and mildew. I had to breathe through my mouth and NOT THINK ABOUT IT. I almost hurled right there in the kitchen. But at the same time, that trailer was full of the most amazing things, things I would like to use for *Final Grrrl!* My uncle was arguing with the two old guys who were already inside when we got there. I moved away from them and started looking through the stacks of newspapers and trashy novels and magazines from decades ago.

Pretty soon, my uncle is really having it out with this other guy. They're in some kind of bidding war. I've never seen my uncle like this. He's a quiet guy, usually. A nice guy. But he was furious and unstoppable. He came stomping out of one of the back rooms with a big tin can in his hands. It was one of those big red white and blue cans that potato chips used to come in before they came in bags. He shoved the can into my hands. It was obviously filled with something other than chips, because I almost dropped it. My uncle whirled around stomped back to the others, waving a wad of $20s at both guys. While they argued, I popped the lid and found a small collection of worn paperbacks stood on their ends and curled around each other so that I could only see the curved tops of their bindings. I grabbed one and pulled it out. The cover had been ripped off, but the brittle and stained title page said it was *The King in Yellow*.

The King in Yellow. I had only heard about this book. I read about it in C.C. Waite's memoir of Tina Mori, and I've heard older kids claiming they read it. No one can ever show you their copy. It's the play that made such a scandal in France a hundred years ago and then was translated into other languages and offended governments and churches and even people who usually do the offending, like punks. Banned everywhere. Passed from person to person. Found on dusty shelves and in packing boxes and now in potato chip tins. You can tell the people who have read the totally normal first act, the boring opening to a musty old play. They're the ones who brag. You can also tell the ones who kept reading, whose dreams are now filled with nights of black stars that hang above Carcosa, whose prayers include Cassilda and Camilla now. They are the people who serve the Pallid Mask and wait on the shores of Lake Hali. They watch the waves swell to more than just the pull of the twin moons. I guess you can tell us apart, too.

I grabbed at the other books. They were all copies of the forbidden play. It sounded like the argument was petering out, so I jammed the copy in my hand into my jacket and closed the lid on the tin. My uncle stormed out again and told me to come with him as he burst out the flimsy storm door. There was still arguing coming from the back of the trailer. I was out of that place before I could make out any more of it. My uncle sprayed rocks and dirt against the two other cars as he sped us out of the trailer park.

He didn't drive back to the shop. He headed farther into the industrial parks and warehouses in this part of the city. He turned into an open gate and drove more slowly. He picked his way through the debris that littered the area as he drove behind a huge warehouse. He parked the wagon, shoved another wad of $20s at me, and grabbed the tin out of my hands. I didn't say anything. I could feel *The King in Yellow* in my pocket, burning a hole there. I was confused and elated and ashamed and scared. I had a copy of *The King in Yellow*. Jen was gonna shit.

My uncle got out of the wagon and opened the back. I turned around to see what he was doing in time to see him unscrew the cap from a gas can. He held the cap in one hand and poured out the gasoline into the open tin of moldy paperbacks with the other. I could smell the fuel as it hit the books and filled up the potato chip tin. I got out of the car. By the time I reached the back of the wagon, he was tossing a match into the open tin. Something—not exactly something inside me—made me lunge for the doomed copies of that dreaded play. The WHOOMPH of the gasoline igniting, and the mushroom cloud, black and sharp, pushed me back, singeing my already black nails.

My uncle stared into the fire in that tin, stared as the potato chip company logo bubbled and melted and the can itself began to warp. I held my hand to my mouth and nose, trying to keep the smell out. His hands remained at his sides, opening and closing into fists over and over again. I think he was crying, but maybe it was just the gasoline fumes.

THE MASK REVIEW: I don't usually spend too much time watching Creature Feature movies on the weekend. They don't have what it takes for me anymore. But I was feeling kind of sick a couple weeks ago, and so I didn't go into the copy shop on the weekend. Instead, I caught this totally weird horror movie called *The Mask*. It's not the Jim Carrey thing. This one is black and white and maybe Canadian. It is about a cursed mask, but that's as far as the similarities go. In this one, putting the mask on doesn't give you superpowers, but it does make you see these nightmare visions. The story was pretty stupid and the acting was mostly horrible. I mean right off the bat it's a pervy killer in a raincoat stalking a screaming woman. Yawn. But those nightmare sequences were pretty wild. They were done in 3D and kind of in color, too, even though the colors were washed out. There were some cheesy effects, like the snake that comes out from between the fingers of this giant hand with flaming fingers. (Pay no attention to the masturbation symbolism!) Most of the nightmare images were kind of amazing, though. I wanted to watch them over and over again. I didn't think to tape it. (Maybe the guys at the video store can get it in for me. Or maybe *you* can. Hook me up!) The best part wasn't what the movie showed you through the mask. It was that the movie made you want to see the visions. It made you sympathize with the characters who were addicted to the powers of the mask. The visions were cool. That was cooler.

ONIBABA REVIEW: Just after Thanksgiving, Jen and I went to the Dryden Theater. Her parents give the theater money or something, so they get season tickets all the time. The employees know her. They don't say anything if the movies are maybe rated R. The Dryden was running a series called Japanese Masters. We went to a double feature on Saturday afternoon. They were showing *Rashomon* and *Onibaba*. Maybe I was full of turkey sandwiches or something, but I fell asleep during *Rashomon*. Really, I think it was because of the music. Those drums and strings put me right to sleep! I mean, the story was cool, though. It was about how everyone has their own story and you don't know what the truth is. They even used a medium to get the dead guy's story!

We were there to see *Onibaba*, but you have to come for both, I guess. Jen was getting lonely, so she woke me up before it started. I kinda felt bad. Jen invited me and Craig to the screening, mostly because she wanted Craig to come. She thought he would want to see a Japanese movie about demons. Craig doesn't like subtitles, so he didn't come with us. But I was game for anything called DEMON WOMEN, so I ignored the many hints she tried to give me. I was feeling kind of guilty for sleeping when Jen woke me up, but I was excited for *Onibaba*.

Holy shit! So much sex. I'm not sure Jen knew what we were in for when she brought us. Maybe she did, and that's why she wanted Craig to come along. Crazy kids. Whatever. I was having a great time. I mean, it starts right out with the two women, one young and one old, who kill some samurais, steal their weapons, and then throw their bodies into this deep dark hole in the middle of a grass field. So brutal. Here I was, watching this black and white Japanese film, and my horror sense was getting tickled like I was watching some Argento. Maybe better! It got boring for a little while after that, but then suddenly there was the sex and lots of it. At first I couldn't figure out where the younger woman was on the whole messing-around-with-the-neighbor question. Pretty soon it was obvious she was totally into it. Good for her.

But then her mom tries to ruin everything. The older woman has previously run into a weird samurai who wears a demon mask that he is unable to take it off.

Cut-out from Paperback:
Camilla: You, sir, should unmask.
Stranger: Indeed?
Cassilda: Indeed it's time. We have all laid aside disguise but you.
Stranger: I wear no mask.
Camilla: (Terrified, aside to Cassilda.) No mask? No mask!

She kills this guy like the other samurai and takes his stuff, mask included. In order to scare her daughter straight, the woman uses the mask to pose as the demon of the grass field. Now, the daughter runs into the demon every time she tries to run through the grass to get some nookie. She falls for this Scooby-Doo trick over and over. To be fair, it's pretty creepy. I don't think *Onibaba* is supposed to be a horror film. It's probably not like any horror film you've seen lately. If you get a chance, check it out and tell me what you think.

SCREAM REVIEW: One of the better presents I got during the holidays was *Scream*. I'll bet I'm not the only one here who was waiting for that one, right? I mean, we can probably all agree that most of the Freddy movies suck after the first one (except maybe *New Nightmare*) but I still like Wes Craven. If I can't have a *Final Grrrl* written and directed by a woman, then I will take Wes's leading ladies, I guess. I know a lot of people like his goofy sense of humor (I do laugh at some of the jokes), but it's a guy's sense of humor. It's Freddy's sense of humor, which is what makes it work. It's like adding insult to injury to face your death while this scarred asshole makes fun of you. "Welcome to prime time, bitch?" Really? Bad enough you're gonna die.

Well, *Scream* is kind of like a love letter to horror fans. Since I'm a horror fan, it was like the letter was just for me, you know? Did you feel that way? That's not to say that I liked everything about it. Are love letters ever perfect?

Well, I don't want to ruin anything for you if you haven't seen it yet, but if you haven't seen it yet, what is WRONG with you?! No, just kidding. There's nothing wrong with you! God, I'm horrible sometimes. Okay, movie! There's a lot about it that is rad, truly rad, and maybe some things that are really fucking annoying. Tons of good kills scenes. Death by garage door? I may not be afraid of the garage yet, but that one was pretty good. Lots of great inside jokes for horror movie fans. And I think Wes must be reading Carol Clover, because our *Final Grrrl* has a totally androgynous name: Sydney. She's maybe not completely alone, though, which is a twist, and a good one. Courtney Cox's Gale Weathers is also a pretty good character. She's not quite a double *Final Grrrl*, but she's close.

I think the best part of the whole thing is the ghost face mask the killer wears. Is it scary? Hell yeah, it's scary. I couldn't tell you why. I mean, maybe I'm on a mask kick lately. You can tell that ghost face belongs right there with Jason's hockey mask and Michael Myers's Shatner mask. I know it's commenting on those masks, right? Obviously. But it works on its own, too. It's good that it does, because the black robes that go along with it are pretty cheap.

What's your favorite mask? Do you think masks are scary? I want to say that I don't think all masks are scary, but I'm not sure that's true. Aren't they all creepy? When I was little, my parents put this African mask on the wall of my room. My grandma called it a Ubangi mask. I never liked it, but my mom and dad laughed at me when I mentioned it. I think my mom referred to it as a fertility mask. Later I had a different idea about what they must think "You-bang-y" means. Gross. It was still in my room, so I hid it away after that. I looked for it not long ago, but I couldn't find it, and I remember thinking at the time that the mask had gotten loose somehow. Like it was hiding somewhere in the house. I still have nightmares about that mask sometimes. I will dream that there is a face on the wall. Not a mask, but a face. It watches me. It smiles. No, it *leers*. Yeah, it leers like an old man, or like Mr. Delyle, our bio teacher (who's not *old* old, but is totally creepy).

So you should see *Scream*! Oh, and one more weird thing about it. Some of the same people in *The Craft* are in *Scream*. Neve Campbell and Skeet Ulrich. It's like I want to smoosh together these two films. I think *The Craft* is about stuff I care about more (revolution Grrrl style now!), but *Scream* is smarter but it's not about stuff that matters to me as much. I'm not complaining. Most movies are the bad combination: they're about stuff I don't care about, and they're stupid. But maybe someday we can have another movie that does both? Maybe Tina Mori is still out there. Maybe she'll make another film.

MORI SCREENING REPORT: Okay, so you're never going to believe this. I wasn't sure I should write about it, but he said I could *IF I WAS CAREFUL*. No shit! That's got to mean he wants me to write about it, right? I've got to calm down and get it straight in my head. It's weird, though. It keeps shifting around in there, like it's hiding in the corners of my BRAAAIIIINNNN!

I got a note at work a couple weeks ago. "I can show you a genuine Tina Mori reel." A phone number. No name. I was creeped out, because who wouldn't be creeped out? This was the Billie Jacobs stalker equivalent of driving up to me in a van and asking if I wanted some candy. But goddam, a genuine Tina Mori reel. Whoever this was knew my candy.

I called the number. I had to let it ring for a long time. Long enough that I had to decide two separate times that I was going to stay on the line until someone answered. Eventually he did. Soft, wheezy voice. I tried to be smart. I kept my head enough to refuse to come to his place. I demanded some place more neutral. I didn't have any suggestions of my own. I didn't think I could get him into the copy shop after hours. He offered another place. The community room of St. Genesius's downtown. He could reserve it. I don't know if it was the fact that it was a church or what, but it did make me feel better. We set a time and date. I was supposed to come alone. I didn't like that, but I did it anyway. A genuine Tina Mori reel! Come on. You're reading this now, aren't you? Everything basically turned out okay.

I was nervous for the couple days leading up to the meeting, so when the evening came, I showed up early and hung out down the street. I guess I thought I was casing the joint, but I didn't see anything. What are cops looking for when they do that? No one came in or out, and there was only a dim light showing through the stained glass windows. It looked like a big medieval church, even though nothing in this town is that old. It was creepy enough that I was kicking myself for not going with something safer or for not bringing someone to wait for me. I was too excited or too scared.

I didn't want to be late. I found the glass doors to the community center around the back of the building. The community room was obviously a recent addition to the church, and the unlocked door made me feel calm. It felt like going into school for a musical performance or something. Inside, there was some security lighting, but the entryway was mostly dark. There was a small office with a ticket window off to the side with posters for community theater plays. A flash of movement caught my eye, and that's when I saw him.

I didn't know what to expect, but it definitely was not him. I've never seen any pictures, but my first thought was that this guy looked like Dr. Holly from C.C.'s memoir. He was tall, covered in a dark and tattered cloak with odd multi-colored patches, and wore a porcelain mask. The movement was his hand gesturing toward a set of double doors. I asked him who he was. In that wheezy voice he said he was sorry but that he wanted to stay anonymous. This was where I finally thought to ask, why me? He said that he often used my uncle's copy shop and that he was aware of my zine and my interest in Tina Mori. He was impressed with my work and wanted me to carry on, whatever that means. It didn't sound right to me, I guess, but I wasn't about to bail. I moved past him and through the doors.

I was right. It was a theater. It was pretty small, and it had the musty smell of old carpet and cleaning fluid and community theater nerves. Our high school auditorium is bigger, but this place was still pretty cool. There were plaster statues and murals on the walls that had a lot of masked people showing the lives and deaths of martyrs. A cart in front of the stage had a projector pointed at a portable screen set up on the stage. I chose a seat in the front row near the projector. The screen wasn't all that big, and I wanted to see as much detail as I could.

The guy followed me down the aisle, keeping his distance. He knew I was worried. He went straight for the cart and pulled a single reel film can out from under his cloak. It was a metallic blue can. He opened it and quickly and expertly mounted the reel on the front arm of the projector and threaded the film through the pulleys and gate. He secured the leader to the take-up reel and then asked if I was ready. I nodded. It felt like I couldn't stop nodding.

He flipped on the projector.

Leader text and a red processing mark flowed down the screen, and then there was a Christmas tree in full color filling the frame. Tinsel hung from the branches. A few balls with glitter. No sound except for the projector and my heartbeat. Cut to a wider shot of the room, tree off center, and a blonde girl in a night gown sitting on the floor among presents. Oh my god! I realized this was C.C. My doubts suddenly disappeared. I couldn't ever remember reading about a holiday short, but that was C.C., no question. She picked up boxes, hefted them for weight. Another cut brought us into close-up as C.C. shook a gift and listened to what was inside. A look of frustration as she put it back. Her eyes fixed on another present; she paused. A quick insert of a Jack in the Box. It was a tin box with a metal handle, but it looked hand painted and weird. There was a clown, but there were also snakes and galaxies and tombstones and the ruins of lost cities. C.C.'s hands entered the frame, picked it up. Back to a medium shot of C.C. with the box. She turned it over, inspected it. She turned to the camera, said something. A reverse shot of two costumes laid out flat with cardboard masks. Mom and Dad in robes, as though they were sitting on the couch. Mom had curlers. Dad had a pipe. Creepy grins. Back to C.C. whose smile was beaming. She turned her attention to the box and began grinding the crank. I was convinced as she did this on screen that I could hear the plinking of "Pop Goes the Weasel," but that's impossible. It stretched and ground on, off-key and out of time, as the camera cut quicker and quicker between closer and closer shots of C.C., the box, the parents. C.C., the box, the parents. C.C.'s face went from eager to frustrated to exhausted to filled with dread. Did the cardboard faces change, or did they only seem to? Grind, grind, grind. Cut, cut, cut. The box never pops.

It wasn't until I heard his wheezy voice asking what I thought that it sunk in the reel was done. He flicked the switch on the lamp like a punctuation mark to his question. I said it was great and asked to see it again. He said no, reversed the film, and said he would show me out. I didn't get ahold of myself again until the cool night breeze hit me. I looked back as he closed and locked the door behind me. He turned away. We never said anything else.

I've tried the phone number again, but it's disconnected.

Well, there you have it. I'd love to be able to tell you more or offer you a frame enlargement or something, but we're all going to have to get used to disappointment.

Cut-out from Paperback:
Along the shore the cloud waves break,
The twin suns sink beneath the lake,
The shadows lengthen
       In Carcosa.

Strange is the night where black stars rise,
And strange moons circle through the skies

But stranger still is
    Lost Carcosa.

Songs that the Hyades shall sing,
Where flap the tatters of the King,
Must die unheard in
    Dim Carcosa.

Song of my soul, my voice is dead;
Die thou, unsung, as tears unshed
Shall dry and die in
    Lost Carcosa.

[Handwritten note: "Cassilda's Song" in *The King in Yellow*, Act I, Scene 2]

LETHAL CHAMBER LYRICS: Last month, my history teacher Mr. Jarvis gave me a failing grade on the big end-term-report. I did this huge and totally awesome paper on Tina Mori, but he said it wasn't important enough, even though Jake half-assed his report on the Red Hook massacre and still got an A. I was going to share my report with all of you, because I think you'd like it, but it's too long to put in one issue. So, I think what I'm going to do is put in pieces. I'll start with some Lethal Chamber songs. If you don't know them, Lethal Chamber was a punk band in the late 1970s. Tina showed her first longer film *Imperial Dynasty of America* at one of their gigs in New York in 1979. Their stuff is harder to find now, but it's so cool. I've copied out the lyrics for a couple songs here. Enjoy!

"Past the Fates" - 1978 – 45rpm

In the city that never sleeps,
On the shady south side of the Square,
If it's oblivion you seek,
You'll find the answers over there.

You'll find the marble portico
Just three steps up to the bronze door
But first you pass the weird sisters
The Fates gathered forever more.

Step into my lethal chamber.
Welcome to my lethal chamber.
Leave behind your fear of danger.
Welcome to my lethal chamber.

Step into my lethal chamber.
Welcome to my lethal chamber.
Leave behind your fear of danger.
Welcome to my lethal chamber.

Final curtain has fallen
Out of money, out of friends.
Most never see it coming.
So this is how it all ends.

The whispers say that it's quick,
That you won't feel any pain
But that just seems like bullshit
It's been pain since I was five.

I've seen the Yellow Sign,
But I'll miss the king,
Reputation beyond repair.

Step into my lethal chamber.
Welcome to my lethal chamber.
Leave behind your fear of danger.
Welcome to my lethal chamber.

Step into my lethal chamber.
Welcome to my lethal chamber.
Leave behind your fear of danger.
Welcome to my lethal chamber.

"Washington Scare" - 1977 - EP

How was the play Mrs. Lincoln?
Have you seen *The King in Yellow*?
It's like a splinter in the mind.
I bet that Boothe's a fine fellow.

Some say they bowed before the King.
None of us saw the pallid mask.
Was it the stranger in tatters?
None of us remembered to ask.

No requests for Cassilda's Song
While we're rockin' on
Washington Scare

No requests for Cassilda's Song

While we're rockin' on
Washington Scare

Do you know the Yellow Sign,
A script of no human tongue?
Can you read it with your eyes,
Or only when bells have rung?

On the shores when black stars rise
We'll drink to lost Carcosa
With our souls full in our mouths
We'll sing to old Carcosa

We're not there yet, on dim shores
Of Lake Hali.
So don't bring it up, for fuck's sake.

No requests for Cassilda's Song
While we're rockin' on
Washington Scare

No requests for Cassilda's Song
While we're rockin' on
Washington Scare

NIGHTMARE JOURNAL: I am five again. I wake up in bed. I see the face on the wall across the room. It is dark brown, and even at night I can still see the white lines gouged into the cheeks and forehead. The teeth are sharpened to points. The mask wants to bite chunks of flesh out of my tummy and my thighs.

The thought of the bites tearing parts off my stomach and legs makes me burn, and when I look at the mask again it is the ghost face mask from *Scream*. It is still on the wall, but it is also not. When I look at the pale and warped face with dark mouth and eye holes, the mask shakes its head from side to side slowly. It won't talk to me. I can tell that Craig is wearing the mask. His face is behind it, but maybe the ghost face mask is the real face behind Craig's mask. I want to make out with Craig, but I know the rules, and he will kill me if we do. He will jam his knife way below my ribs and twist it around. He will laugh.

I look over and I see Jen on the day bed where she sometimes spends the night. Her pajama top is unbuttoned and she has been slit open with an "I" incision, the two huge flaps of skin pulled back and pinned open like one of the worms in Mr. Delyle's class. It makes me think of Myrtle in *The Great Gatsby*, with her breast torn away. There is blood everywhere. I can smell Jen's death. My head swims.

The mask is still shaking from side to side, but it's a different mask. It's pale, but it's not the ghost face any more. This one is like a shroud, a curtain. There is a strange symbol embroidered into the material on the forehead. The mask swishes left and right. I think it might be yellow, but it's too dark to tell.

The mask is coming toward me across the room. At first, I think it must be someone in a black robe and yellow mask, but I don't think there's a body. There's only a mask. Jen's blood-spattered face moves with the mask. Her eyes are wide with terror. She is afraid for me. For her. It comes closer.

At last, I wear the mask. The walls of my room are gone. I can hear the cloud waves break in my ears. Jen reclines on her throne, and below her crimson chin, beyond the Hyades, I plunge into the cool waters of Lake Hali, in search of her song.

MEMENTO MORI

By C.C. Waite

CHAPTER ONE

I have been meaning to write this book for years. I have answered thousands of questions about Tina Mori and told hundreds of stories about our time together when people asked about it. I used to be a lot more enthusiastic. I told stories rich in detail and love. I still feel that love for Tina and maybe even a certain kind of nostalgia for our time together, but more and more often I found myself resenting the burden of telling the story again and again. I wanted to outsource it, and so I decided to write it all down. That was years ago.

You have probably come to this book because you are interested in knowing more about Tina Mori. But I think about my own history with books and I can't help but think that you might have found this book because of other motivations or circumstances. Maybe you have heard of me through your interest in ethnobotany, or maybe you know me through some other means either professional or personal. Maybe you found this book in a library or a bookstore and something about it caught your eye. Maybe it was on a friend's bookshelf, or it was recommended to you. In any of these cases, you likely don't know who Tina Mori is. You may not be aware that Tina directed some of the most frightening movies ever made. She is not widely famous. In fact, outside of the underground film world, it's probably correct to call her completely unknown. But her films have left an indelible impression on all those who have seen them and even on some who haven't. Tina has become a legend. I don't resent that legend. I don't have any desire to tear it down. But I know that many people want to know about her and about her films, and I am maybe the best person to tell that story.

I met Tina Mori during the most intense high of my life. I had just placed a tab with a pink stamp of the comedy and tragedy masks on my tongue. A friend of mine had been trying to get me to try it for a week and I finally relented. I knew well enough that I shouldn't have tried it alone my first time, especially a drug I hadn't used before, but I don't always trip well around other people. Even if it was a bad trip, I figured nothing too dangerous would happen in my dorm room. I was sitting on my bed, Pink Floyd on the record player, when Tina opened the door. At that same moment, my view of the room cracked into long, iridescent shards that began to spin like a kaleidoscope. Tina was less interested in me and more interested in something that she saw on or through the cinder block wall above my head. She peered beyond that wall and fixed her gaze on something distant, her nostrils flaring. I thought I caught the slightest nod from her at whatever it was that she was seeing, and then she finally looked at me, right into me. It felt like a secret had been revealed to me in a language I had never heard before.

Tina quietly swung her bag off her shoulder, set it down on the floor next to the door, and slipped out of the room, shutting the door behind her. For whatever reason, she must have thought that I wanted or needed to be alone. SUNY Red Stone had forgotten that I was in a double room, and I had spent the first week of classes alone, though only on paper. With the place all to myself, I got to work. I had experiments to run. The college thought that I was a double major in anthropology and botany. My adviser took great pleasure in saying that he was training an ethnobotanist for the first time in his career. That was all fine, but I only had a passing interest in their view of science. I was there to experience things. I was at a stage where I thought of my body as an instrument for the experience of life, and I was dedicated to having as many intense experiences as I could. I found all sorts of different ways to have new and more intense reactions to the world, and a lot of those ways had to do with various kinds of drugs.

Tina returned to the room a few hours later. She didn't knock this second time, either; she quietly and matter-of-factly opened the door and walked in like she had been living there for a week already. I felt like I had marked the room, and so I wanted to give Tina a chance to get as comfortable as possible after our strangely intense introduction. I found my towel and robe and said that I was going to take a shower and that we could talk when I got back. Tina only nodded with a small smile as I slipped out. I had been vaguely worried that the college was going to give me a roommate at some point and that it was going to wind up being some uptight girl from the middle of nowhere who could seriously cramp my style. I had a very pleasant feeling that Tina was not going to be like that at all. I wasn't attracted to her yet, not at that point. At least, I didn't have that familiar reaction when I looked at her. It was more like I felt that there was the promise of sharing secrets, things that nobody else knew.

When I got back to the room, Tina already had her clothes put away and her bed made. She had very few knick-knacks to put up on the wall or on the desk on her side of the room. But she did have a curious tin with unusual designs painted on the sides. She opened it up as I closed the door and asked if I wanted some tea. She was gesturing toward my hot plate with a kind of inquisitive arch of her eyebrow. My smile launched us into a freewheeling conversation that took us through the boiling and steeping and drinking until we knew the essentials about each other. She knew that I was a priest's kid from everywhere, because my parents were constantly going on missions around the world, bringing God and music to tiny villages whose inhabitants displayed little interest in the one and mostly polite tolerance of the other. I learned that she was an indifferent pianist who wound up at Red Stone's conservatory because she didn't quite have the talent for Juilliard or Berklee, and her family in any event didn't have the money for Ithaca. She was at college on a scholarship, but she almost never talked to me about piano. It was like the bus that brought her to northern New York; I knew she had been on it, but it wasn't worthy of note. I remember wondering later how someone like her could spend so much time and energy on something she didn't care about. It was a while before I understood. Right then, we were two people who didn't know each other very well.

"Do you have any more of that?" she asked me. She appeared to stare into my forehead in a way that made it clear she was asking about the psychedelics.

"That was my only tab. I can get more."

Tina smiled and gave her head a little shake. At first, I was embarrassed; I felt like I should have known she wouldn't really want to try it, even though she had asked. Or maybe it was that the moment had passed. If I had another tab on me, would she have taken it? Would things have been any different?

"What's it like here?" I thought for a minute before answering her, wondering what she wanted to know about the most. I shrugged.

"Small town. A lot of the people I meet want to be teachers, so go figure." Tina sipped her tea and nodded, looking at my wall hangings and carvings. She stared longer than anything else at the carved ceremonial mask I had hung above my desk.

I was watching her, too. I have always thought that Tina was beautiful, but sometimes I have been reluctant to focus on her looks. So many people focus on her looks for all the wrong reasons. I guess like a lot of people, when I first saw Tina, I saw her as Asian, as Japanese. But that was only the first instant, taking in her face and hair and eyes and attempting to categorize her before I consciously knew what I was doing. Before I could ask *why* I was doing it. In the second instant, I saw more clearly. I saw the way that she didn't meet the expectations of the first instant. She looked Japanese but wasn't, at least probably. I had been all over the world with my parents, and I was a good enough biologist (though a novice and leaning toward botany) to understand the basics of phenotypes. I could often tell the difference between a person of Japanese and one of Chinese or Korean descent without any additional information, like names. My first guess, which turned out to be accurate so far as it went, was that she was partially Japanese; one parent was Japanese and one was, what? English? Scandinavian? That was always harder for me.

"What do you want, C.C.?"

"I want to make sure I don't miss out."

"Miss out on what?" I thought about that. The answer was so vast, that I couldn't wrap my arms around it. I think I just shook my head and smiled.

"Me too," she said. I didn't know whether she meant it the way that I meant it, but it did feel like we shared some understanding.

We settled into the semester's routine fairly quickly, and we didn't talk very much for a couple of weeks, because Tina had already arrived a week later than everyone else. She had a lot of catching up to do in her classes, and it took a while for some of her professors to calm down and not see her as the troublemaker they originally thought she would turn out to be. It's not that they were far wrong in their assessment; it's that they had no real idea the kind of trouble she could get up to when she put her mind to it.

I didn't try too hard to corrupt her at first. There was plenty of pot and beer and liquor around and more than enough parties to give us ample access to them for not a lot of money. I found out quickly that Tina stayed away from pot unless by smoking she could gain access to a place or a group of people that interested her. She was by no means straitlaced, so I asked her what her aversion to marijuana was, and she said it simply didn't work for her. She smoked and all that happened was that she got a distracting buzzing behind her eyes. She said it felt like her eyeballs wanted to get out of her head, and since she liked them where they were, she didn't feel the need to encourage their wanderlust.

That woman could drink, though. She said she liked wine, but she probably preferred better wine that we had access to, because she rarely went for the great glass jugs that made the rounds at the orchestra parties or at the writers' pads. She knew how to shotgun a beer, and she could throw back the hard stuff like she was drinking orange juice. When she did this, her eyes got bright and her smile became generous, and she developed a disturbing tendency to laugh at the wrong moment. An earnest sophomore might be delivering the setup for a joke or a story, and Tina let slip a giggle that soon sent her falling over on her side in hysterics. At first, I thought that she had heard the joke before, and knew how it was going to end, but no. She insisted that she knew none of the jokes she heard. But there was nothing funny about the setups, so I started to wonder if she was coming up with her own punchlines; was it possible that she was projecting ahead and seeing a path to a different joke entirely and finding there something grim and sardonic to laugh at in her disquieting way?

I did get some sense that Tina had her own methods of finding a good time. A couple of times she stumbled into our room very late at night, or early in the morning. She didn't smell of anything in particular, not pot or beer or even cigarettes, but she was on something. She was ecstatic and eager and utterly present all at the same time. It was tremendously attractive, but I don't mean that she was attractive in these moments. I didn't want her when she was like this; I wanted what she *had*. I was curious about it, but she was never able or willing to articulate what it was she had been doing, or where I might be able to find it. Until one night.

I was fast asleep one night in October, dreaming about crawling vines of the strangest purple color, when Tina burst into the room and jumped on my bed. She loomed over me, one foot on either side of my hips, and then she bent down at the waist and mussed my hair as a method waking me up.

"C.C., get up!"

"Why?"

"I'm taking you out."

"Out?"

"Dinner and a movie."

"Are you nuts? It's almost three in the morning."

"No time, C.C. No time! We need to go, and you need to come with me." She seemed to lean in even closer so that the breath from her lip tickled my ear. "You want to come, don't you?"

To this day, I don't know if it was me and what I probably already desired from Tina, or if she knew what she was doing, but I was suddenly filled with desire for her and for whatever it was that she wanted. At the time, I thought that this might be my chance to see where she sometimes went late at night and came back so curiously charged. I was out of bed and throwing on clothes and brushing my hair while she clapped and jumped from bed to bed.

She took my hand and led me into the night before I was ready, forcing me to toss my brush back into the room and slam the door on our way out. A couple people opened their doors and peeked out bleary-eyed and angry at our noisemaking, but Tina didn't care, and honestly I was already excited for wherever it was she was taking me. Outside our dorm, an older man in suit and tie sat in an idling bronze sedan. He wore a tweedy hat and sunglasses, even though it was the middle of the night. He turned his head slowly as we skipped out the side door of the building and headed for the car. Tina swung the door open and ushered me into the middle of the front bench seat, nearly pushing me up against this total stranger.

"C.C., this is Horace. Horace, C.C."

The man said nothing. Tina closed the door, and we took off into the darkness.

SUNY Red Stone is situated north of the Adirondack Park in a rural stretch of land between those mountains and the St. Lawrence River. There are only small villages and towns and vast stretches of farmland and wilderness along the Canadian frontier. In no time, we had left the asphalt boundaries of the college parking lots and entered into the dirt and gravel by-ways of the surrounding farmland. I remember stars and a cool wind and the oddly meaty stench of the driver's cigarillos. I couldn't place the tobacco. I wanted to ask him about them, since they piqued my interest as a botanist, but I couldn't work up the courage. There was something forbidding about him. Tina hummed in the seat next to me as she watched out the window.

We drove a few miles out of town and eventually pulled into a sprawling homestead with one of the old farmhouses built from fitted blocks of red sandstone that gave the area and its reputation and the college its name. A wooden plank fixed above the front door was carved with the legend FROSTWOOD. Behind the house was an enormous barn. Enough light was present to reveal that, though it might once have been painted, the barn was now silvered gray like all weathered wood. The great sliding door was open, and I could make out a small crowd within and could hear a strange pulsing music coming through a PA system. Tina squeezed my hand and was out the door before I could even ask her what this was all about. I wasn't at all sure that I wanted to be at a strange barn party in the middle of the night, but I was relatively sure that I didn't want to be there on my own. I was out of the car and after her without even looking back at the driver and his weird cigarillos.

"What's up with Horace," I said as I got closer to her. I could hear the driver's door close behind us as we approached the barn door.

"He's a guy I ran into back in the city. He told me about this."

"Where?"

"Riley Hall. I was practicing."

"This guy happened to run into you in one of the piano practice rooms in Riley Hall?" Tina stopped at the barn door and turned to look me square in the face. Lots of alarms were going off in my head, alarms I often don't listen to, but something was telling me to listen this time.

"I'm here on a piano scholarship. He knew where I'd be. It's not that mysterious. He was up here for the party, he knew I went to school here, and thought that I'd be interested. He's being nice." That last was said with a kind of finality punctuated by the man brushing past us and disappearing into the throng of people inside.

"Just be cool, C.C. We're going to have a good time. Lots of people here from New York, some from Montreal. There are even some from Akwesasne."

Tina offered that last bit as an enticement. She knew that one of things that I had been most interested in lately was the nearby Akwesasne reservation. The prospect of getting to talk with some tribal members was exciting. At the time I took this as an indication that Tina was being thoughtful and that she didn't want me there for her own reasons; later I realized that was probably not the case at all. This was an extra detail she used to sweeten the deal.

I smiled, though, and followed her inside the barn. I had attended barn parties before, at least a couple, and there are some things that never change. There are always people trying to use a large central space for dancing, there are always people trying to sneak into lofts for some not-too-secret screwing, and there are always too many shadows. All of that was true of this night and more. This party was a little classier than some. It was like whoever was throwing it was interested in transforming the barn into some kind of beatnik scene. It was barn-cum-coffee house at this point. There was a long folding table at one end of the space where a woman in her twenties with white spiky hair and a cigarette dangling spun records on a turntable connected to the amplified speakers we heard when we arrived. She slipped another disc out of its cover, and I could see that it had no label on either side, just shiny black vinyl. Though there were people who lingered in the middle of the barn's open space swaying in a sort of numb imitation of dance, most of that space was given over to tables made of doors laid across saw horses and surrounded by folding chairs. And at the end of the barn opposite the turntable was a large white sheet or canvas that had been stretched tight between the timber framing of the barn to form a movie screen. That's when I looked up and back to see that the only shenanigans visible in the loft at the moment were the two young men who were setting up a 16mm movie projector next to what looked like a smaller 8mm projector. They had a small collection of cases for reels, and they were making very precise adjustments to the projectors, making sure that they were angled perfectly.

That was a new one on me. I had never been to a barn party that also included a movie, and for some reason this actually calmed me down immensely. As the tension slipped from my shoulders, I realized that I was thirsty. Almost every table had two bottles, one clear and one brown, along with a collection of short glasses. I didn't see any beer cans or bottles or any of the usual jugs of wine that you see at college parties. This was a different kind of do. The barn was also filled with a miasma of different smokes, from white to gray to blue, that at least at this early hour didn't strangle the senses. I was, very suddenly and somewhat confusingly, excited to try all of it.

I surveyed the floor again and found Tina sitting at one of the far tables, talking to an older woman in a blue-gray turtleneck sweater. She was wearing sunglasses and had fabulous hair from the previous decade, sort of a Jackie Kennedy thing. The man who had driven us there was sitting at the same table. I couldn't tell if he had any interest in the conversation at all, but Tina and the woman were debating something if not quite arguing. I started to move toward them, planning to use Tina as my in before I branched out with all of the strangers, but I had only made it a few steps when she glanced in my direction and warned me off with the tiniest shake of her head. I stopped in my tracks and turned my attention to the table in front of me as the older woman turned her head in my direction.

The table I was next to also had a man and a woman at it, sitting almost across from one another. The man, obviously tall though he was seated, had both his long dark hands wrapped around a glass of the clear liquor (I assumed it was liquor). The woman had a glass in front of her that only had some dregs of the brown liquor at the bottom of it, she was holding a cigarette to her lips and staring at the flame of her lighter that she held several inches too far from the end of the cigarette. She remained like that, fascinated.

"There won't be any invitation," said the man without looking directly at me, though I noted that he wasn't looking at his companion either. I smiled and nodded as I sat down and reached for one of the empty glasses in the middle of the table.

"Which do you like better?" I had nothing to go off of. I wasn't a liquor drinker in particular, but that was what was on offer, and I didn't want to appear impolite.

The woman's lighter flicked off and she turned to me with infinite slowness. She was a mannequin come to life, or some carnival automaton that had a coin settle into its gut. She said nothing.

My first reaction was to groan and call them on their beatnik bullshit, but there was something about both of them that made it impossible. If they were pretentious artists, then they had somehow wrapped me in their canvas. I could still tell that something was not quite right, but I didn't have the power to do much about it.

I looked at the two bottles again and decided to go for the clear liquor in the clear bottle, thinking that at least there were no visible impurities. I put about a finger of crystal fluid into my glass, re-placed that the bottle, and sniffed it. A vapor rose from the tumbler that brought one word to mind: octane.

I looked up from the glass to see not only my table companions staring at me but also Jackie Kennedy and Tina. Tina's eyes were apprehensive. I couldn't see Jackie's eyes, of course, but her tongue dashed out over her lips as she looked at me holding the glass. I was suddenly and crushingly self-conscious, and I knew that the only way out of that horrible feeling was to throw the drink back and satisfy everyone's expectations. This was a familiar moment of initiation for me. I had been through dozens of similar ones with my father in villages all over the world. Why, then, was this one different? Why did it feel dangerous?

The thought that I might be in danger pushed me into action, because I realized that Tina might be in danger, too. Since she had warned me off from approaching, but she wasn't warning me off from this, I assumed that I was helping her by drinking whatev-er was in those bottles. And though I might have felt like I was surrounded by zombies, no one was dead and lots of people were drinking. I tossed the drink back.

In the moment before I tasted it, before it reached my stomach and started its dark work, I noticed the odd symbol molded into the bottom of the glass. Like any American, I was used to seeing the script "L" of Libbey Glass or the anchor of Anchor Hocking, but I had never seen this symbol before. It was a glyph that looked like it might be a letter, but from a language that I had never seen. Or maybe it was an imperfection rather than a trademark, but if the glass was marred in some way, it was having the unusual effect of making me even more frightened. This is difficult to explain, but it was as though the mark was a symbol whose meaning I did not know, but I somehow still vaguely understood.

As I was puzzling over this strange sign, the drink plowed into me. It felt like the lights in the barn dimmed all at once and the sound slowed down. I became fluid, barely contained within my skin. I had this sense of expanding further and further, and the immensity of it filled that old space with dread. In some corner of my mind, I was worried about losing myself. I felt like I was not in control, and I thought that at that point, anyone could probably do anything to me. Despite this worry, it didn't cloud the majority of my thinking and feeling. I might have been scared, but I felt expectant, too.

There was a supremely confusing moment when the movie projectors turned on. I wasn't sure, but I decided later that the barn lights had dimmed, either when I took my drink or at some point shortly thereafter. Now, I could see the white square at the end of the barn lit up with the bright white of the film leader. I could also see the dozens of faces illuminated by that screen. My tablemates weren't looking at me anymore, and neither was Jackie. But Tina still was. I couldn't quite tell what was in her eyes. Regret? Worry? And then she turned toward the images splashing across the screen.

How do I describe what we saw? In some ways, it is easy. There is a level of reality in which the film that those two young men showed first was simply Maya Deren's famous film *Meshes of the Afternoon*. I had never seen it before, so I didn't know that this is what I was watching, but I have watched it since, and I can recognize many of the images as the same ones I saw that night in the barn. I remember the beautiful Deren, the disappearing and reappearing key, the dark robed figure and its shocking facelessness. But when I see *Meshes* now, which I rarely do, but when I do, there is something missing, something that was certainly present on that night. I'm aware that all of us were watching that film under the influence of any number of drugs. And it's true that I have never been able to watch *Meshes* while under the influence of anything after that night. I have only re-watched it while stone cold sober. But I swear that what I saw was a different film in fundamental ways. I never again saw Deren run after the robed figure on the curving drive of her Los Angeles home, only to see the concrete change quickly and subtly into gigantic blocks of fitted gray and black stone; never again saw the roof of the house become the battlements and towers of an oddly alien fortress. And that water, what should by all accounts be the Pacific Ocean, I have never again watched it and seen the foam-dripped reflection of twin moons rippling beneath the black stars that hang in the smoky firmament. And when Deren finally confronts the robed figure, how is it that the robe is no longer black? How is it that even with the black and white print, I have the terrible sense that the tattered cloth is rather yellow than sable. Unaccountably, mercifully, it has never been that way since.

When I felt that I could no longer endure my soul's crescendo, the film was at an end. There was a darkness that descended on the barn before the film leader rolled again, and the light from the naked projector lamp filled the room once more. In that darkness, I grappled with my mind as it slowly spun back into what felt like its accustomed orbit. I felt rather than saw someone sit down next to me, and then I felt Tina's hand slip into my own.

"Isn't it amazing?"

"Amazing."

The light pulsed from the lamp as the end of the reel flapped against the projector. In no time, though, that projector was off and the other was turned on. This film was also in black and white, and it was titled *At Land*. In it, Deren washes up on a beach and then climbs some driftwood roots into a fancy dinner party, where she crawls down the long table, which happens to also be a dense forest, toward a chess game in progress. I have not seen this film since that night, so its remaining images are more jumbled in my memory than *Meshes*, but I do remember the final image of Deren running along the beach, away from the camera, her arms held aloft and a chess piece in one hand. Here again were those black stars hanging in the sky as the foam spreads across the beach near her feet. Beyond the waves that break on the sand, something large and dark swells beneath the surface of the water. Tina squeezed my hand again, but this time she did not let me go. Instead, we sat there and watched the film together, sending secret coded symbols back and forth using the electric sweat of our palms.

When the film was done and the lights came back on in the barn, the tall black man was still at the table, but the smoking woman was not. I had not seen her go, but her absence felt complete. Erasure. I couldn't tell you why, but I felt with absolute certainty that she was lost, and that if anyone were to go looking for her, they would never be able to find her anywhere in this world.

CHAPTER TWO

A fter that night, Tina was fascinated by film. She had never wanted to go to the movies before that, but from then on we went every chance we could. There were the regular Hollywood movies playing at the two theaters in the little village of Red Stone, and there were the two drive-in theaters nearby. Neither of us had a car, but there was always someone going to the movies, and we pretty quickly got a reputation as the girls who were always up for a show. Up until that point in my life, I wasn't a particular fan of movies. They were all right, and some of them were fun, but I could take them or leave them. I preferred live music if I could get it and musical theater if I couldn't. Movie musicals and Disney cartoons were probably my favorites, but I liked a lot of the music documentaries to come out of the 1960s, too. In fact, documentaries were my guilty pleasure. I think this had to do with all of the informational and training films that I watched while growing up as a missionary's daughter. The narrator's voice in these films was familiar and reassuring, telling me what I should know. Of course, this is also the very same voice, or at least the authority that it represents, that I rebel against at every opportunity.

The films that Tina reacted to the most—aside from the ones we saw that night at the barn party—were the films played at the

college's Art of Cinema screenings. Two local professors and an interested student had been trying to find a way to see the films that
they heard were playing in places like New York and Boston, and
they decided that the only way it would work was if they could
get other people to help them pay for the print rentals. Foreign
and art films were pretty easy to see in a city of any size back then,
but a little village like ours wasn't likely to ever get them in their
normal popcorn theaters. There was interest, though, because of
the college community and all of the people who were intrigued
by these films and all of the people who wanted everyone else to
think that they were intrigued by them. This was over a decade
before we got to SUNY Red Stone, but the Art of Cinema series
was still going strong when we arrived. It was 50¢ for a ticket to
see Godard or Kurosawa or De Sica, but you were just as likely to
get a brief film noir retrospective. This was easier for Tina and me
to get to, since the films screened in the auditorium on campus,
and she sometimes went back without me after we saw a film that
she particularly enjoyed. She saw *The Cabinet of Dr. Caligari* twice
when it ran and *The Third Man* at least that many.

Tina was serious about her viewing, too. For most films, you
couldn't talk or even move around her. She never ate or drank anything from the concession stand, and had no trouble telling other
patrons to be quiet. It was like she was meditating. She got very
quiet as the lights went down, and her breathing became steady
and deep. I remember the first time I noticed this, at a screening
of *The 400 Blows*, her rhythmic inhalations and exhalations almost
put me to sleep. I had to concentrate on paying attention to the
screen. That's what she was doing, after all. Tina wanted to open
herself up fully to the flickering shadows that jumped across the
screen. More than anything, though, she wanted to learn, because
she had finally discovered that she wanted to be a filmmaker.

It wasn't even an aspiration in the sense that we normally talk about it. It's not exactly that she wanted to be a filmmaker. It's more accurate to say that she finally discovered that she was already a filmmaker, that moving pictures were the language of her soul. She was not a musician, and this revelation made her profoundly happy, because she was able to understand fully why she had felt like such an imposter. Her family and the people around her wanted her to be a great musician, and they wanted this in the mundane way that Americans want things. They want things to be different, maybe because they continually fail to perceive the world the way that it actually is. They are not satisfied with the world they see around them, but this doesn't mean they have seen accurately. They see the world as reflected in a grimy mirror, clouded by shame and ignorance. In reaction to that image that they wish they could erase, they set up programs and shrines to their desires. They go to school and they exercise and they buy makeup and clothes that will all transform them into the thing that they want to be. We all do that to some extent. But Tina had her moment when she saw very clearly for the first time in her life what she already was. Motion pictures reached out to her across a vast gulf of suffering and confusion and wrapped her in certainty. Movies spoke to her, even when she wasn't entirely sure of what they were saying. She was somehow aware that this was the language that would make sense to her if only she could remember it, and she believed the best way to remember that speech was to try to forget what she had already learned about the false person others wanted her to be.

She didn't stop going to class immediately, but she was no longer as attentive and her work quality dropped precipitously. But she wasn't idle, and she wasn't always going to movies. She spent hours and hours in not only Red Stone's library but also the libraries of the other local colleges and even the public libraries nearby. She was getting every book she could find on photography and filmmaking, sponging up all the information she discovered. It was dizzying to watch her blaze through a British book on how to make home movies, alternately laughing at the silliness of the scenarios they suggested and making extensive notes. She didn't want to make home movies, but that's what most of the texts she found were geared toward. Even back then, there were precious few books on how to be part of the avant-garde. That's how it always is. You can read the books written by the critics and the historians, but the artists themselves rarely write. There were some manifestoes, of course. She read Breton, and she eventually found Bresson and Bazin. Some of these she found because she was able to work backwards from what she had already seen of Maya Deren's work.

I remember the moment when Tina found out that Deren was dead. I know that she had hoped Maya was still out there somewhere, making movies. I watched Tina's search with both jealousy and dread. I could feel her wheeling away from me and spinning into the orbit of artists far from our little campus north of the Adirondacks, not that I felt any need or desire to stay there. But she was moving so quickly. She felt acutely the years that she had already wasted, and she had no patience for more of the same. The moment when she read Deren's obituary silently—I was sitting at a library table next to her, reading along with her—I felt elated, as though I had vanquished a rival. Or no, that's not right. It was more like finding out that a legendary rival is a kind of powerful figment of my imagination. And Deren was powerful. I think more than any other filmmaker, Maya was the one who held the most power over Tina, the power to inspire and to intimidate. It changed Tina when she discovered that she was listening to the dead.

The biggest change wrought by this discovery was the intensification of the search for her own film camera. Part of Tina's research so far had been into the kinds of cameras that were available, their capabilities and costs. Tina was on scholarship, for now, but that didn't mean that she could spend freely. She was in many ways a poor college student like most of the rest of us. But she was serious about getting a camera and being able to pay for film and processing, and she was budgeting her money accordingly. Tina wasn't sure what camera she wanted to get. From her reading, she could see that a lot of the avant-garde filmmakers of the past couple decades were using 16mm and 35mm film cameras, but these were expensive, both to buy and to get film and processing for them. The alternatives were smaller 8mm home movie cameras. She was already hearing about the weird films being projected at rock clubs in New York, and those were mostly done on cheap 8mm cameras. The older wind-up 8mm cameras that used spools of film were very cheap, but she decided that the newer Super 8 cameras made more sense for her. The self-contained Super 8 cartridge was easier to load, and the images they produced were better. You could even get Super 8 cameras that recorded sound right onto the film, but she decided to let that option go at the beginning. Maybe later she would want to make movies with synchronized sound, but for now she didn't care enough about dialogue to spend the extra money on a sound camera and film and a special projector.

As it turned out, though, she got her first camera for free. In her search for books on cinema, Tina had also asked around at all of the local colleges as to whether there were any professors with an interest in cinema. She started, of course, with the faculty adviser to the Art of Cinema series, but he was simply an aficionado content to consider himself more cultured than many of his colleagues because he had seen four films by Yasujiro Ozu. The break came when Tina requested a copy of Sergei Eisenstein's *Film Form* through inter-library loan, and the librarian at the circulation desk asked if she was doing a paper for Professor Peters.

"Yeah," said Tina after a brief pause.

The librarian, an older woman whose Farah Fawcett do put most of my classmates to shame, took a pencil from behind her ear and scribbled down a string of authors. "If you are cross-registered in Dom's class, you're supposed to have library privileges at WC. He usually keeps the required texts on reserve there."

"My paper is kinda weird, so I needed to get different books."

"I'm happy to request this, but I'll bet they have a copy over there. Do you want me to call?"

"I'll be over there tomorrow for class. I can check then."

It took more searching than she expected at first, but Tina eventually located Prof. Dominic Peters on the faculty of Woodbury College, the smaller liberal arts college in the next town where all the rich kids who came from other places went to school. Tina and I hadn't had much contact with WC people at this point, so we only knew the school by reputation. You could sort of tell when you were talking to a WC student at a bar or a coffee house or a movie theater, but it was harder to tell with older adults. You might be confident that you were talking to a professor or a dean or something, but there was no way to guess which school employed them.

Peters was a member of the Art Department at Woodbury, and this got Tina excited that one of the nearby colleges might actually teach filmmaking. She was a rare self-starter, but even I could tell that years of formal music lessons had impressed upon her the sense that students were taught by teachers. She had not yet taken it upon herself to provide her own education in film technique. That came later. So, it was with fairly high expectations that Tina dragged me along to Professor Peters's house instead of to his office on campus. Her argument was that we weren't Woodbury students, so we didn't have any business showing up to his office hours. When I pointed out that we didn't have any business showing up to his house unannounced either, Tina shrugged off my objections. I don't know if she had done any extra digging but my worry was that Peters was married with a family or something, and Tina was counting a little too much on the surprise effect of two young women showing up unannounced at a bachelor's house. I mean, there were two of us, so I wasn't worried about any kind of danger, but this was treading into some potentially embarrassing territory if she miscalculated.

Peters lived in a tiny bungalow on a shaded street that dead-ended into the river. In the few warmer months in Red Stone, his place was invaded by mosquitoes and black flies, but we were well into the fall semester. It was only the occasional warm evening that prompted the mosquitoes to mount offensives in any real numbers. Things had already cooled enough to hold the flies at bay, so we were unmolested when we arrived at the professor's door at twilight. Tina rang the doorbell, and we didn't have to wait long for the porch light to come on and the door to open.

"I'm probably not interested," said the cadaverous man with the jutting slate hair and patchy beard.

"We're not selling anything," said Tina. Peters raised his eyebrows, unconvinced. "We want to talk film."

Peters's eyes flicked from Tina to me and back before he glanced down the street and at his neighbors' windows.

"Film?"

"Yeah," I said. "Movies?"

The fingers of his left hand twitched at his side. He was obviously doing some pretty heavy calculations in his head at that moment. I had no idea how it was going to go, but Tina had a better sense of how to move things along.

"We can talk about it out here, if you want," she said. Peters stepped back and held the door.

"No, you better come in. I'm already letting in too many bugs." Tina grinned at me and stepped inside. "I'm expecting a phone call soon, so I hope this won't take long?"

"Not long," said Tina. I entered, and Peters shut the door behind me.

The living room we found ourselves in wasn't nearly as creepy as

I worried it might be. A few windows were open to let the fresh air and scent of pine needles into the house. But the place wasn't without its warning signs. The living room walls were hung with some of the strangest art I had ever seen in a home. There was a photograph of a hideous hag leering back at the camera over her shoulder. There was also a painting—an oily soup of dark tones punctuated with bright yellows and oranges—that depicted a multi-headed dragon rising from a lake. A couple were framed pictures of nude witches preparing for a sabbath. I couldn't tell at first whether these were photographs or paintings; they looked weird. I'll admit that my attention was drawn to the nakedness in the photos, not because I was or am particularly prudish, but because Tina and I had entered this guy's house of our own accord. It confirmed some of my fears at the same time that it made me pause. Peters dropped into a padded arm chair and gestured toward the threadbare sofa.

"So, you want to talk about cinema…?" We recognized the pause was for us. I looked nervously at my roommate.

"Tina," she said. I tried to hide my frustration with her as I introduced myself, too.

"Have you made movies?" asked Tina. Peters held her gaze for a long moment before his eyes flitted over to me. He must have found something more familiar or reassuring in my face, because he smiled slightly before he answered.

"I've dabbled. I'm more of a photographer, but I've had my flirtations with motion pictures. I wrote an article on Russian montage theories and techniques. That was a few years ago, when I was experimenting a bit more with a couple different kinds of film cameras I had picked up along the way."

"Along the way where?" I asked.

"Well, here I suppose. Would either of you like a drink? Sometimes it takes a few minutes for my manners to catch up with the rest of me."

"I'd like a drink," Tina said, and I nodded along with her.

Peters rose from his chair and stepped over to a small alcove where he collected his liquor. The shelf above the wet bar held tumblers and martini glasses, but the one above that had a small collection of handheld movie cameras. Tina nudged her knee against mine. Peters brought three tumblers and a bottle of vodka over to the coffee table in front of the sofa. He set the glasses down and poured sloppily.

"*Zazdarovje*," he said before sliding the liquor down his throat. I was a bit leery after my experience with the last batch of clear liquor, but this bottle looked legitimate. Tina tossed hers back moments before I sipped from mine. "What's your interest in film?"

"Artistic," she said. Peters considered Tina for a moment before pouring two more glasses of vodka. Tina picked up her refilled tumbler before adding, "Transcendental."

"Transcendental?" Peters said this word almost to himself, staring into his own glass and mulling the implications. "What is it that you want to transcend?"

I was looking around the living room, mostly at the pictures on the walls, and Peters noticed. "Do you know Mortensen?"

"No."

"Very interested in beauty and monstrosity. Desire and the grotesque. I like him, but these pictures hold a different meaning for me, or at least I come to them from a different place." He stood up and went over to a picture of a woman rubbing salve on the lustrous nude body of a witch. "These pictures remind me of Bulgakov's greatest work *The Master and Margarita*. Have you read it?"

I shook my head. "A play?"

"A novel. A masterpiece. In it, a member of the devil's entourage gives Margarita the opportunity to serve as Satan's queen at his annual ball. To prepare for the ball, she rubs a magical cream all over her body, turning her into a powerful and beautiful witch."

"What does she do with her power?" asked Tina.

"She becomes invisible and flies over Moscow, terrorizing some idiots before she continues on to fulfill her promise."

"She transcends society," I said. Peters nodded.

"But not her own code."

I sipped at my first vodka and thought about that. Not breaking rules for the sake of breaking rules, but breaking rules in order to pursue some other more immediate truth. I wondered what it took to see that kind of truth, to be sure of it. Peters swirled some vodka in his mouth and swallowed.

"I'm still not sure I know how I can help you ladies."

"Do you teach filmmaking? Would you?"

"Are you students at Woodbury?" We shook our heads.

"State." Peters nodded, sipped thoughtfully.

"I have helped some Woodbury students with some projects. Nothing too formal. I don't teach filmmaking classes; the school would never go for it. But when students want to make movies, as they have once or twice, I'm usually happy to let them try it. But you're not my students."

"Would you consider some kind of private tutor arrangement?"

"All right, come on. Who put you up to this? Ashe? Gutjahr?"

"What do you mean?"

"This doesn't smell right to me. Two coeds come knocking on my door one evening, asking me to teach them how to make movies."

"Really, Professor Peters…"

"I think you better go," he said, though even then I wasn't convinced by his tone. He was signaling that now was the time for us to convince him once and for all that we were real. He wasn't being clear about what sorts of assurance he would believe, but I could guess.

The phone in the kitchen rang, thwarting whatever momentum Peters was trying to build toward our sordid doom. With a grunt of exasperation, he excused himself, putting his tumbler on the table.

He pushed his way through the strangely incongruous saloon doors that separated the living room from the kitchen, and before they had stopped swinging completely Tina was off the sofa and snatching a shapeless black leather bag off of the camera shelf above the bar.

"Come on," she hissed, and I launched myself off the sofa and toward the door, adrenaline flooding my body in utter surprise at what she had done.

We were out the door and off down the street at a dead sprint. I think I heard Peters at the door when we were a few houses away, but he wisely chose not to call out after us. I was looking around, too, as we ran. I expected the police to jump out at us at any moment, though of course there was no way they were going to. It was unlikely even that Peters knew precisely what we had done, it had happened so quickly.

"What the hell are you doing?" I said once we turned the corner at the end of the block.

"I needed a camera, and I saw the one I wanted."

"That bag?"

Tina zipped open the bag, and inside was a blocky metal camera, black and silver.

"I can't believe you. He's going to call the cops on us as soon as he figures out what we did."

"I don't think so." Ultimately, I had to agree. It was a weird evening, and I think Tina had gotten a free camera in exchange for enduring a few minutes with a supreme creep. She had that kind of courage.

Over the next couple of weeks, I still felt the lingering echoes of fear about whether or not Peters was going to report our crime to the cops, but no one came asking about the camera. Tina found out pretty quickly why we had nothing to worry about from Peters.

When she got the camera back to the dorm, she took it out of the bag and inspected it. It was not exactly what she expected it to be. It was actually a Soviet Super-8 camera, a wind-up design. It wasn't made of plastic, and it didn't run on batteries. (It did have batteries to run the internal light meter, but we didn't know that until later.) The mechanism was entirely spring-driven and loud. There was no way we were going to record dialogue while we were using this camera. But the two things that made sure that Peters wasn't going to send anyone else after his camera was that it was covered in Cyrillic, and it had a partially used film cartridge in it at the time Tina stole it.

We never did develop that film and find out what was on it. I've occasionally wondered what secrets it held. But I'm with Tina in thinking that it was probably something that Peters wasn't interested in sharing with the outside world. If he had sent the cops to campus looking for us, he would have had to answer questions about why he owned a commie movie camera. That was still a tricky question to answer in 1978. Now, of course, Tina and I had the same question to answer if anyone ever found us with that camera, so she came up with an interesting solution to the problem by covering the camera with painted designs, intricate work that covered up most of the Russian writing and distracted from the marks on the lens rings that were necessary to her work. Now the camera was hers, and she was ready to start making movies.

Months later, when Tina started to show her Super-8 movies at some of the rock shows and coffee houses around the village, we sometimes saw Peters there in the back of the crowd. He was always good at lurking. If he was angry with us, he never showed it, and he never tried to come up and talk to either of us, as far as I know. If I had to guess, I think he was even pleased with the work that Tina was doing, though he and I remained in a relatively small group of people who thought so.

CHAPTER THREE

It was hard to shake the feeling after Tina stole her first camera that the whole enterprise was cursed, or maybe it was just that camera, or just her. She spent a week staring at the thing in our dorm room, doing her best to discern what all of the knobs did. Most of them were pretty easy for her to figure out, but that camera wasn't designed for the American consumer market. It was designed for Soviet film school students, who were all being taught filmmaking in some mechanistic totalitarian way that never varied (or so we thought back then). They probably came out of the womb knowing how all of those buttons and knobs worked, and if they didn't they could read the manual, which of course was in Russian. Peters didn't have the manual, or at least he didn't have it in the black leather bag with the rest of the camera's accessories, but Tina was convinced that it wasn't all that hard to learn. There were only so many things the buttons and knobs could do, after all. She was happy that the damn thing actually used Kodak Super 8 film cartridges. We both had a moment of wondering whether we had stolen a camera that we couldn't even get film for.

Getting the film was very easy, and so was getting it processed, but only if you had the money. It wasn't exactly expensive, but we were college students. And neither of us was particularly rich. You went to the drug store and asked the cashier for the kind of film that you wanted. It came in these small square boxes, mostly yellow and red, because most drug stores only carried Kodak film. In some cases you could also pay for a processing envelope, so that you mailed it yourself once you had shot it, but a lot of people also brought it back to the drug store or the camera shop. Not that they had the lab in the back or anything, but they were set up to send the film out and get it back for you to pick up. This is how most people got their regular film and photographs, too.

Red Stone didn't have a dedicated camera store back then, and I doubt it does now. I think the closest one was probably up in Ottawa, or maybe over in Lake Placid. But there were still plenty of drug stores and grocery stores where you could get film. I used to notice that once you got close to any sort of tourist destination, like Niagara Falls for instance, you could buy regular and movie film almost everywhere. They had these big diamond-shaped wooden racks on the wall, and the rectangular film boxes were stacked inside them just so. After her week of poring over all of the functions on the camera and making sure she knew how everything worked, Tina went to the drug store downtown and bought two cartridges of black and white film. I asked her why she bought the black and white, since I would have gone for the color film, but she wasn't entirely certain why she had chosen it. She was surprised at herself for not knowing, but she was also surprised at me for asking. This was the question that plenty of people asked her in the years to come, and she was always unprepared to offer a solid answer. She only made a couple of her shorts in color, as far as I know, though she often had at least one cartridge of Kodachrome on her as she got deeper and deeper into filmmaking. She didn't like talking about her process the way that other artists were at least trained to be able to talk about it, whether or not they actually liked discussing it.

Tina was always mystified by that; it was something that she did, though it was also clear to me that she spent a lot of time contemplating what she was doing. It wasn't that she was developing logical reasons for what she wanted to do. Tina was in no way analytical about her art. She was communing with her visions, like there was an entire universe inside her head that she was exploring, and sometimes she was able to push the button on her camera and capture some of that universe on celluloid. We usually think about these universes as fascinating and magical and safe, but they aren't always safe.

Tina came back with these two film cartridges and told me that we were going out. She grabbed the black leather bag with the camera and pulled me out the door of our dorm room. I barely had time to grab a coat and put on my boots, as it was November already and in Red Stone you needed to be fully prepared for winter as soon as you had cleaned up from Halloween. When I asked where we were going, all I got from Tina was a vague reference to the art building. We made our way across campus, the wind already starting to bite into our skin this early in the season, toward the building that had the art studios. This was a place where I had spent a considerable amount of time already, hanging out with some of my artist friends and scoring some grass. They didn't usually have the best pot, but theirs was abundant and less expensive. Mostly I hung out with them because I had some sense that I belonged there, though I'm not so sure that was true when I look back on it. It was where I thought I *ought* to have belonged, but there was a lot more posing going on there than just with their life models. Outside of the music conservatory, State attracted more than its fair share of posers, who were dedicated to living an artist's lifestyle while knowing next to nothing about art. I think it is fair to put me in that category, though I never thought of myself as an artist.

It's true that I started to think of myself more and more as Tina's assistant or partner in crime. The incident with Peters had been deeply exciting. I had never done anything quite so taboo, and certainly I had never had someone else make the decision for me. It was like suddenly finding oneself on a rollercoaster without having known that you were even at an amusement park. It would have been easy for me to be afraid of or disgusted by Tina and her antics, but I felt like I was alive and incredibly lucky to be in her presence. It's not only that she was exciting, because she wasn't always; it was that being around her made it feel like your whole life was exciting, like anything could happen at any moment. A lot of nineteen-year-olds are looking for that, for evidence that the world is not quite as boring as their prematurely jaded judgment tells them it is. They desperately want the world to be more interesting, for it to have a meaning that they have spent the last few years discovering it doesn't have. You lose your faith in God and Santa Claus and Abe Lincoln, and part of you wants it all back. Not having that solid ground of meaning and security is pretty hard, especially when all of the adults around you are asking you what you want to do with your life.

Not that they asked us girls that very often. It was pretty obvious what they expected from us. The real question is how what we wanted to do was going to result in the marriage and family that everyone assumed we wanted. Sure, we could go to college, and we could even have some fun and be a little rebellious, and we could even get a job and make some money—this was the tail end of women's lib, after all—but no one seriously thought we were going to be anything other than wives and mothers. I don't think Tina thought that way, and I know I didn't, so both of us felt a little bit like explorers, like we could do anything, but that also meant that we spent a lot of the time drifting at sea without any reference to land. In those cases, the best thing to do is to look to the stars.

We reached the art building and entered through a side door, taking the stairs up to the second floor where there were a few studios, but most of the space was given over to the offices of the professors. I had an irrational fear in that moment that we were going to run into Peters, even though that he didn't even teach at our school. Maybe he would be there talking to other art professors that he knew. But he wasn't there, of course. That wasn't what we had to worry about.

Tina was walking normally until about halfway down the second-floor hallway, where she started looking around to see if anyone was looking at us. There were a couple open doors to offices and studios, but everything was pretty quiet. She found the door she was looking for, the office of Professor Amelia Van Rhys, and turned to me, whispering.

"Take these and keep a lookout here, like you're sketching the quad." She handed me a small hardcover sketchbook and a pencil case. "If anyone looks like they're going to come into this room, start talking to them really loud."

"What am I supposed to talk about?"

"Ask if you can talk about what classes they're going to offer next semester."

"What if it's not a professor?"

"You're smart. You'll think of something." Tina looked up and down the hallways again and then slipped into the office.

A thrill of fear shot up my spine when I heard voices from the open studio door next to the office. I edged closer to get a look. It was a painter's studio with tall windows and layers of canvases leaning against the walls. The door was open a few inches, and I heard a woman's voice and then nervous laughter from a man. I saw the woman from the back. She had on a long sweater and full, dark hair pulled back away from her face. And then I saw the guy. He was young, a student probably, though I didn't think I had ever seen him around, and he was shirtless and unbuttoning his jeans. Like I said, I'm not prudish, but I was also not used to being the secret voyeur, though it also occurred to me at that moment that I was not the secret voyeur. Tina was. The guy looked up at that moment, maybe alerted by the roar of blood to my face as I blushed, and that caught the woman's attention, too. She whirled around and saw me look away before she closed the studio door against prying eyes.

I'm not sure what I thought was happening there. I guess after our encounter with Peters, I was in a place where I was thinking more about professors and students, and flirtation across generations. I could understand it, even if I wasn't interested. I had been in classes where the professor was magnetic in one way or another, and it had been clear to me for years that there were professors who could not help but leer at their students. You hear rumors about those sorts of things, and I had been on the receiving end of some inappropriate and unwelcome suggestions, but I had never witnessed anything myself. What occurred to me immediately after those thoughts is what turned out to be the real situation. Professor Van Rhys had hired a nude model from among one of the local colleges, and she was going to draw or paint him in her studio. This was, in fact, her job, in addition to teaching. This realization was punctuated by her turning on music, probably a tape deck. I never heard a radio DJ, and I was out in that hallway for a couple hours.

It was all a mystery to me, and my imagination worked hard to fill in all the gaps while Tina was doing whatever she was doing in Van Rhys's office. The situation was so unusual and exciting for me that I started drawing what I imagined that the model looked like as he lounged on some chair or even on the floor. That's what I was sketching when Tina finally slipped quietly out of the office, making eye contact with me but still looking both ways down the hallway before she came out and closed the door again behind her. Just then, the studio door opened, too, and the music from within got louder.

"You did a great job again," Van Rhys was saying to the young guy, now fully clothed again. "Can I keep you on my list of models?"

The guy saw us first as he came out into the hallway. He looked at me in recognition (a smile, somehow both sheepish and proud) and then at Tina. Van Rhys smiled and said hello before returning her attention to her model.

Tina nodded in a friendly way and turned to me. "Do you think Bren is still at the library?"

"She said she would be," I said.

She was training me, subtly, to always be acting. I was getting better and better at improvising when she came up with these off-the-wall sentences that demanded utterly boring and plausible replies. It was mostly about the timing and the delivery. You could say almost anything in those moments. In any case, it worked, and we were off down the hallway in the opposite direction from Van Rhys's model. Once we were out of the building, Tina told me all about what happened in the office.

"I knew what was going to happen," she said. "I'd been walking around campus for a couple days looking for interesting places or things to film. On one of those days, I was walking through the art building, hoping that the student paintings and sculptures on display offered at least good background for some kind of scenario.

"I found this group of three guys in that hallway outside Van Rhys's office. One of them, a skinny guy with long, feathered black hair, had a camera around his neck, and he instantly spotted my movie camera. I was carrying it in its leather case, but he saw the handle sticking out of the bag. Skinny guy called out to me and asked me if I made movies. His friends weren't so sure about talking to me, I could tell, but he calmed them down.

"Skinny guy asked if I was cool, and I tried not to sound too eager when I shrugged and nodded and said, 'sure.' He explained they were in a band, Copperhead Mouth, and they were going to take some candid photos for a slideshow that they wanted to have on a screen behind them while they played at a gig in a couple weeks. Skinny guy—he said his name was Vic—thought a movie was even better. I asked what they were going to shoot 'candidly.' And one of the guys put his hand on Vic's arm, but Vic blurted it out anyway. The guy who hadn't said anything yet was Donny, the guy that had been naked in Van Rhys's office/studio. He was also in the band, and he had already scheduled his session with the art professor. This was the second time that he had posed for her; that's how they got this idea. Donny already knew that there was a door between her office and the studio, and that she rarely stepped away from her easel at all while she was working. They figured that they could have someone hide in her office and take photos that they could project as slides during the concert. But movies, man, that was awesome.

"I was instantly on board, and I let them know it. Donny got a little bit shy; it wasn't just the professor and the other guys who were going to see him naked. It's like the reality of how many strangers would see him nude finally hit him when he looked at me. He tried to back out, saying he wasn't so sure about it anymore, but Vic and Jeff, the other bandmate, urged him on. They told him it would make them famous locally, maybe even more. This was exactly the kind of exposure that could help them break out. How else were they going to get out of the North Country without some kind of real plan? This was a real plan, and anyway, couldn't he see how excited I was to see him naked? He was gonna be a hit. 'Yeah, man, but what about Ginnie?' 'Are you kidding? She's going to be the one who gets to say she's with you. She's gonna love it!'"

There was fire in Tina's eyes as she told me this story. Her words were tumbling out faster and faster.

"I could tell that Donny wasn't entirely convinced, but he wanted to be. I was grinning at him, hopefully not too creepily. I didn't want to give the guy the wrong idea, but this was better than anything that I had come up with. When he finally agreed to the whole thing again, I more or less blurted out, 'so what's in this for me?' Vic was a little miffed at first, but he understood. He said that I was in for a full share, like everyone else in the band, as long as I delivered on time. I said there was no problem with that. He asked if I could bring a projector, and I told him, unable to hide my embarrassment, that I had a camera but no projector yet. This was fixed right away when Jeff (the drummer, I later found out) said that he could borrow his parents' projector for the gig with no problem. 'Well, all right,' said Vic. 'It's a gig?' I nodded and left after we exchanged numbers.

"This was two days ago. Yesterday, Vic called and told me when Donny would be at Van Rhys's studio for his next appointment as well as the date and time of the gig where they wanted to show the film. I wrote it all down and said that it was no problem."

The truth is she was totally excited to do this thing. Her first real film was going to be this secret voyeur film with nudity and power and all that. She was aware enough of what was going on with feminism that she understood the dynamic that she was the one shooting this secret film of a woman seeing and drawing a nude man, appreciating his body. Tina had never seen Donny (the band's lead guitarist) naked before, but he was a good looking guy in clothes; she assumed he was likely also a good looking guy out of them.

Tina gave a lot of thought to how she would shoot the film once she got there. She had a sense that sound would be a factor. She even talked about it with Vic. She told him that her camera was a wind-up model, that it wasn't very quiet. If Van Rhys liked to draw or paint in complete silence, then there was a good chance that the whole plan wouldn't work. They would both be able to hear the camera running. Vic said not to worry, that the model had talked all about the fact that Van Rhys couldn't draw unless she had the right music playing, the right ambience constructed.

The other thing that Tina tried to think about beforehand was how she was going to frame the film. She was going to be hiding in a darkened office, shooting from a single angle. She wouldn't be able to arrange her "actors" at all or do anything about the lighting. She knew it was going to be during the day and that the studio was built to let in a lot of natural light, even if Van Rhys didn't choose to use the overhead lights. Tina figured that she would look for the most interesting framing that she could get from her hiding place once the whole thing was underway. Still, she was very nervous about being caught in the office and having the whole thing fall apart before there was even a film. She said that the nightmare version of events was that she could be discovered by another professor or by Van Rhys or even a campus security guard, and that she would be kicked out of school and have nothing to show for it but a stolen Soviet movie camera. Tina never said so, but I'm pretty sure that all of this made it even more exciting for her. She wasn't an adrenaline junky *per se*. I mean, she didn't go and seek out other kinds of thrills while I knew her. But she did love the idea that there was some danger wrapped up with this art of filmmaking. That inspired her and made her even more eager.

To calm herself down, she grabbed me and dragged me along as her lookout. While I was out in the hallway with the sketchbook, keeping my eyes peeled for all of those nightmare scenarios, Tina said she crept up to the communicating door that was already open slightly, as she had been promised. She had the foresight to load and pre-wind the camera before she even came and got me, but she didn't think that maybe the best thing in this instance was to have a tripod for the camera. She was still learning all that stuff, and it hadn't even occurred to her until she was in the middle of shooting that roll of film. She knew that if she was going to shoot the whole roll, she would need to rewind the camera while she was hiding there in the dark. In preparation for that, she had practiced winding the camera as slowly and quietly as she could while not losing too much time. There were all sorts of opportunities for it to go wrong, but it didn't, at least not until sometime later.

When Tina got to the door and knelt on the ground, trying to find a comfortable position from which to film, Donny was already out of his shirt and was taking off his cowboy boots. Then came the moment when the model must have seen me in the hallway, prompting Van Rhys to shut the door to keep out prying eyes.

Tina thought at the time that there was no jealousy or any sense of the proprietary about her gesture of closing the door. If anything, she was trying to put her model at ease. Donny looked a bit nervous or maybe embarrassed, but Van Rhys was a total professional. She moved quickly to set things up the way that she wanted them. She almost tripped over Donny's cowboy boots as he was shimmying out of his blue jeans and then slipping off his underwear with only the slightest hesitation. Van Rhys grabbed a boot to move it out of the way, but then she held it and thought about it for a long moment. He apologized for his boots being in the way but Van Rhys handed it to him and told him to put them back on.

Donny laughed a bit and said, "What?"

"Yeah, put them back on."

She handed him the other boot and then began moving some canvases out of the way. Behind them, she found a wooden pallet that she had placed against the wall at some earlier period, and this she dragged out to arrange behind him like a fence. She then waited for him to get his second boot back on and directed him to lean against the pallet with one boot up, hooked on a slat. When Van Rhys finally had him posed the way that she wanted him, Tina was struck by the familiarity of the image, but she was a bit too distracted by this guy's proximate nakedness to place it. A few moments later, when she started filming and was then engrossed in the problems and worries of the camera and her shot, the thought came to her that Van Rhys had posed him like the Marlboro Man.

Tina was right: the filming itself was the most harrowing part of the whole ordeal. When she finally saw the arrangement of the studio, she had some choices to make. She was lucky enough that no one was looking directly at the office communicating door. Donny could see it easily, if he turned his head, but Van Rhys was clear about wanting him to keep his gaze down at the ground in that pensive smoking man stare from all of the magazine ads and billboards. And Van Rhys herself had to turn around to see the door. To be as invisible as possible, Tina wanted to position herself a foot or more back from the door, but still not have the door and doorframe crowd the frame of the film. This was the hardest bit to manage, and once she did that, her framing choices were limited. She could either film as wide as possible and get most of Van Rhys's shoulder and arm, the easel with paper, and Donny in the background, or she could go in tight and focus exclusively on the drawing itself while the artist drew it. This second framing immediately suggested itself as the far more interesting one, and it also had the advantage of not requiring very much depth of field.

Once Tina had made this decision, it was a matter of keeping her hand steady and keeping as quiet as possible. She said that once she finally got the courage to press the trigger on the camera, she was astounded by how loud the camera was in the darkened office. But she kept her finger on it for a full ten seconds before she realized that she had to take her time. She only had about three minutes of film in a single cartridge. She had no idea how long this session was going to take. This made her wonder if she was squandering the opportunity that was in front of her, but she wisely stuck to her plan. The second time she pushed the trigger, Van Rhys stopped her pencil to listen.

"Do you hear that?" she asked.

"What?"

"Sounds like a clicking or something."

Donny shook his head. Van Rhys shrugged and leaned in closer to her easel.

"Maybe it's the heater or something." Donny observed, somewhat petulantly, that he was pretty sure it was not the heater.

The artist got back to work, and Tina began her process of anticipating when were the best times to get a few seconds of footage here and few more there. Every few shots, she turned the key slowly and steadily to wind up the spring motor in the camera. She was thankful that winding the motor was actually much quieter than running it. It worked perfectly right up until the end. She knew that virtually all of the shots she had gotten featured Van Rhys hard at work; there weren't more than one or two shots that were essentially dead time, but those were easy to cut out of the reel, and they wouldn't reduce the overall run time by much.

She was very happy with how everything was going, when all of a sudden Van Rhys and Donny were done. The artist sat back from the easel and put her pencil down before she had gotten to the head of her figure. The rest of it was recognizable if not fully detailed, though Tina noted that Van Rhys had been sure to capture the shallow curve of an appendectomy scar above the Donny's toned pelvic girdle. Tina wasn't sure exactly what the band was looking for. Would a film that didn't fully reveal their bandmate satisfy them? She thought from their initial meeting that the model would not mind this turn of events at all, but Vic might be disappointed. As all of these thoughts were running through her head, Tina got up from the floor with screaming knees and slipped from the office into the hallway as quietly as she could. We left and walked straight to the drug store, where Tina sent it off for processing.

The wait was long but not without its own exciting events. The entire campus was thrown into turmoil several days later when a freak car crash resulted in one student fatality and another severely injured and indefinitely hospitalized. The rumors built up steadily around this morbid story. Two lovers were joyriding in the girl's little British sports car, a Spitfire, and the boyfriend was at the wheel. They were speeding through the Adirondack Park, supposedly on the way to a bonfire (there were rumors that it was a midnight gathering at Barron Circle), but they missed their turn and headed down the wrong dirt trail. The police, and the rest of campus, speculated that the girl must have screamed at the last moment when she saw the privacy chain stretched across the trail, and the boyfriend must have turned to her as she ducked. How else to explain why he was decapitated but she had the gearshift knob wedged in her left eye socket? Though her injuries were extensive, and at first, the doctors at the hospital were not sure that she would survive, it quickly became apparent that she would pull through. However well her body eventually healed, she had gone utterly insane.

It was in this grim atmosphere that Tina took delivery of her developed reel of film, so tiny in her hand for all of the work and danger that had gone into making it. The box came with a piece of paper, folded in quarters. Tina unfolded it and read the angular print etched in pencil.

> My boss says I have to send this back to you, since
> it is film of a drawing and not a real person, but I
> think it is disgusting and pornographic.

The note was unsigned. She handed it to me without comment. Whether or not the note affected her, her films did not contain any racy content until later, when she had also learned how to process her own film.

Tina had thought about trying to edit out those couple of shots on the reel that weren't absolutely perfect, but she didn't have the right supplies, and she knew it was better to make sure that the screening went off without a hitch.

When the day came for the gig, Tina and I went to the giant Victorian house in the center of town that for years had been given over to use as a fraternity house. When we arrived, there was a lot of drinking going on, but the partying was heavily tinged with a marked somberness.

Vic found us within a few minutes.

"Hey, have you got it?" Tina handed it over without comment. Vic looked at the little reel of film in his hand and nodded. "Thanks."

Vic waived over Jeff, the drummer, who took the reel from him.

"The gig's in the basement," Vic said. "We're going to start up pretty soon and get this over with."

The next few minutes were confusing and shocking. I was confused when we got downstairs after detouring to the beer keg and we saw the band tuning up, but they had a new guitarist, an embarrassed-looking kid with red hair and a yellow flannel shirt. Donny was nowhere to be seen. I thought maybe he was too embarrassed. Tina wanted to be near the projector while her film was screening, so we both took up positions near the middle of the room where it was set on a small card table. Jeff was showing another kid how to work it, but the kid was swatting the drummer's hand away, protesting that he knew all about it. I was confused about what the flyers that were posted here and there around the house had the word "memorial" added in after the fact.

But then I got it, I think around the same time that Tina knew. Vic got up on the low stage and started rambling about his best friend, Donny, who was the heart and soul of the band and who would never play with them again, who left behind two parents who didn't understand him and a girl who maybe would never understand anything ever again. Vic was laying down the bass line for their opening tribute song to Donny's memory when the kid at the projector turned it on, and the screen behind the band flickered to life with Tina's film.

For the next three and half minutes, Tina and I were the only ones who knew what was going to happen. At first, the white screen was broken only by the artist's sure hand, her pencil, and a spray of dark twinkling spots, imperfections in the black and white film that looked like a field of black stars rising behind the unfolding scene. They looked like the same stars from the screening of *Meshes of the Afternoon* and *At Land* from the barn party. When I made the connection, I looked at Tina, whose eyes glittered with the realization of what she had done. As Donny took shape under Van Rhys's hand, his lean nakedness slouched comfortably against what looked like a ranch fence and not the simple wooden pallet from the studio, even as some people began to recognize Donny's scar and point and shout at the screen and then suddenly also at us, we were the only ones who knew that the film ended without Donny's head.

CHAPTER FOUR

I felt an acute desire to lay low after the concert. People had been shouting at Tina as she yanked the small reel of film off the projector while it was still snapping its acetate leader over and over against the projector. I didn't think anyone was going to hurt us, unless we stayed around long enough to insult them in some new way, so I hustled Tina out of that basement as fast as I could. The adrenaline of fear mixed together with the adrenaline Tina was already feeling from seeing her work on screen and from seeing the effect it had on a live audience. It was one thing to be inspired by a filmmaker like Maya Deren, but it was something else to make a film of your own and see it work on people in a similar ways. Tina had been bitten, and she had no intention of applying any kind of antidote.

For a little while, I wanted to distance myself from it. Tina's orbit was more powerful than any I had been in before, at least in terms of an individual. I had been around groups that had such a strong pull, it almost made you cry to want to do something other than what they wanted you to do. Just as I was scared of those groups, I felt a little scared of Tina after the concert, too. There was no confrontation or argument. I didn't say anything to her about it, but I did get back to my studies. I was still attending class and doing my homework at this point, but my attention had strayed since the barn party. Now, I tried to redouble my efforts at school.

I mostly liked my classes, too. My English class was pretty standard stuff, and world history felt like shaking cobwebs off of things I had learned already, but the botany class I was taking was exciting in all the right ways. There weren't any true revolutionaries on SUNY Red Stone's faculty at that time, but you could tell that some of the younger professors were interested in shaking things up, and Prof. Duprey was one of them. He was teaching introductory botany, but he wanted to keep his students interested, so he built the entire course around plants as medicine, with a large unit on psychoactives and two weeks on poisons. We were limited in what we could incorporate directly into our lab work, but he kept things engaging by assigning books like Louis Lewin's *Phantastica* on the use and effects of dozens of plants. I remember keeping a tally on the inside cover of my copy of all the substances I had already tried. A small group of my classmates and I compared notes. I was more proud then than I am now, but I was ahead of my nearest classmate by at least half a dozen species. I was surprised that this barely put a dent in Lewin's catalog. I assumed that most of the substances in *Phantastica* were unobtainable in Red Stone, and I'll bet they were in 1978. That was my experience, anyway.

At the same time, Tina had thrown herself into filmmaking. I can only describe her enthusiasm as feverish. She went to class, too, mostly out of habit. But when she took notes in class, she was usually writing about the films she wanted to make. She wrote out scenarios and jotted down phrases that captured the images that sometimes flitted through her mind. Where other students sometimes doodled in the margins of their notebooks, she drew storyboards. These were usually not detailed or especially adept. Tina was not a gifted sketch artist, though her skills developed over time. However, these sketches were most often a shorthand for herself. She could sketch out the fundamentals of a shot, a mere

rectangle with additional scratches inside, and still be able to trans-
late it into magic on film.

She spent the better part of a week working on these notes and
ideas before she decided she was ready to make another film. She
caught me in a moment of boredom. I still wonder if she was
watching me and gauging my mood for a couple of days, waiting
for me to be restless enough that she could enlist me in her schemes
again. She said she wanted to go out and get some outdoor shots,
and she needed an actor. She knew I wasn't really an actor, and I
guess I knew she wasn't really asking for one. She wanted someone
she could point the camera at, and that was going to be me.

I brushed my hair after she made me change my clothes—something about contrast—and we took off on what seemed like a long
hike at first. When I asked what the film was about, she only said
that it was about being watched in the woods. I thought we would
head for one of the busier spots on campus like the student union,
but Tina said she wanted the setting to be more natural. I didn't
have to do anything, she insisted, other than hike through the forest and occasionally look off into the distance. I was up for a walk,
so I relaxed and enjoyed it, mostly.

Tina had her camera in its black leather bag slung over her shoulder as we left campus and struck out into a wooded area to the
south. The leaves were still mostly green at this point, though here
and there were bursts of bright orange and yellow. It's one of the
only things I miss about Red Stone. The summers were often lonely, and the winters brutal and long, but the autumn was always
glorious. When we had walked deep enough into the woods that
we couldn't easily see out of it, Tina readied the camera and then
briefly described what she wanted me to do. As she had promised,
I was a young woman hiking through the forest. She set up ahead
of me on a trail as I walked toward her, or she followed behind or
beside me as I sometimes looked at the ground and other times

looked ahead into the distance. Most of these shots must have been very short, because she only had one film cartridge with her that day. Fifty feet of film goes pretty quickly, unless you know precisely what you are doing.

Tina kept giving me brief instructions on where to look and whether to walk or not. She never told me what sort of expression I was supposed to have, or what sort of things this girl hiking through the woods was supposed to be feeling. And yet, the farther we hiked into the forest, and the more I looked around, the more I sensed that there *was* someone watching us. For one shot, I walked where Tina told me to walk, but in the middle of the shot I thought I heard something behind me, opposite from where Tina was positioned. I swung my head around, and of course there was nothing there. She asked if I was okay, and I said I was. What else was I going to say? But it got worse from there. I think back on it now, and Tina stopped telling me what to do. I walked on, keeping mostly to the path, but sometimes venturing off of it, seeking out something that I could only feel, never see. Tina stayed with me, her shots obviously coming in closer and closer all the time.

I felt compelled to scramble up a slope that brought me to a ridge line overlooking a river valley. Tina held back a bit as I did, shooting me from behind. When I crested the hill, I looked out over the valley, above the trees on the other side of the river. I was looking at the sky, which was gray and misty that day, not very beautiful. But I wasn't enraptured by it; I was terrified of it. Something in me needed to get to the top of the ridge where I could see the thing that dogged my steps through the woods, and for some reason I was sure that thing was hiding behind the gauzy gray in the sky above. A moment came when I began to doubt, when I realized that I was searching for something in the sky when that made no sense at all. I heard the wind-up motor of the camera running to my left. Tina was shooting me in profile as I stared into the air, looking for my pursuer. I understood then that this is what she wanted. I didn't look at her, though I felt the urge. I kept giving her what she wanted. Mostly, I always did.

I saw *The Eye* sometime later. The sequence of shots convinced me that it was mostly edited in camera; that is, she was shooting precisely what she wanted in exactly the order she wanted it. What this meant was that she was also capturing my growing dread at whatever it was that I felt was following me. It was a good performance, because the paranoia she captured is utterly genuine. Nothing happened, of course, and I felt pretty silly as we walked home (though I remember Tina as being especially happy), but you can see the fear on my face in those close-ups. What I can't account for is the eye. As I climb the slope to the ridge, there is a cut to a shot that must have been taken from roughly where I stood when I reached the top. It also looks out across the valley. Above the trees on the other side is an immense, staring eye. The first time I saw this effect, my stomach fluttered with a hint of queasiness. I could both see that it was an effect, a superimposition of some sort (it must have been), while I also failed to see any imperfections to suggest how it was done. It was just there, this eye, for a couple of lingering seconds. Suddenly, my ass filled the screen again, as the shot of me climbing the slope resumed. I reached the crest in a couple more seconds, and I stood there staring, my back to the camera. Cut to a close-up of me in profile, still staring into the distance. Another cut of the eye, its pupil pulsing ever so slightly, as though hungry for me. And then the eye gradually dissolves into nothing but the gray of the autumnal sky. The final shot is of my profile as I decide quite deliberately not to look at the camera. You can see the fear pass from my face. The muscles on the back of my neck relax. I exhale.

I asked Tina later how she did it, but she only smiled and evaded with a remark about movie magic. I remember thinking that she must have made friends with the home movie club. They called themselves the film club, but they mostly had older 8mm and some newer Super 8 cameras. Supposedly, there was a literature professor who had a 16mm camera, but we never met, as far as I know. After the Copperhead Mouth concert, I got a lot of subtle cues that we weren't seen as socially desirable, so I thought that Tina more or less stayed away from the club. They were the only people I knew who had any kind of editing equipment or who could have helped Tina figure out how to have the lab process her film the way she wanted it. As far as I knew, there was no way she could have done the composite work on her own. And then there was the question of how much special processing cost. Tina had proved herself willing to steal film cartridges here and there, though it wasn't something she could do all the time. But there was no way for her to shoplift processing. She needed to be able to pay for that, at least. Given how her notebooks were bursting with film ideas, she needed a way to finance her movies more reliably. So, she got a job.

Tina wasn't looking for a ton of money, so she wasn't very picky about the job. The only real criterion was that she needed to be able to walk to work. By the time she started looking, most of the work-study positions had been snatched up, so she needed to look off campus. A couple of applications at local stores didn't pan out; Tina wondered out loud if they knew that she had stolen from them. But she soon had luck at a roadhouse a mile or so from our dormitory. Barnstormers was a regionally famous restaurant back then. The owner came from a farm family, but he had no interest in farming. He didn't particularly have an interest in cooking either. His real interest was business. He was fascinated by franchises, and he thought the market was ripe for something bigger and more elaborate than the usual fast food. He sold off the family's acreage but kept the immense barn, which he converted into a flying circus-themed restaurant. In addition to the restaurant's sign, painted directly onto the side of the barn, the tail of an antique plane jutted up from behind the peak of the roof. Inside, a vintage Jenny biplane hung suspended upside down from the rafters, and a strange mix of aviation and carnival memorabilia cluttered the place. The fact that it sat across the road from Red Stone's tiny airfield probably both inspired the idea and lent it a certain weight of authenticity. Barnstormers never became the restaurant empire its owner hoped, but I understand it stayed in business until he retired a couple of years ago.

The owner started Tina out on the floor as a server; she had applied for that position, hoping to make as much money as she could with relatively few hours. He probably thought Tina was an exotic addition to his wait staff, where she might even be taken for someone of indigenous heritage. He should have known better. A significant number of his clientele were middle-aged World War II veterans, some of who had served in the Pacific. I think it only took a handful of shifts before Tina was given the option of leaving or switching to the back of the house, where the only open position was dishwasher. I never asked her about that choice, but she traded her waitress's half apron for the full version. Her hands suffered for it, but in the end she wound up making more money. That was her main goal.

In two or three weeks, Tina had balanced the hours at Barnstormers with her film needs. Her calculations didn't leave any time for studying, and eventually they even started to eat into her class time, too. She had fewer regular classes than I did, but she was supposed to be putting in studio hours, and those were the first things to go. Tina was good enough that she could skate by with little practice at first, but eventually her instructors were going to start nagging her on general principle. She was completely unconcerned. When her first paycheck came, she cashed it, bought three more film cartridges (two black and white and one Kodachrome this time, just to try it), and got to work.

Tina was out most days working on her films, as long as the weather allowed it. The film she usually bought could be used indoors with enough light, but she didn't often have the resources for that. Like early filmmakers, she was mostly restricted to working with large amounts of natural light. Luckily, Red Stone's location offers a lot of natural beauty, and it was easier for Tina to figure out a ride somewhere than it was for her to arrange for intense artificial lights or a cast or crew of more than two people. She stuck to what she knew she could arrange without much difficulty, and she let her creativity and inspiration run free within those bounds.

Her ability to get the composite effects she wanted was breathtaking. In her short *The Stairs*, I sat on the shore of Barnum Pond reading a dog-eared collection of Poe's stories and looking out over the water. Like she had on *The Eye*, Tina flitted around me, shooting from different distances and angles. She didn't have a tripod yet, but she had a wooden fruit crate with her that she could rest the camera on. She sometimes spent forever finding small rocks that she could use to prop the box just so, in order to achieve the framing she wanted. Though this could sometimes be frustrating, I was enjoying reading about the Red Death and thinking about the masquerade and all those decadent Italians who thought they could hide away from the end. I wasn't quite done with the story when Tina said that she had all the shots she needed. As we hitched back, I asked her what else she needed for that film, but she said it was done. Sure enough, she sent the cartridge off for processing the next day, since we didn't make it back to campus until after the drug store was closed.

When I got to see *The Stairs* later on, it was exactly what I expected for the first couple of minutes. There were establishing shots of the forest and the pond, shots of me walking along the edge of the road that skirts the water until I find a nice log to sit on. In the short, I make myself comfortable, and then I pull out my book. As I said, I had a paperback copy of some of Poe's short stories. I don't have that book any more, but I remember its cover distinctly. It was a blocky, almost cubist painting of a man with piercing eyes. There were several flights of impossible stairs, and a strangely jointed black cat. However, in the film, the cover seems different. It's never clearly in frame, but what you can see is not at all what I remember. Instead, there is a black cover with a muddy abstract design, but not cubist. There is one shot in the short, though, taken from behind me. Over my shoulder (or over the shoulder of some girl with hair like mine), you can read the same page I'm reading, only it's not "The Masque of the Red Death." It's not even a Poe story at all.

It's the first page of Act II of *The King in Yellow*.

It's only on screen for a second. Probably less. Maybe thirteen frames. But in that moment, what was merely a stomach flutter from watching *The Eye* becomes a vast emptiness. My gut feels so hollow, I can hear a dreadful wind inside. I can't read the words. But I have. I know what it is. I think it's only because I don't have the book in my hands that I am not consumed to a cinder on the spot. I have seen enough superstition to dismiss most legends of this kind, but I have never had a similar experience with the object of any other legend. I had heard of that evil play before, but just heard of it. No one had it. People said they did, but no one did. Just like people said they partied at Barron Circle, but no one really did.

And that's why what happens next in *The Stairs* somehow didn't shock me as much as it should. I look up from the banned book I hold in my hands and stare out across the water. In a point-of-view shot, we see Barnum Pond, but now there is a dark rectangle floating on the surface of the pond. It is difficult to estimate distance in the film, but the rectangle seems to be about fifty feet away and maybe six inches to a foot above the surface of the water. It is perfectly motionless; it does not bob on the water or float toward either side of the frame. The shot cuts back to me briefly as I stare at the rectangle. There is a sudden cut to an extreme close-up of me as I inhale. It seems like it could be a natural inhalation, but the sudden cut makes it seem apprehensive.

A return to the POV shot reveals a robed figure rising up out of the rectangle. The emergence of this figure forces the viewer to re-assess what she is seeing, and now it become more apparent that the rectangle is not floating at all. It is a stairwell from the bottom of the lake. *To the bottom of the lake.* This figure in its light-colored robe, its face hidden in a cowl, has risen from the murky depths of Barnum Pond to greet me. The film cuts back to the normal close-up of me. I smile now, warm and genuine, as I close my book and stand. I tuck a strand of hair behind my ear, and the film cuts to black.

CHAPTER FIVE

While we were making films and skipping classes, Tina's reputation grew. If she had been at all interested in dating any of the people we went to school with, it's possible that her first screening might have represented her social death at SUNY Red Stone. She had become the morbid filmmaker, the dark artist who had nothing but the most gruesome feelings for the tragedies of the world around her. Some of the speculation about her went beyond idle and fantastic gossip. There was a vicious racism to it, as well. Those sorts of comments weren't relegated to her shifts at Barnstormers. More than once, I heard the slurs and stories that were making the rounds about the "chink" or the "jap" that I lived with, and how she was a soulless, crazy "dragon lady."

When I first heard these characterizations, I didn't know how to respond. I think it's been hard for me to recognize that. I saw Tina as different, and I think some of that had to do with her ethnicity; I'm not beyond or above these things as unconscious reactions. Maybe none of us are. What pains me more is that it took me so long to become aware of how Tina must have felt about it. She had to have seen the looks and heard the comments, felt the invisible repelling force some people emit when it comes to race. When I heard about or witnessed these slights, I was confused, and hurt, and angry, more or less all at the same time. But even though I counted Tina as a good friend, and we had certainly been through a lot in the several months we knew each other, there was so much about her that I didn't know. In the fall of 1978, that extended to her ethnicity and family history. We like to think that we are living in an enlightened age with regard to race, even now, Rodney King and the L.A. riots notwithstanding, but let me tell you we thought that in the late 1970s, too. We had been through the civil rights movement, or our parents had, and feminism was all around us. There had been the AIM movement. We felt very aware. But what many felt at the time, and what many of us still feel, is the paralyzing fear of talking about race openly with each other, especially across ethnic divides. I had not asked about Tina's background at that point, and if you asked me why, and I had been inclined to be what I thought was honest, I would have told you it was because that didn't matter to me. Maybe there is some truth to that, but the bigger truth is that I didn't want it to matter, so that we didn't have to talk about it. What I didn't stop to think about was that it obviously mattered to Tina. She may have not talked about it all that much, but of course it touched her. It couldn't help but touch her.

I learned the details that I was allowed to learn over the course of the next couple of years. Tina was American by way of Japan, Peru, Texas, New Jersey, and finally New York. Her great-great-uncle had come to Peru from Japan in 1899 on the *Sakura Maru*, and a few years later encouraged his brother, Tina's great-great-grandfather, to do the same. These brothers remained in Peru and eventually were able to bring over wives-to-be and start families within the Peruvian-Japanese community that was thriving there. But by World War II, Peru threw in its lot with the United States, and as a condition of their alliance, the U.S. demanded that they be allowed to deport most of the Peruvian-Japanese population to internment camps in the southern U.S. Tina's family was interned at a camp in Kenedy,

Texas, until they were sent to work on farms in New Jersey in 1944. At the end of the war, Tina's family chose to stay in New Jersey, where her father grew up, though he had been born in Peru. The older members of the family mostly socialized within the relatively tight community of former internees who remained in New Jersey, but Tina's father grew up in New Jersey public schools. He did his best to turn away from their insular community and fit in with the other American kids. In some ways, Tina's father is the one who shouldered most of the burden of the family's assimilation. He was the one who other kids picked on mercilessly and blamed for Pearl Harbor and taunted about Hiroshima and Nagasaki, even though none of those events meant anything more to him than they did to any other American kid. He found himself not Japanese and not American in what appeared to be conspicuous Japanese skin.

Tina's father's reaction to all of this was to fight hard to be seen as American. He shunned his parents' advice and culture as a teenager and did his best to emulate some of the people who were treating him the worst at school and around the neighborhood. Shuichi had an aptitude for piano and applied himself eagerly in his music classes, but his classmates were merciless and his performances suffered. He eventually drifted into his school's vocational program where he discovered that his ability to learn and in some cases master machinery earned him the indifference of other students and his teachers, if not their respect. This was better than the treatment he got in many of his other classes, so he took the first opportunity that came his way when it came to work. In his junior year of high school, he got a job on the factory floor at a South Jersey manufacturer of pre-fabricated diners.

It was sometime during that first year of working at the diner factory that Shuichi must have caught the eye of Joyce Fitzgerald, the teenage daughter of Candace and Theodore Fitzgerald, who owned the factory. Tina tells a family story that her father heard

Joyce playing the piano one day as he passed by their house on his walk from the factory to a bus stop a few miles away. He stopped for a moment to listen, because her playing was so beautiful, and then he caught a glimpse of her through the window. Joyce saw him, too—saw him wave as if in a trance—and she smiled back at him. And that was it. By the time he graduated high school, they were in love and planning to elope.

The Fitzgeralds were broad-minded enough to employ Shuichi in their factory, but contemplating his marriage to their daughter was too much for them. They did not approve the union, and for years the couple was on their own. They tried to stay on in Bridgeton, but the community was too small, and the Fitzgeralds loomed too large. The Moris moved to Queens within a year. Shuichi worked odd jobs at first, but eventually found steady work in a factory uptown where no one cared about his background.

And this, in 1960, is when Tina came into the picture. As with many interracial couples, concerned parents and friends and strangers on the street say to "think of the children." This is simply racism. It is the fear of the mixed blood child, the fear that boundaries will weaken, that categories on which the world rests will tumble and fall, and then where will we be? Tina's father was all for giving his new daughter as American a name as they could think of, but his young wife was still fascinated by her husband and his family's unusual history. She suggested a compromise. She felt destiny had brought them together in New York, so she wanted to name their daughter Destina out of respect for his family's multiple generations of history in Peru. They settled on Destina Junko Mori, and they called her Tina for short. Shuichi initially bristled at the thought that his daughter's name was used to honor his parents' and their parents' choices, but in his private moments he saw how shrewd the choice was. To the extent possible, it allowed Tina the chance to be accepted by all of the people in her life at that time.

She could be Destina or Tina, as she saw fit.

She used to tell me that she preferred Tina not because it was the more familiar version of her name in American culture, but because she always cringed from the implications of her full name. Destina was an even bigger burden to bear than her ethnicity, which was something that she had been born with and was able to get to know as she grew up. She learned to be aware of how people might treat her based on how she looked and what they thought that meant. But being named Destiny is a reminder that we are all sentenced to hurtle toward some unknown fate.

This is all to say that things got a bit more difficult for Tina in Red Stone after the incident at her first screening. But not everything was bad then, and we wound up with an opportunity that got us out of town for a while. I came back from class one day not long before fall exams to find Tina reading a card she had received in the mail.

"What do you think of this?"

Tina handed me the card. It was bigger than a business card, but it wasn't a folded greeting card. This was a single card with an embossed and filigreed design on the front that held the name Dr. Jean L. Holly in calligraphic script. On the back, was this note:

Ms. Mori,

I have heard wonderful things about the film you screened last month at the rock and roll concert. I would be honored to make your acquaintance and to have the opportunity to discuss your work at greater length. Please call on me at your earliest convenience any day after 9:00pm at the back door of the Resurrection Cemetery gatehouse. I

should be very grateful if you would bring the film
with you.

Yours,
Dr. Jean L. Holly

"I have no idea," I said.

"Me neither. I looked up the name. He's not faculty at Red
Stone."

"Woodbury, maybe?"

"Maybe," Tina said. "I kinda think probably not, though. He
could be a doctor doctor. Not a professor. He might not even be
a *he*."

I had seen the gatehouse once or twice before. It was an elaborate
Victorian pile made from the signature red sandstone from the local
quarries. It was actually built right into the extensive red sandstone
wall and wrought iron gate that stretched across the front of Resurrection Cemetery, which itself lay on the outskirts of the village in a
heavily forested section of the riverbank. It was a great place to take
a walk in the nicer weather, but I always got there by taking a path
through the woods along the river's edge, and so I rarely entered
the cemetery past the gatehouse. Though it was obviously a house,
and a rather large one, I never thought for a moment that someone
actually lived there, and certainly never thought that person was
some kind of doctor. That seemed, I don't know, perverse.

"Are you going?" I said.

She shook her head slowly, almost absently, but then she suddenly stopped and put the card down on her bed.

"I'm going to go," she said with a firm nod. "Tonight. Will you
come with me?"

Since the screening, I had been wondering if I was simply getting
into too much trouble hanging out with Tina. It's not very honor-

able, I know, but I was thinking of ways that I might be able to ditch her next semester. It's not that I thought she was doing any of this on purpose or that she was even a bad person in any way. It was more that I thought bad things or bad energy surrounded her, and in that I'm not sure that I was wrong. I think there was something that hung around her, unbidden and unseen.

"Of course, I'll come." I had to say yes. It felt like she was asking for help, and no matter what my misgivings were at the time, I felt acutely that people were giving her a lot of shit that she didn't deserve, and I wanted to be there for her when she needed me.

The wait until we could go to the gatehouse was excruciating. We had picked up our mail in the afternoon, and both of our classes were over for the day. It was too early for a movie, and the only thing we could do to pass the time was to eat some dinner. Tina wasn't hungry, or so she said, but she stayed with me while I ate. We didn't stay long, though, as both of us became aware of the stares and the whispers. I felt like there had to be somewhere else we could go, but there wasn't. Nowhere else but our room. So we went back and put on the radio, listening to WQRY (We Know Rock), the college's station and their list of rock music for the kids. This was working well for me, but I could tell that it wasn't doing much to help Tina. I tried to get her to play silly games with me, but she was somewhere else the whole time.

"You're not nervous about this, are you?"

She shrugged. "It's not this exactly. I mean, I'm not nervous about Dr. Holly or whoever he is, but...I don't know. I think a lot about Donny."

"It's not your fault—"

"I know. It's not that. I don't know if I can describe it. It's like electric current or something. I feel this power surging between me and Donny's death and the film I made. I didn't kill him. I don't feel responsible. But I do feel this connection. I feel it all the time."

"Do you feel it with other things? Other people?"

She nodded.

"Tina, have you made any films without me?"

She didn't answer immediately. She got up from the bed where she had been laying and paced around the small room. She went over to her desk where the small spool of film containing the film of Donny's last modeling session rested in its little cardboard box. She picked it up and held it, turned it over and over in her hands.

"I feel like I should get rid of this."

"You mean throw it away? Destroy it?"

"No, I mean I think I need to give it away. I feel like I shouldn't have it anymore, but I don't think I could destroy it."

"Well, maybe this Holly guy will want it. He wants to talk to you about it anyway. This might be your chance."

"Let's go," she said.

"It's early, but we can take the trail and walk around in the cemetery for a while, if you want."

Of course, not everyone wanted to walk through a cemetery under those circumstances, let alone stroll around aimlessly to kill time, but Tina and I weren't most people. It was dark and cold. There was a lot of moon visible that night as we walked from our dorm all the way into the village and across the bridges that stretched from one shore to Mill Island to the other shore. Just past the second bridge, a small trailhead opened along the river, disappearing into the tall and leafless trees that stretched into the sky, black or silver as their share of the moonlight dictated. From the bridge, we could see the tombstones that dotted the sloping verge of the cemetery about a half mile up river.

The trail took us pretty close to the Diaper Hill apartments where some of the younger faculty lived. I usually didn't think much of it, but in the winter, the greenery didn't conceal you from their windows or vice versa, and the moonlight made it more likely that someone in those apartments could see moving silhouettes on the trail. It's not that the trail was private in any way, but I wasn't interested in even a friendly stop by the police, and I was pretty sure that we were not allowed in the cemetery after dark. Tina wasn't saying anything as we walked, so I did my best to imagine myself as invisible as we trudged along the path toward the graveyard.

It took very little time for us to reach the edge of the forest near the red sandstone wall that divided the groomed space of the cemetery from the back road. At the far end of the wall from where we were, the dark stone chimney and peaked roof of the gatehouse rose above us, and between the house and us the wall was pierced by its great stone and wrought iron gate, with its enormous Celtic cross. It was a dramatic piece of architecture for such a sleepy little town. At the moment, I'll admit that the incongruity struck me as more sinister than absurd. From where we were, I could see a weathered plywood sign painted a thin coat of white with the hand-painted word NIGHTCRAWLERS scrawled on it. When I saw it, I immediately read it as an advertisement, and it took my mind a while to realize that it was far too late in the season for someone to be selling worms to fishermen. By the time we were well away from the house and walking into the grounds of the cemetery proper, I had dismissed the oddity as a sign of neglect. Surely nightcrawlers were only available during the summer months. The ground wasn't yet frozen, but neither was it yielding up very many worms, I thought.

I breathed easier as we came to the first intersection in the paved paths that ran through the cemetery. The frequent trees meant that there was a thrilling zebra-like pattern of shadows cast over the ground and the tombstone.

We could soon see the few and feeble lights from the center of the village, the spire of the great sandstone church on Mill Island as well as the truly impressive monuments that some families had erected for their loved ones. We stayed mostly quiet while we walked, though I suspect that some of this had to do with a kind of superstitious respect for the dead. I don't think either of us was scared to be in a cemetery at night. Other people might have been, and we had heard the occasional scary story about this one, but the stories weren't much different than a hundred other stories that teenagers might tell one another about graveyards in their town. Campfire tales. There are creatures that roam there after dark. People have gone missing. Lovers, usually.

We gained the porch of the gatehouse, warmed from our fearful exercise. I hadn't noticed it before, but a dim light glowed from behind the front door.

"The note said come to the back door," I reminded Tina.

She nodded and we turned to go back down the short stairs. I could tell that neither of us wanted to go around back, closer to the woods, where there were certainly no lights glowing.

There were actually two back doors on the gatehouse; both of them were round-topped Gothic-style doors. They looked like they opened onto the same space, so Tina knocked on the one closest to us. We heard nothing for more than a minute, a long minute. Tina was about to knock again when we heard some rustling from behind the door. I looked at Tina and took a deep breath. Maybe I am trying to make myself feel better, but we did feel like we had left something behind in that cemetery and we were unsure of what we were running to in this house, no matter how fancy his notecards were.

Dr. Holly answered the door himself. When he did, he failed to turn on a light in the back space, which we soon learned opened into the kitchen and pantry spaces of the gatehouse.

"Please forgive the darkness, but I'm very sensitive to the light. Come in and give your eyes a moment to adjust, then I think you will be able to find your way to the sitting room."

His voice had the force of intelligence behind it, you could tell, but there was a disturbing quality to it, a sort of breathy squeak that grated on my nerves like nails on a chalkboard. We did as he said and waited in that space near the pantry and off the kitchen until the moonlight streaming through the uncovered windows was enough to guide our way without injuring ourselves.

"Ready? Then please follow me."

Holly led us through the kitchen into a dusty room that had once been a dining room but whose oblong table (probably big enough to seat twelve) was covered in boxes and scrapbooks and record albums. Here there was a faint odor of the same cigarillos smoked by the man who drove us to the barn party. At one end was an ancient typewriter with chipped black paint in between two unequal towers of typescript pages. He opened a set of French doors and led us into a very comfortable sitting room. When we were inside, he closed the French doors and drew a pair of heavy curtains.

"I know this must seem strange to you. Please forgive the lengths to which I am forced to go to preserve my nerves." He closed the doors behind us. "I will sit here. When I am seated with my mask on, please feel free to turn on the small table lamp behind me."

Holly lowered himself into the roomy wingback chair, the back of which rose well above the top of his head. Tina wasn't moving, but I was craving light, so I moved toward the table as our host took a carnival mask from the small table next to his chair and slipped it onto his face. At his signal, I switched on the light.

The sitting room was also evidently a library, or Holly wanted as many discussion pieces as possible, because the room was lined with floor-to-ceiling shelves that were themselves filled with books and busts and several exotic pieces that I had never seen anything like before. There was a lot of the place that I could see was straight out of the Victorian era, mixed in with some Gilded Age decadence and shot through with the strangeness that I came to associate with Holly.

"Did you bring the film?"

Tina reached into her coat pocket and took out the small cardboard box that held the reel. Holly leaned forward and reached out his hand.

"May I?" Tina hesitated a moment before she also leaned forward and placed the box in his hand. "It feels so light, don't you find? Too light for all the heavy emotions that are wound around this core."

"What do you want with it," I said.

"I am a collector. I want to collect it."

"How did you know about it?" Tina said.

"Though I don't ever leave this house, I do have assistants to go out into the wider world to do my business for me. One of these assistants was at the event where your singular film was screened—on some other unrelated matter—and told me about it. Whatever we might say about Copperhead Mouth's music, they were quite willing to give you credit as a collaborator." Holly produced one of the flyers that Skinny had printed and spread all over town that did mention Tina Mori as the creator of the cinematic accompaniment. "You were not especially difficult to find."

"What's your interest?" I asked. Tina looked at me, but Holly's masked face revealed nothing at all.

"Are you willing to sell this film to me, Ms. Mori?"

"I don't know. How much?"

"I am prepared to pay seventy-five dollars for this film."

"Right now?" I asked.

"Immediately."

"One hundred and fifty," said Tina. Holly's mask dipped slightly as he chuckled.

"Ms. Mori, let's not speak in absurdities. I am interested in acquiring your film. I am offering you a frankly exorbitant sum for it. How much does a single cartridge of film cost these days?"

Tina shrugged. "Three bucks, if you actually pay for it."

"Seventy-five dollars is a lot for one reel of film, but you lead with that offer, so I doubt you think it's too much," I said. Tina looked at me again, this time with some surprise. "Obviously we're here because of the value that Tina has added to this reel of film through her talent. For that kind of talent, I don't think one hundred and twenty-five is out of line."

"I most certainly do. However, I am willing to offer you one hundred dollars for the film, if you will also promise to do me a favor."

"A hundred?"

"And a favor."

"What favor?" asked Tina.

"As I said, I often employ assistants to do things that I am unable to see to on my own. I have a task which requires travel to New York City, and none of my current assistants is able to help in this matter."

"What do you need in the city?"

"A former associate of mine took something from me, a keepsake of considerable sentimental value to me, and I need someone who can go down to the city, locate the item, and bring it back to me."

"You want us to steal something for you?"

"The object is mine. I am asking you to retrieve it, not steal it. Though my former associate has chosen to discard our friendship over this matter, I daresay that he and his friends are people that you might like to know. They are currently engaging in some rather exciting experiments in avant-garde cinema not unlike the one that brings you here. I imagine that you have found it difficult to meet like-minded artists here in Red Stone. I find it very easy to believe that you would have much to learn from one another."

"You pay for our bus tickets, and you have a deal."

"I will pay for one such ticket." Tina and I looked at each other.

"Okay," I said.

Holly took a scrap of paper and a fountain pen from a nearby table. He unscrewed the cap slowly, and I noticed his delicately shaped and rather long nails. They shined in the muddy lamplight as though they were polished. Holly scribbled on the paper and showed it to me. It was the same sign I had seen on the bottom of the glass at the barn party. The moment I recognized it, my stomach lurched as though I were on a roller coaster. I exhaled sharply so that I could take a deep breath and steady myself. I was worried I was going to be sick, but it never tipped into nausea.

Dr. Holly moved the paper to show Tina. She stared at it, seemingly unmoved.

"No problem," she said.

CHAPTER SIX

Tina and I hadn't fully discussed what we were doing when we got on the bus to New York City, but neither of us thought that we were leaving school for good. Maybe the college would have preferred it if we never came back. It's not that we were particularly troublesome, but I got the impression that there were people who worked for the college administration, often glasses-wearing squares who thought that anything that smelled different was somehow a threat to their way of life. At the very least, both of us felt that we could use some time away from campus to let the things die down and for us to get a better sense of perspective. I don't know that we needed that perspective, but I'm sure that a lot of the adults in our lives at the time thought that we did.

There was something very freeing about that trip for both of us. We had enough money to get down there and stay a little while if we were careful, and if we managed to get Holly's bauble back for him, there was the vague promise of a reward on top of what he had already paid us. I guess I should say what he had already paid Tina. There was an unspoken agreement that we were a team, but when it came to the actual films and the money that came from them, it was always Tina who was being paid. No mistake there. She never skimped on me or asked me to pay for myself. Neither of us was rich, but there was a kind of sisterhood about our adventures for those couple of years. It wasn't that we pooled our money, but I think that we were both always aware that there were two of us who needed to eat and who needed a place to sleep and so on. Later on, there were times when I was the one who was bringing in more of the money, but neither of us was ever making so much that there was any room for resentment to seep in. Our jealousies came from sources other than gold.

The bus from Red Stone down to the city was a rusty death trap until we changed buses in Albany. The broken seats kept us awake through the first half of the trip, so that both Tina and I slouched against one another on the more open roads of the second half of the trip. We slept fitfully through the Hudson Valley, both of us wanting to be as rested as possible when we arrived in Manhattan. We had both been around—me probably more so than Tina—but neither of us could fully shake the sense we had of our destination as a dark and rotting canyon of danger. Tina had grown up in Queens, but she spent very little time outside the borough, and even then it was rarely in Manhattan.

The address that Holly had given us was in Alphabet City, which would be easy to find, but it was in the center of a part of the city that was run down and trash-filled. The fancies that Tina and I built in our minds before we got down there were far worse than what we actually found, but they weren't different in kind, only in degree. In so many ways, the city fathers had abandoned that neighborhood, and a whole society of immigrants, misfits, and outcasts had turned it into their home, their playground, and their stalking fields. We didn't know what we were getting into, but we had told ourselves stories.

Our bus slid into its Port Authority berth in the middle part of the afternoon, and the gray overcast that promised but perpetually withheld snow gave us twilight far earlier than it did in the North

Country. I could feel the night coming, and we still needed to get down to a few blocks beyond Union Square. Tina and I hurried for the subway, finding our way down to 14th and then over to Union Square, where we came out of the underground station. Only the pale blue of the sky between the buildings let us know that it wasn't night yet. Both of us were apprehensive when we topped the stairs, and we stood on the sidewalk letting the reality of the scene we had been imagining sink in before we stepped off toward our goal. I hoped we weren't gawking, but anyone who stands on the sidewalk in Manhattan and looks around at their surroundings is likely to be taken for either a tourist or a crazy person. Tina grabbed hold of my sleeve and tugged me in the direction of our destination.

If I had taken a photograph of the streets that afternoon, there would be a lot about it that was precisely what both of us expected. The buildings were mainly older and falling into serious neglect when they were not completely burned out or demolished. There were certainly shady characters moving about on missions that only they knew, and we rarely saw a police car or a uniformed officer on the beat. But the busier streets also had a kind of energy that I didn't expect. There were people, most of them immigrants, making a home out of this place, and they were living their lives the way that millions of people lived their lives in other places. Though there were empty store fronts, there were also many open stores, and people came and went and congregated in delis and bodegas and locksmiths and pawn shops and bars. There was something vibrant there amid all of the trash that we expected to find.

The less-traveled streets were different. Here is where we found something less inviting than the more romantic shops and convivial atmosphere of 14th or 4th. These were the streets where sudden vacant lots yawned into blackness between crumbling tenements. Trash was piled everywhere, and the stench from it was harder to avoid, or it was less mixed in with gasoline and diesel fumes. There was more shit and piss in the air, and fewer lights anywhere to promise respite from the dimness and dankness that pervaded everything. We saw fewer families and more solitary figures, talking to themselves or to no one, floating through this world even though they looked like they were seeing another world entirely. This is where we were going, and I'm a bit ashamed to say that the increasing gloom was getting to me the farther we got from the busier streets. Tina did her best to project confidence and familiarity, but we both knew that she had never walked these streets before. Growing up in Queens didn't make her any more comfortable than I was.

The growing sense that we were not entirely safe on these streets ensured that neither of us slackened our pace, though. We kept on until we arrived at the front door to the building where Holly had said we could find his precious *objet d'art*. It was a yellowed six-story apartment building with dozens of blank windows overlooking the street. Here and there on its facade, the windows had been boarded up, while others were open to the elements. A small handful emitted dim light from behind makeshift blinds or curtains fashioned from old sheets or newspapers or posters. From somewhere inside, we could hear music, its screeching chords cutting through us like knives.

There was no trouble getting into the building, since the front door had been removed long ago. The first-floor entryway was carpeted with the dried sludge footprints of people who had come in from the winter, though we could only tell this by the feeble light from the street. There were no lights in the first-floor lobby, though there was a naked bulb in the stairwell that we could see from where we entered. As we turned toward this light, an enormous fart, raucous and wet, erupted from beneath a pile of trash heaped beneath a bank of mailboxes built into the wall. Tina and I nearly sprinted to the stairs when we heard it, but we were laughing by the time we were halfway up the flight. I don't know about her, but I was rapidly losing context for whether or not I should be afraid. It looked dangerous, smelled horrible, and sounded like some medieval fair. My adrenaline was up and I was wide awake. I remember taking the third and fourth flights of stairs with a bitter metallic taste in my mouth, and wondered if I had bitten my tongue or cheek somewhere along the way, but it wasn't the coppery taste of blood.

We didn't see anyone else until we reached the sixth floor where we expected to find the apartment we were looking for. On the very top step of that flight, there was a couple, maybe a little older than Tina and me, kissing each other, their hands appearing and disappearing about their clothes with a serpentine fluidity. The lights had become a bit more reliable on the fifth and sixth floor so that we could see more or less everything, or at least we felt that there were no shadows deep enough for anyone or anything (larger than a rat) to hide. For that reason, we took these lovers as a welcome rather than a warning, and we set about looking for #6D.

The doors we found may have been numbered and lettered in some past life, but they had long ago lost any coherent sense of alphanumeric identity. Some had fragments of numbers and letters so damaged and partial that they looked more like alien hieroglyphs, but even these were in the minority. There were now more apt to sport graffiti or fully realized paintings or shellacked magazine cutouts as the only way to help strangers find their way. But all of this turned out to make a certain kind of sense. Architecturally there may have been multiple apartments on the sixth floor of that building, and I'll bet that's what you'd find there today. But that night and for the time that we were there in the city, that floor was all one space. No one had a sense of this place is mine and that place is yours. We were simply at the place itself, and somewhere inside was the person we wanted to see.

The one clue we had that helped us to navigate our way into this looking glass world was that of all the doors on the sixth floor hall, only one of them was open and emitting the screeching music that we had heard down below. When we reached the doorway, I immediately thought of what I saw as a party, but as we moved into the room full of smoke and bodies and sound, I wondered if it was an orgy or a hell or someone's living nightmare. It took me a couple of weeks to realize that this was just like any other day.

At first, no one paid much attention to us. There was no friendly welcome or hostile confrontation. No one took any notice of us at all. From the front room, where about half a dozen people sat on chairs and a couch and the floor smoking and nodding out, either listening to the blistering music or doing their best to live through it, we could see the kitchen. Tina and I both moved toward it as a place where we could regroup and try to figure out what to do next. Mercifully, the screeching ended before we reached the kitchen doorway, though the ringing in my ears continued.

The kitchen at first felt like a refuge, but that feeling slipped away in moments. A man in frayed black formal wear sat at a small aluminum and linoleum table. His hair was big and black and wild, and his face was painted white with theatrical highlights around his eyes and cheeks. Those eyes held deep reserves of instability. He stared straight into Tina and me as he took a deep drag on a yellow cigarette that I could smell from across the room. I felt as though I was transfixed. I couldn't have moved even if I wanted to.

"Who are you?" He affected this accent that careened between faux-British and laughable German.

"I'm Tina; this is C.C. A friend of ours told us that we could find Paul here." The guy took another deep drag and blew out the smoke so that he should watch us through a screen of his own making.

"Paul who?"

"Steiner." In order to look away from his eyes, I forced myself to inventory the items laid out neatly on the table in front of him. I couldn't guess what everything was that I saw, but I quickly guessed that he had an entire pharmacopeia at his disposal.

"Paul's working right now. What do you two want with him?"

"A friend of ours from Dorchester said that we should look him up when we got to the city. She said he was the guy to talk to about the real movie scene."

"Did she?" Now he looked at me. "Movie scene?" I nodded; I knew that Tina was signaling me to give her some help. The Dorchester reference meant that I should get in on this and that we should lie about why we were there. "You are fans, one presumes?"

"Haven't seen any of his stuff yet, so how should we know? That's why we're here," I said.

"Paul's work is singular in the extreme, but to truly see what he sees, you need to be in the proper frame of mind." He stood up from his chair and grabbed a tea cup from the kitchen sink. The handle had broken off, and the cup was obviously far from clean. "Paul's work is like a house with many windows. If you look in through the wrong window, you won't see anything interesting. I can help you find just the right angle."

He moved back to the table, opened a small leather drawstring pouch and grabbed a clump of some kind of tea leaves or vegetable matter of some other kind, dropping it into the cup and then drowning it in wine from a large glass jug. He held the cup out to us.

"You'll need this first before we go see Paul." I took the cup from his hand, though I had seen Tina begin to reach for it. I lifted it to my mouth, inhaled. Though instantly more on guard, I was not shocked. Behind the syrupy smell of the Gallo, there was a peppery aroma battling it out with a sharper chemical one.

"The kava is a nice touch," I said. "A traditional welcome to strangers. Good for smoothing awkward negotiations. The quaaludes are a bit much, though." Tina shot me a look before glaring at Crazy Eyes.

"Trying to drug us?" she said.

"Normally, I'd be cool about it, but this is a little overdone," I said.

"What's going on in here?" A tall guy with dark curly hair and a shaggy beard had slipped into the kitchen with us. His lips were thick and friendly, and his eyes, though refracted through bottle-bottom glasses, were eminently sane. "Everyone doing all right?"

Crazy Eyes looked away, back to his pharmacopeia on his little table, and you could tell that this was an exchange they'd had before.

"Swayne-o sometimes has an over-developed sense of hospitality," he said. "Did you guys just get here?"

Tina and I let ourselves be led out of the kitchen and back into the front room. I still had the cup in my hand, and for some reason, I kept it. I think maybe I felt more comfortable, even knowing what was in it, having a drink in my hand in that squat.

"Yeah," Tina said. "We're looking for Paul."

"What's your name?" I asked, wanting to do a little better this time around.

"Well, it's not Paul, unfortunately." It was a line; Shaggy was working us, too, or he was working Tina. I felt his eyes move over both of us as he maneuvered us away from Swayne, but his gaze came to rest on her face, and it only moved to mine a moment after I said something. He reached out his hand to Tina. "I'm Hack."

I introduced the two of us, and Hack gestured around the room and named some names. Only one or two of the people he named looked in our direction, but it felt good to have a little bit more context for where we were, who we were with. Even so, still no Paul.

"Swayne-o said that Paul was at work," Tina said to Hack. He smiled.

"At work, huh? Yeah, I guess so. Come on."

Hack led us out of the main room and down a narrow hall back to what we supposed must have been the bedrooms and maybe a bathroom, even if only a cold water one. We did pass rooms, though at the time I thought of them more as booths or dens. The tableaux I saw in them reminded me of carnival sideshows or dioramas at a natural history museum. In one room, bodies lay motionless on the floor, covered in tattered blankets, extra clothes, or in some cases newspapers and other trash. I had to give it a double-take to see that they were sleeping, or completely passed out. The next room held two young men sitting cross-legged on a mattress on the floor; they were talking intently to one another, but when we walked by, the one facing toward the door nodded to Hack. We were about halfway down the hall when we came upon an opening in the other side of the hallway. Until that point, the rooms had all opened from one side of the hallway, but here the wall had been forcibly knocked down with sledgehammers. An irregular archway had been opened in the brick, wood slats, and plaster. As we passed through this opening, we got a momentary glimpse of the dark and chittering world that exists between the rooms, between the walls, and I shuddered as I wondered what exactly these people had unleashed into their lives by opening up the walls in this way.

Our trek through the labyrinth of the squat continued, and I started to worry about whether or not I could find my way back. For the first few minutes, I was paying attention to our turns, trying to remember landmarks in this place, but it didn't take long before the things I saw and heard and smelled distracted me from that task, and the alternating hot and cold rooms (we occasionally entered a space that had windows open to the night air) worked to make me sleepy and a bit nauseous. The sights and sounds were

blending together. There were people eating and talking and singing and dancing and pissing and fucking and reading poetry to no
one in particular. And when we finally got to the room where Hack
was leading us, we found Paul and three other people making a
movie.

Steiner was a guy of middle height but powerfully built under
his cowboy shirt and blue jeans. However, his obvious strength was
mitigated by the golden fast food paper crown he wore. He was in
the middle of this apartment's living room, though all this room
held in the way of furniture was a rickety dinner table, four mis-
matched chairs, and a handful of photoflood lights in shiny metal
reflectors clamped here and there. Even the table was not standing
on its own accord, but had two extra pieces of wood nailed in place
underneath it to stabilize it. The walls were filled with graffiti and
what looked like sketches for murals, or they might be the musings
of a single person with a lot of room and no shortage of crayons.
The actors sitting at the table were doing their best to offer game
portrayals of a stereotypical family. The dad had blocky glasses and
a pipe, the mom had a torn dress that fell off her shoulder and
lipstick smeared across her mouth, and their daughter was older
than either of them, but her pigtails and skirt hinted at who she
was supposed to be.

Hack motioned for us to stay still and watch from the doorway,
since Paul was in fact still working. He was orbiting the melodrama
with a newer and far more American Super 8 camera than the one
that Tina used. The father character was reading a newspaper and
chewing on his pipe, while the mother hammed up her desperate
yearning for a more interesting life, a better-hung husband, and a
prettier kid. And then, very suddenly, everything went sideways.
Paul stopped moving around the table and zeroed in on the daughter who reached her hand under the hem of her skirt. She had
turned away from the table enough to be able to flash Paul if she

wanted to, or if he wanted her to. While she was moving her hand around in her crotch, she smiled and rolled her head in ecstasy before she ultimately pulled a long and wicked-looking fish flaying knife with a white plastic handle out from between her legs. With a lightning fast arc and a terrible shriek, the flaying knife scribed a perfect line across her mother's throat. The mother didn't react at all at first, but a moment later, an arterial rush painted the back of the father's newspaper red, and that's when the mother screamed.

I was about to let loose with a scream of my own when I realized that Tina was giddy and nearly bouncing up and down, trying not to laugh. Hack was grinning ear to ear, and Paul was zooming in on the streaks of blood on the newsprint first and then panning to the look of exaggerated shock on the dad's face and then on to the triumphant sexual joy of the daughter.

"Fuck! That's it."

Paul backed away from the gory family, as though the spell had been broken. "Reel's done," he explained to the daughter, who was acting out her disappointment in the same melodramatic mode.

As Paul opened the camera and removed the film cartridge, Tina grabbed my hand and nodded at him. A small onyx medallion with the symbol we were looking for shone darkly between Paul's collar bones. The item that Dr. Holly had sent us to retrieve was dangling from his neck on a black cord. I had the same visceral reaction to it when I saw it that I did at the gatehouse, and that made me think back to the barn party and its strangeness. I hadn't realized until that moment how far off track I had been feeling in the city. Every step we took led us further and further away from what it was we were supposed to be doing, not that I could have articulated what we were supposed to be doing. Life is weird like that sometimes. But seeing that symbol dangling around Paul's neck brought it all back and made a weird kind of sense. We had been sent to New York to find Paul Steiner and retrieve this little item that both Tina and I were staring at right then. It simultaneously brought things into focus and frightened me.

"Now's our chance, I think," Hack said to Tina. He led the way into the room.

"Paulie, do you want me to save this blood?" The mom was languidly turning toward us as blood continued to shoot out from her neck, but as we got closer to them I now noticed her left hand down in her lap that was squeezing a bag filled with stage blood. Paul set the expended film cartridge on the table and then went over to the corner of the room where I could now see that there was a battered doctor's bag on the floor. He opened that up and rummaged around a bit before swearing under his breath.

"No more film?" This from the daughter, whose voice gave away that she was a man in drag.

"No more Kodachrome. All I have left is black and white."

"I've got some," said Tina.

Everyone turned to look at her. The dad looked over the tops of his blocky glasses. Paul looked at her through his camera's viewfinder as he walked over from the corner of the room. Tina reached into her bag and pulled out the yellow and red box.

"It's my last one, though," she said.

Paul looked at Hack.

"Got any cash on you?"

"Sorry, man."

"We could use a place to stay, though," I said.

Paul looked at me and smiled broadly.

"Plenty of room! Is it a deal?" Tina nodded. I think she wanted to see him keep working. She would have given him the film, but she was aware that it was her last roll at the time, and she thought about those cartridges like gas on a road trip. She was always aware of how much was left in the tank, and she was always trying to figure out where the next gas station was.

"Cut that out," Paul said to the mom, who was seriously depleting her supply of plasma.

In moments, Paul and his troupe were back at it. There were more close-ups and reaction shots that he wanted to get, and he needed some shots of the ruby red arc, if he could get them. While we were standing in the doorway, still doing our best to stay out of the way of the shoot, two girls came up to us from behind and dragged Hack away from the makeshift movie studio. He made gestures toward us as though he intended to catch up with us later, but I could tell we were essentially on our own. This was not entirely a bad thing, as we needed to figure out how to get that necklace away from Paul. Tina was so enthralled by watching him work, that I wasn't sure she was even interested in the whole reason we were there anymore.

A number of ideas occurred to me, but none of them were all that appealing. Did he have to be wearing it? I mean, even if we got his clothes dirty, maybe sprayed some of that stage blood all over him, he could easily leave the necklace on while he stripped down and jumped in the shower, and that assumed that there was even a functioning shower in this place. I had yet to see one. This left a few different permutations on the story in which I or Tina or both of us try to seduce him and while he's distracted or unconscious afterward, we steal the damn thing and get out of there. I had no interest in doing anything like that. I don't think either of us were sure what Holly was going to pay us for the return of that thing, but it wasn't enough to get me to do that unless I wanted to already, and there wasn't anything about this scene that was making me horny.

But sometimes a problem will resolve itself without you doing very much to help. Paul spent a few minutes getting the close-ups and inserts that he wanted for whatever it was that he was doing. When he was done, he pointed his camera at the two of us and let it roll as he swayed toward us. When he reached us, he dropped the camera down to his side, reached out and grabbed the tea cup from my hand, and, over my startled protests, downed the whole thing in one gulp.

"I know where we can find more," he said as he handed the cup back to me and then grabbed the doctor's bag from the corner.

Tina looked at me and said, "Sounds like a great idea."

The actors were splitting up now, some of them moving to what we assumed must be a bathroom somewhere nearby, while the daughter went back the way we had come, twirling the flaying knife in her hand. Paul snaked his arm around Tina's shoulder and gently grabbed my elbow and led us off in a different direction. He said he wanted to drop his stuff off in his room, but his knees were giving out in a couple of minutes. He might have been making excuses or asking us what was going on, but frankly all we were hearing was slurred words and the scraping of his boots along the floorboards. Tina and I had to carry him the last few feet to his room and then drag him onto his bed, where it was the easiest thing in the world to remove the necklace, slip it into a pocket, and then go back into the hall to try to find our way out.

Once again, Tina and I had stolen something together, even though Holly did insist that we weren't stealing it. Regardless, Paul might have tried to stop us if he had been at all conscious, and we both felt guilty as we worked our way out of the rooms in that sixth floor squat. Tina and I whispered our fears and our plans as we went. Even though we had an invitation to stay the night, we were not interested in being anywhere near Paul when he woke up.

We agreed to get out as soon as we could, and it wasn't all that long before we were dodging an inquisitive Hack as we regained the main room from the first apartment we entered, then we were out in the stairwell again and on our way down to the street. When we exited the building's dim entrance, Tina and I turned in opposite directions.

"Where are you going?"

"Back to Port Authority," I said. I was honestly surprised that she had anything else in mind.

"You want to leave already?"

"We can't stay here. Let's get back to the station and just stay there until the next bus leaves for Red Stone."

"That could be all night," Tina said. I could tell that the whine in her voice wasn't really about spending the night in the bus terminal.

"I know it's not comfortable or glamorous, and it might even be sketchy, but it's free. We'll be able to look after each other there a lot better than we could down here." The two of us were moving now, because I think we both sensed that we still weren't far enough away from our petty crime to stop and have an argument. We went back and forth about it as we made our way back to 4th and 14th. I thought there was still probably time to catch the subway from Union Square again. "Maybe we can find a diner and grab some coffee."

Tina was still moving down the sidewalk with me, so I started to relax a bit. We were both scanning our surroundings, trying to peer into the darkest shadows, sizing up the very few people we did see, never making eye contact. But I could also tell that, as Tina looked around, she was really looking back toward the scene we'd just left behind. I took pity on her.

"As soon as we get the necklace back to Holly, as soon as we get paid, I'll come back with you."

Tina stopped and looked at me. She wasn't smiling, but her whole face lit up with gratitude. There was a lot about the city that I did find appealing, and I knew that Tina was awash in excitement at having found more people who were making movies like she was.

"I don't think we'll really have to worry about Paul," she said. "I mean, I don't think he'll remember much about tonight after I gave him the film."

"He *was* drunk and thought he was going to score."

"Maybe he won't even notice it's gone."

CHAPTER SEVEN

It turned out to be a lot harder than we thought to get out of the neighborhood and back to the Port Authority. We left the building and turned what we thought were the same corners on our way back to Union Square, but the blocks of abandoned and bombed out buildings appeared endless. The night's cold was bracing at first, and no doubt we were also shivering from all of the adrenaline, but I don't think we were that disoriented. And yet we could not find our way.

It felt like hours that we walked block after block, took turn after turn. I half expected that we would reach one river or the other at some point. We started to cut through vacant lots and down even darker alleys, trying to strike out in some new direction that might lead us to a place we had been before that was not the apartment building where we had stolen the necklace. But time and again, we started down a new block only to see the dim shape of the squat rise up out of the gray winter street.

We were both frustrated and a little scared, I think, but it was Tina who got angry first. She accused me of having taken something back at the party, of being on some kind of trip that was leading us astray. We were both cold and wondering where we were going to sleep, or even if we were going to sleep, if we couldn't find our way back. I told her that I hadn't taken anything; neither of us had. There was something else going on that made it impossible for us to find our way, but both of us were afraid to talk about what that might be. It was after the first of these brief spats between us that I first noticed the terrifying silence that had fallen over the neighborhood. There was a lot about our situation that was disturbing, but that was the first moment that I began to feel absolute terror. This was Manhattan. Sure, it was after midnight on a cold December night, but we should have heard cars and sirens and people and even some damn pigeons, but there was nothing moving on these streets to make any sound except for the wind blowing in from wherever.

The air that moved through those streets and crept across the vast vacant lots brought with it strange smells, too. At first I didn't think too much of it, because the breeze was displacing the pervasive smells of garbage that were occasionally punctuated with something worse. The new odors were a mix of diesel fumes, coal smoke, the reek of humans in endless toil, along with a sublayer of sweet fermentation. It smelled old but not stale, like an artifact out of time but not an antique. People will tell you that smells are the strongest carrier of memory, but if that's true it wasn't my own memories that these smells were evoking.

I didn't begin to lose it until we came out of one alley and found ourselves on a narrow curving street. At that point in time, I was not intimately familiar with the city. I had not spent enough time there, especially at night, to feel like I could find my way wherever I wanted to go. However, traveling the world with my parents had honed my sense of direction and orientation. I could study a simple map or a detailed one and have the general layout well in hand whether or not I actually had the map with me. On our way to the apartment, I had looked at a handful of transit posters with maps of Manhattan; I felt more or less oriented to the island. Certainly, our senses of direction were failing both of us that night, but I was pretty sure that there should be no curving street like this one in the East Village. There was the grid of the island that even the greenest of tourists could use for orientation, and then there were the occasional streets that cut across the city on the diagonal.

The street we had found curved or meandered through a canyon of brick and wood buildings much older than the ones we had been passing, but maybe not in quite as bad of shape. At first, I thought that we had stumbled into a kind of unmapped space behind the buildings that made up a city block, a sort of service alley. I thought the various footprints of the buildings to either side had simply created a street that was not entirely straight. But it was a real street, if not one that you found in modern Manhattan. It was cobble-stoned and a bit warmer than the wider streets, because the stones were wet and slick, but there was no snow or slush to be found here. Even the gutter running down the center of the street was only damp. Looking up, I could see occasional rickety stairs coming down from second or even third-story doors, but there were no fire escapes that faced onto this street. And none of the windows were lit. There were doors facing onto this serpentine alley, but there were all closed tightly against us. Some of them had small plaques or numbered signs revealing addresses, but I couldn't read any of them. They were all in an alphabet that I had never seen before and could not read. Even when I looked around in frustration and then back at a sign that I had spotted previously, the writing appeared to have changed.

I've had a lot of time to think about that night, and I know many people will read this and immediately think that I was dreaming or high. All I can do is assure you and myself that I was awake. I was lucid. I was frightened. It was in this curving street that I noticed a subtle change come over Tina. She was still upset, still frustrated with our inability to get out of the neighborhood, this new and eerie place notwithstanding. But as we looked on those forbidding doors and their strange signs and plaques, I could tell that Tina was more curious than scared now. The look on her face was the same one I saw at the barn party when we were watching *Meshes of the Afternoon* and *At Land*. It was a look of wonder. She was thrilled to be on this adventure. I think she felt like she was in a Maya Deren film.

I like adventure, and Tina and I had been on several together so far, but her attitude worried me. Whatever it was that was happening to us and wherever we had found ourselves, I was convinced no good would come of it. If we had passed through some kind of enchanted wardrobe, I wanted out. I might want to come back later, but at that moment I was convinced we needed to get back to something more familiar. Even the party at the apartment was better than where we were. Maybe Paul had not yet come to. Maybe we could slip the necklace back around his neck like we never took it and then somehow get back to a world that was real. Tina still had plenty of money to get us back to Red Stone. We could tell Holly that we got down there but couldn't find the stone. Sorry. No dice.

Our path bent through the night, first to the right then the left and so on, slithering away from what felt real and right. After a time, the street ended in an irregularly shaped court. Here, the old stone gutters that ran down the center of the alley split into two and then circled around the court before meeting at an ancient muck-covered iron grille. Across the court, an arched doorway was filled to the top with utter darkness. We stopped, unsure of whether to proceed or try to go back and retrace our steps or find some new way.

I was going to suggest that we go back when we both turned at a new sound. It sounded like heavy boots approaching us from the direction we had come. It was one set of footsteps, but the steps were slow, deliberate. The echoes in the alley were odd, probably because of the irregular surfaces of the buildings facing it, so it sounded like the steps were almost upon us and then they suddenly sounded farther away, but they always sounded like they were getting closer. Tina touched my hand—I almost jumped two floors straight up—and jerked her head toward the black archway. Nothing made a great deal of sense at that moment—maybe we should have stayed where we were, called out to the approaching person to ask for directions—but I had to admit that her unspoken plan was the best.

"Do you have the Yellow Sign?"

We both nearly jumped out of our skin as we whirled back around to the court with the shadowed archway. Between us and that dark opening stood a figure, tall and indistinct in the gloom of the alley. The figure wore a long coat or cape and what looked like some kind of featureless mask, though it was difficult to make anything out in that moment. Tina had a better hold on the situation, or at least of herself.

"Dr. Holly?" she asked.

"Do you have the Yellow Sign?" The footsteps still sounded behind us with their maddening dislocation. The figure reached out a hand.

"We're supposed to give it to Holly," I said, and my voice broke when I said those words. I was terrified.

"I am with him," said the figure. I had no idea what that was supposed to mean, but Tina reached into her pocket and took out the necklace we had lifted from Paul. She stepped forward hesitantly and held out the stone by its cord. The figure took it from her and placed a thick envelope into her hand in return.

The footsteps suddenly stopped behind us, as though the person had skidded to a halt. I turned, again expecting to be able to make out someone within sight of us, but there was nothing. When I turned back—all of this in mere seconds—Tina still stood there in the court holding the envelope, but the figure was nowhere to be seen. Tina appeared dazed.

She hadn't turned at all, as far as I could tell, and she didn't even notice that we were now alone in the alley.

But apparently we weren't. With a heavy scrape, the footsteps came running at us. My instincts kicked in, and I sprinted toward Tina, grabbing her hand and pulling her into the darkness of the archway.

I did not want to confront whoever it was that was following our steps down that strange alley, and if we were forced into some kind of confrontation, I didn't want it to be there. Not then. I wasn't ready. The darkness of the archway may have been a poor choice, but neither of us was thinking straight.

We held hands and plunged into the dark, using our free hands to stretch out and try to feel the walls as we fled blindly. Now our footsteps became the only ones that I could hear, and soon I could also hear my ragged breath, gasping for air. Fear will tire you out pretty quickly, and there isn't too much scarier than running full-tilt into the void, hoping to escape an unseen pursuer. Our senses were heightened to an unbelievable degree, and we were jolted by every piece of information that came our way, which was largely relegated to sound. We could hear our gasps and our footfalls echoing in the close space, but then we heard the creak of a door or perhaps a window opening, then the growl or shriek of some animal that we had disturbed at its feed. We could not have run far; it was no time at all, though seconds also stretched on into infinity. I heard Tina call my name at the same instant that I crashed into a door that gave way under the force of impact.

Though it was actually dim, I was nearly blinded by the naked bulb that lit the passageway where we found ourselves. Just after I tumbled to the ground and began scrambling to my feet, Tina came through the door to help me up. The door slammed behind us, shut by a small Hispanic woman with long, stringy dark hair escaping in tendrils from a baggy woven cap. She was draped in successive layers of long garments: a smock, an overcoat, very wide pajama pants that still couldn't conceal her chipped and weathered combat boots. She smelled like dirt—or no, soil—and that was a welcome smell at that moment.

"Runnin' from the law?" she whispered as she put her ear to the door we had just come through. She waited only a moment before she scurried away down the passage, either gesturing us for us to follow, or swatting at non-existent bugs. Tina and I exchanged glances with each other, looked at the door, at the receding form, and chose this new and more tangible mystery.

We soon found ourselves in a comfortingly normal if shabby stairwell that had a familiar air. One flight of stairs brought us into the ground floor entryway of the squat we'd left some time before. Hours? Days? I still had no idea, and I couldn't swear to it now, but our guide acted like she recognized us and didn't appear to think that we had been gone long at all. She led us to the darkened second floor, down the hall, and beckoned us into an apartment on the opposite side of the hallway from the one we had entered four floors above.

Once inside, we could see some street light seeping into the tall windows at the front of the room we were in, and soon she found a wall switch in the dark, illuminating strand upon strand of Christmas lights that snaked their way up one decorative but scarred wooden pillar, over the entryway into what must have been a dining room at one time but was now an empty space, and into a wide and carefully arranged spiral on the ceiling of the living room. The colors were comforting, and it looked like the furnishings might be, too, until I realized many of them were piles of trash. Nothing smelled too horrible, though to be honest the smell of soil in here was nearly overwhelming. I chose to be grateful for it, and once the several locks on the door had been thrown and she had positioned a piece of lumber under the doorknob (kept there for that purpose), I let myself relax and breathe.

"I saw you come and go," said our host. "Most stay longer."

"It wasn't for us," Tina replied. Tina looked around at the room and its piles, the lights. "Thanks for helping us."

I added my thanks, too, but the woman waved us off.

"Us sisters have to stick together in the city. It's bad on the street, but it can be worse inside." She came up to me very suddenly, making me cringe back. She looked into my face searchingly. Satisfied, she moved on to Tina, who stood her ground better and let herself be surveyed. "You two don't seem bent. My name's Lur. You wanna wash up, can's down the hall. Water in the kitchen. I ain't got nothing to steal."

Tina shot me a look.

"We're not interested in stealing anything," I said. The woman grunted at that.

"I'm gonna go dream. Do not disturb," she said with a finger held up to admonish us. "You can leave tomorrow, if you want." With that, she turned around and headed down the hall. Tina and I watched her go until she was out of sight and we heard a door close.

Alone in the festive heap of the living room, we looked at each other, and then down at the package in Tina's hand. She had been clutching it the whole time, and I wondered if that was the reason that the woman thought we might be thieves. You couldn't see the bills, but stuffed envelopes are unmistakable. Tina stepped to the center of the room, where the light from the multi-colored spiral was brightest, and she opened the envelope for the first time. I stepped over as she did and saw her eyes go wide. It was filled with bills, of course. In that light, they seemed unreal in some way. They looked like cash, like a lot more cash than Holly had paid for the film of Donny, but they still looked different in that light.

"There's got to be hundreds of dollars here," Tina said. "Maybe even a thousand."

"Maybe we shouldn't have given it to that guy."

"Are you kidding? It felt creepy just having it on me. It was like all I wanted to do was get rid of it. I think that's why I didn't ask for the money first." Tina closed the envelope back up and tucked the package away inside her coat.

"What should we do?" I said.

"Stay here tonight. Try to get some rest. I'm exhausted," she said, as if she was only just realizing it. "We'll get out of here when it's light and ask how to get out of the neighborhood, if that's what it takes."

I nodded and started giving the heaps around the room a closer inspection. If we were going to spend the night here, then we should see about making ourselves as comfortable as we could. I wasn't sure if I was going to be able to sleep. I was exhausted, too, and my body wanted to collapse. But my mind was still in flight mode. I was over-excited and scared, though I could feel myself relaxing slowly.

My initial impression was mostly right. The room wasn't filled with trash. It was more like an odd assortment of things that nobody else wanted. Other people's trash, Lur's treasure. It certainly was arranged as though it was some kind of hoard. It made me think about that dragon from Tolkien's book, the one that slept curled up on top of all its gold, and also of the dragon in Peters's living room. Instead of gold and gems, though, we found dusty tarps, large woven baskets that smelled vaguely of some spice I couldn't immediately place, and heavy bags of potting soil. There were other smaller items strewn about, but nothing to sweep away the sense that we were actually in a storage room instead of a living room.

Tina and I moved some baskets and found the least dusty tarp we could and arranged a halfway decent bed on top of some of the soil bags. It was warmer inside than out, but the two of us still huddled together under the tarp. When we both finished squirming our way into some kind of comfort and things quieted down, I could tell that Tina's heart was still racing. I was pretty keyed up, too, but the ritual of making a bed and a growing feeling of at least relative security started to work on me like a sleeping pill. I remember thinking that I was grateful for her warmth and closeness, and then there was nothing until I heard the boots coming up the stairs.

In a flash, I was awake but completely disoriented. The room was much brighter as daylight streamed in through the tall windows at the front of the room, though the Christmas lights were still on. The boots coming up the stairs in the main hall brought me back to the events of the night before, and I nudged Tina several times until she surfaced from wherever she was right then. I felt her tense at the same sounds I was hearing. She looked at me, and I held a finger to my lips for her to be quiet. I didn't hear our host coming out of her room. Maybe she was hunkered down where she was, or maybe she was leaving through some other door. Maybe she didn't hear it, or maybe she didn't care.

Tina lifted her side of the tarp and very slowly rolled out of our makeshift bed and crawled quietly over to the bright windows. She kept her head down and away from the glass, inching closer and higher until she could see what was happening outside the front door of the building.

"Ambulance," she whispered, as the boots continued up the stairs and then past our door. "And cops."

I crawled over to where she was and looked for myself. There was a single squad car on the street parked in front of a white ambulance, but I quickly saw that there was no red light on the roof. I stood up a little more and could read CORONER on the side of the door.

"Someone's dead," I said.

The boots had continued up the stairs, but they were followed by the clanking of something being dragged up the stairs, rattling one step at a time. They were now followed by a lighter pair of steps. I imagined these were men in white coats, carrying some kind of stretcher with a white sheet for the body. We were listening intently, though with less fear than a few moments ago. I thought I could hear doors opening a crack out in the hall, and whispered conversations passing between more residents of this building than I had imagined there could be last night. But without seeing them, it felt like I was hearing the ghosts of the building conferring with one another like students whispering about the new kid. Who will it be this time? A boy or a girl? What will she be like?

We still didn't want to disturb our host, so Tina and I had to content ourselves with the windows. People from the buildings across the street were beginning to appear. I could see people in other windows across from us and above them. They were strange haunted faces, glancing out with some vague interest in the official vehicles but then disappearing into the murkiness of their lives when there was little to see. Perhaps they had seen it all so many times before. As long as there was no blood, no screaming, there wasn't any reason to stay and watch. But it took a little longer, that's all. The blood and the screaming did come. We heard the wailing faintly at first, and I thought that it was actually coming from somewhere across the street, but it must have been echoing off the building from open windows above us. Then it started its way down the main stairway. It grew loud and inconsolable as it passed by the door to the apartment where we were and then down and out the main entrance. Two police officers in winter coats exited with a young woman between them. She had the golden paper fast food crown crumpled in one hand. One of the officers grasped her upper arm, leading her toward the police car. She wasn't cuffed and she was sobbing into her hands, into the bent and torn crown, as she allowed herself to be led.

A few moments later, the two men I had imagined in white coats came out of the building at either end of a stretcher covered with a white sheet that was already stained with growing splotches of dark red. As the officers opened the back door of their car and ushered the young woman into it, she turned back and saw the stretcher bearers, and she unleashed a new and piercing wail. As her face turned up in agony, I recognized her from the party last night. She had played the mother in Paul's film.

CHAPTER EIGHT

Paul Steiner's death was a turning point for Tina and me. It felt like we had been tied together, like a pair of escaped prisoners, running from whatever long arm that was constantly dogging our steps. From the moment we met, our friendship brought us closer than any I'd had before. But on that gray day in Lur's apartment, as the meat wagon slid away from the curb carrying Paul's bloody corpse, we started along different paths that only intermittently twined back around each other for the next few months. I don't want to give the wrong impression; we were still good friends. We lived together and looked out for each other and shared money when we had it, but I think Tina had maybe left something of herself behind in that weird serpentine alley of the night before. She was less present, even when we were together.

It started, as I suppose it often does, because of money. When the scene was over and we left the windows overlooking the street, both of us were trying to wrap our heads around what had happened the night before. I wanted to go upstairs and see if there was anyone who could tell us more, but my worry that someone knew what we had taken, someone like Swayne, kept me from venturing out of the apartment.

To distract herself from similar thoughts, Tina took the envelope from her jacket and held it in her lap. The thickness of it in the morning light had me both curious and on guard. I glanced toward the hall and tried to listen for any sign that Lur was up and about. I didn't want her to barge into her own living room or storage room or whatever the hell it was, while we had a pile of money strewn across her floor. Tina opened the package and slowly flipped through the contents. Her eyes went wide at first, but then slowly crunched into a pensive frown. She looked thoroughly confused.

"What?"

She handed me the package. I looked toward the hall again before I slipped out the stack of bills.

I had never held that much money at one time. There was a crisp twenty-dollar bill on top of the stack, but as I flipped through the stack as Tina had done, I began to share her confusion. There was a mix of bills, mostly tens and twenties, but then I thought I saw a seven-dollar bill. I fanned the stack out, and sure enough I began to see fives and sevens and threes. The intricate designs on the fronts were also different than what I expected, but subtly so. However, the backs, which were green on the normal bills, turned to an icy blue on the strange ones.

"Fake?" I said.

"Play money," said Tina, staring out the window from where she sat on the floor.

I pulled a twenty out of the pile, one of the blue twenties, and inspected it more closely. The paper felt right, normal. It had that scratchy fibrous texture that all new bills have. It still read RESERVE NOTE in the scrollwork at the top of the bill, but above the treasury seal it read THE IMPERIAL DYNASTY OF AMERICA. The founding father depicted in the oval portrait in the center of the bill was unfamiliar to me, and there was no name given at the bottom. I flipped the bill over and found a blue cameo of a classical building, small and columned, in an urban park. Above it were the words THE LIVING GOD and above that another scroll of THE IMPERIAL DYNASTY OF AMERICA. The detail was exquisite, but the images made me dizzy. What the hell was going on?

"Holly tricked us," I said.

"What if we gave it to the wrong person?" I hadn't even thought of that. Tina was scared by this prospect. "We have no idea who that guy was last night. If Holly wanted that thing and was willing to pay us to get it, and someone was willing to steal it from him, then maybe..."

"Do you think someone killed Paul?"

Tina simply shrugged.

"It didn't look like they were arresting that girl. What if he killed himself because we took it?" There was that stab of guilt, plunged into my throat while also hollowing out my stomach. Something about that rang true. I could taste the reality of it, and all I wanted to do was spit it out.

Trying not to think about Paul, I started dealing out two piles of bills, one real (as far as I could tell) and one fake. There was a lot of it, but my zeal to avoid thinking about death focused me. Soon I had a tall stack of counterfeit bills and a much smaller pile of real money.

"There's eighty-five dollars in real money, and over nine hundred in fake."

We both heard a door open down the hallway. I looked up, and Tina was already grabbing bills. She pocketed the real bills and then stuffed the fake ones back into the envelope. When they were all back, she shoved the package into my hands, and I jammed it into my bag.

Lur emerged from the hallway lugging a window with her. It was an old wood sash with pristine glass panels. The paint was chipped from the frame and the crossbars, but the wavy hand-blown glass panels reflected the gray light from the windows behind us and the colored lights overhead.

"One of you help me with this." I jumped up from the floor, tottering a bit with my own sudden and excited movement, trying to conceal what we had been doing. Lur was at the door, moving the piece of lumber and undoing the locks. She looked over at Tina. "You staying?"

"I'm heading out to get some food. Can I bring something back for you? I mean, it's the least we could do for letting us crash here."

"No meat. No junk food. We'll be back before you."

We weren't though. We all left the apartment, and we didn't see each other for hours. Lur and I headed up the stairs, carrying the window between us, and Tina headed down and out onto the street. I was still worried that she wasn't able to find her way out of the neighborhood, but Lur kept my attention focused on our task at hand.

"Where you two from?" she said. I was focusing intently on trying not to get splinters from the window, and so I did not try to lie.

"I'm from all over. Tina's from Queens." Lur nodded. It looked like she was fitting puzzle pieces together and wasn't fully satisfied. "We came here from SUNY Red Stone. You?"

"I came here from Guatemala, but I was small." She pronounced her home country with a hard "g," like a New Yorker. My tentative grip was threatening to drop the window, so I clung more tightly to the frame, splinters be damned, and put my back into it.

"I spent a year in Belize and Honduras with my parents when I was about five," I said.

I was so busy talking with her and trying keep up my end of the work that I didn't notice Hack coming down the stairs until he was right next to me. We locked eyes for a moment, but Lur wasn't slowing down our ascent or our conversation so there was no chance for him to ask about our disappearance or for me to ask about Paul. He looked shaken, though, and I thought about him all day long.

When we reached the sixth floor, the door to the apartment was closed. A hush had fallen over the whole building. If Swayne and the others were in there, they weren't making a peep. We passed on to the end of the hall, where Lur stopped and took out her keyring and unlocked a heavily painted door that led to the last flight of stairs to the roof. The final door opened out onto Lur's workshop.

In the center of the roof was the strangest greenhouse I've ever seen. It was maybe ten feet by fifteen feet and probably only seven or eight feet high with a slanted roof. The entire thing was cobbled together from old windows presumably salvaged or stolen from the buildings on the Lower East Side. You could see that it was filled with green but they were not huge flowering bushes or anything like this, and at least at first glance, it wasn't some inner-city grass growing operation. The thought crossed my mind, but that was too bold, too out in the open. We were on a roof that was visible from any number of buildings surrounding it, and it only took the cheapest of binoculars to have a good idea precisely what was growing in that greenhouse. At least, that's what I thought.

We leaned the window up against the side of the greenhouse very carefully. Lur was no doubt worried about preserving the glass in her new window, while I was worried that the whole thing was going to come tumbling down the minute we touched it. But the hothouse was sturdy; I'll give Lur that much. She had built it herself years ago and rebuilt it more than once since then. She knew every nook and cranny, and she was able to tell just where she might need to look for replacement sashes or panes when any of the glass broke. That was the situation at the time, of course, and once she had unlocked the industrial padlock that guarded the door and we went in, I could see the damage.

Lur busied herself gathering the tools that she needed to replace the window, while I enjoyed the unexpected tropical comforts of the glass house. Long wooden tables stretched from one end of the place to the other along the longer axis. These tables were basically troughs of water with rich potting soil, the kind we had been sleeping on bags of downstairs, at the bottom. From this medium sprang dozens of blue lotus. Their wide green pads floated on the surface of the water, and here and there you could see the gorgeous starburst blossoms opening up to the daylight streaming through the harlequin panes of the greenhouse. It was amazing. The blue lotus is not a particularly difficult plant to cultivate under the right conditions, but arranging those conditions on the roof of a New York apartment building with found materials is something else entirely.

I realized that we were working against time. The broken panes that I had seen when we entered the greenhouse had been covered with a tarp, but they were letting too much of the heat escape. Lur had run a couple of extension cords up the side of the building from her apartment, connecting them to repurposed hot plates mounted beneath the troughs. She was able to periodically warm the water in the greenhouse (mostly at night), and then let the sunlight take over during the day. It wasn't perfect temperature control, but over time she had discovered what worked and what didn't.

"When the lotus is steady and serene, it takes that calm into itself. Its power grows." She waved her hand at the city around us. "It can be hell out here and heaven in there. When the flower is apart from our world, it exists between worlds. That's where the power comes from."

It was all interesting to me, but this last bit especially. The blue lotus is one of these flowers that an ethnobotanist learns about early. You can make a powder from the dried and crushed seed pods that, when mixed with alcohol, can be a powerful mood-altering drug. I thought of Swayne and his own concoction from the night before, and I wondered if he knew about Lur and her hothouse.

I didn't ask her about that right away. We had a task to complete, and though I have spent plenty of time in greenhouses, I hadn't yet spent much time trying to maintain ersatz ones. It took more time than I expected to remove the damaged frame and carefully set it aside, leaning it against the north side of the greenhouse for possible future use, and then prep the hole for its replacement. As makeshift greenhouse panels go, the one we had brought up fit perfectly, but there was still a tremendous amount of shimming that needed to be done before we could get to filling in the gaps and securing the frame to those around it. It was cold out that morning but not freezing, and the work warmed us both up. I was sweating pretty honestly by the time the job was done, and I was starting to wonder how I was going to do laundry without another change of clothes. I already knew that Tina and I were going to stay in the city longer than we had originally intended. It's not that I felt at home, not at all. But working on the greenhouse and later *in* the greenhouse with Lur completely changed my view on things. A lot of my apprehension and fear drained away with the work and with the talks Lur and I shared. It didn't feel like I was out on a limb, even though I most certainly was. It felt like I was at home, but it was a home that I didn't immediately recognize. There was trust without familiarity. I couldn't explain it, but I was grateful for it. I needed it.

Lur and I came to an understanding that day. She appreciated my continued help with the greenhouse as long as I didn't ask too many questions. I thought this was a personal quirk; she wanted to show me how things were done in her greenhouse, and I should keep my mouth shut and pay attention. However, it dawned on me as we went that she didn't yet want to talk about exactly what she was doing with the lotus or why. There was something about the plants and the extract that she prepared on the workbench and in her apartment, something that other people came to her for, paid

her for. And she wasn't selling to health food stores or co-ops or
stale hippies. The people who sometimes came to the apartment
for what she had—visits that required me and Tina to leave—were
strange people. They rarely talked. They hid their faces. It was familiar and unsettling, and more and more, I didn't want to know
anything about them.

Not so the flowers. I wanted to know everything that Lur would
teach me about them. She was very open about their cultivation. I
was a quick study, having some experience with more common lotus plants already, and I picked up the idiosyncratic things I needed
to know about the operation without asking too many questions.
Once she learned about my interest in botany, Lur essentially took
me on as a student or an apprentice (though her first piece of advice was to get rid of my copy of *Phantastica*). I eventually learned
how to watch the weather reports on the news (or listen to them
on the radio) and compare them with a tattered almanac that Lur
always kept on hand. This information helped us to know when to
use the heating coils and when to back off of them. The power line
from the apartment to the roof felt something like an umbilical
cord. The two of us were falling into a kind of synchronization as
work partners. I used to fall asleep and dream that I could feel the
lotuses breathing, dreaming their own dreams. When I had these
dreams, I often saw the greenhouse as if from the roof of another
building a couple blocks away and a little higher. It was always
at night, and there was always a pale blue light emanating from
the greenhouse, though the real house had no lights (the extension cords were already overtaxed by the heating pads). But in the
pale blue gem of the glass house, I saw a woman gliding between
the troughs of flowers, her long yellow robe floating on the air as
though she were submerged. She wasn't Lur or me or Tina. I used
to think of her as the tender of the lotus.

Lur offered us a room in her apartment, one of the former bedrooms down the hall across from her own, in which she had been keeping many of the rest of her possessions. We could each stay for a song (not that a room in Alphabet City was expensive back then) as long as we didn't cause problems and I kept helping with the greenhouse. At the time, I viewed the separate rent for Tina and me as a gesture of respect for our individuality, our autonomy, but I think it was that Lur sensed something about how fleeting our connection might be. She didn't say anything about it; she told us, business-like, and left it at that. I paid mine for the rest of December and said that I would see how things were working out after the holidays.

Later that first day with Lur, an hour or so after the light failed in the city, Tina came back to the apartment with sandwiches and a conciliatory expression. I was glad to see her, and I couldn't find it in me to be angry at her for taking the real money and leaving me with the funny money. I still had some of the cash we had shared from the film that Holly bought, but there was the thought at the back of my mind that she might not have come back. I had made a friend in Lur, and I had a place to stay, but I didn't yet have a way to stay here in the longer term. I felt more entitled to my share of the eighty-five dollars than I did to the film money anyway.

Over sandwiches and some of Lur's wine, we talked about our days. Tina had waited long enough outside the building that Hack met her after he passed us on the stairs. He appeared relieved to see her and asked where we had gone last night. Tina told him that we were staying nearby, but that Paul had given us a weird vibe, so we cut out at the first opportunity. Hack nodded, Tina told us, and then broke the news that Paul had killed himself sometime early in the morning. Slashed his throat down to the bone. Sarah found him in his room, said he still felt warm. Hack had run down to the corner to find a phone that he could use to call the police, but not before telling everyone to get their shit together. Most of the people got out of there before he could, but Swayne had to scramble to close up shop.

Tina and Hack found a diner over on East 3rd where they drank coffee and had some runny eggs. They talked for a couple hours, at first about Paul, but eventually they were talking about Paul's films and then film in general and then Tina's passion for film. Hack's passion was similar, or at least of a similar intensity, and when Tina spoke about her love of the art, Hack listened, nodded. There was something in his eyes, she said. She was sure that he understood what she was talking about.

Hack told Tina about the other work that he and Swayne and Paul had been doing. Swayne was an idea man, he said, while Paul and Hack were the filmmakers. But they all hung out and worked on their ideas together. Sometime last year, Swayne and Paul had been talking about their dreams and how they wanted to film them. Hack spent more time at places like Cinema 16 and a couple of the art theaters, so he had seen a couple of the more famous surrealist films. He's the one who suggested they look into the surrealists and read about what they had done, but Paul was too eager to get started. He wanted to experiment immediately, and he didn't think he needed anyone else's advice, experience, or permission to do it.

He tried to keep a dream journal, but he discovered that he rarely remembered what he dreamed. He didn't even know whether he had dreamed anything at all. Swayne had some ideas for how they might enliven their dreams chemically, and Paul was all for it. A day or two after he consulted with Swayne, Paul started reporting that he was experiencing the most elaborate and inspiring dreams filled with kings and prophecies and far-flung worlds and curious cul-de-sacs of time and space. It sounded like it was all pulled from some kid's book, but Paul's face rapidly became ashen and drawn, and it was obvious that he took his visions seriously.

Meanwhile, Hack was taking a slower path. He ate spicy food

just before bed or stayed up for two days in order to see what effect it produced. Stomach upset and sleep deprivation had results that were similar in degree, though different in kind to Swayne's pharmacy. Hack's dreams were intense and disturbing, but they were always his dreams. One of the things that Paul often said, and Hack suspected it was the cause of his strange wasting away, was that they didn't seem like his own dreams. He felt when he was dreaming like he was visiting someone else's nightmare.

Within a month of the first experiment, Paul was making films inspired by his nightly visions. Up until then, Paul and Hack had both been making more or less juvenile movies inspired by the punk and underground rock scenes. These early works were crass and confrontational and sometimes violent. They were not especially interesting. Paul's new films were something else. They looked different: Gothic, nightmarish, and inscrutable. Paul was doing things with light and architecture and despair that took Hack's breath away and probably made Swayne jealous (this was Hack's suspicion). And it made Hack a little jealous, too. He told himself that Paul's films had simply convinced him that Paul's dedication and courage were well-placed. He decided that Paul had been correct, so he asked Swayne to help him out.

Swayne was a businessman beneath his German Expressionist persona, but he also cared about his customers' experiences. This is something I learned to respect about him. His personality and motivations rubbed me the wrong way and made it more likely that he appeared to be the villain. I didn't understand this until much later, when it no longer mattered. When Hack asked him for something that would help him dream in the way that seemed so easy for Paul, Swayne refused. In fact, he evaded. Swayne had a variety of psychedelics he could have sold to Hack, but he didn't want to. Swayne provided recreational drugs. Hack was asking for something between ritual and vocational pharmaceuticals, and that wasn't something that made Swayne comfortable. He thought Hack was coming at the problem the wrong way, so he tried to help him out by giving him an alternative.

Swayne was an avid reader and his primary interests covered the many ways that humans attempted to alter their consciousness. He read a fair amount about not only Timothy Leary and his experiments, but also about people like William S. Burroughs and Brion Gysin. He was especially fascinated by Burroughs's and Gysin's experiments in alpha waves. He found the schematics for their dream machine, and he passed the instructions along to Hack. Even though I was already disposed to dislike Swayne, I have to admit that I felt a rising warmth toward him when I heard that he had asked Hack if he had any history of seizures before he let him play around with the lamp contraption. Hack had not, and so once he got the twirling cut-out lamp shade affixed to a second-hand turntable, he was off and running.

Hack sat in his room for hours, with his eyes closed and his face pushed up within inches of the dream machine. The pulsing of light, timed to synchronize with alpha wave patterns, plugged into Hack's brain waves and changed what he was thinking. He talked about receiving the most surprising visions, even though he was not chemically altered. He was fully present and completely awake, so he was ready to embrace whatever stimuli came his way. He didn't have to fight his body at all like he might have if he were using psychedelics or hallucinogens.

He usually kept his door closed, but he was interested in sharing what he was learning. His strong desire to goose his own dreams and nightmares did not come from a sense of competition with Paul; Hack simply didn't want to be left behind. He wanted to be part of what they were doing, but he needed help. Once he discovered what the lamp could show him, he was eager to share it with Paul, too. Steiner was interested. It seemed like science-fiction to him, but he could see that Hack was getting results. When Paul tried it, it worked for him, but he felt like it was interfering with his groove. It was probably a good thing that Hack and Paul had different methods. They were both contributing, and that meant that their small group didn't have a hierarchy. They could discuss their shared goals and their diverse methods and take inspiration from each other's progress.

In many artistic movements, infighting eventually spells the end. Though both Paul and Hack could be strong personalities, they never came into direct conflict, and neither of them demanded to be in control. There was nothing to control. By the time Paul started to get a little bit of attention for his new films, Hack was also creating his own style of film fantasy. Neither of them was getting rich or famous doing what they were doing. Would they have eventually? Maybe. There were people in the scene who appreciated their art. Some were eager for every opportunity to be deliciously creeped out by Paul's nightmares, while others began to seek out Hack's version of dark urban fairy tales. What started the crack that eventually ended The New Dreamers was Paul's involvement with Dr. Jean L. Holly.

Unfortunately, I know very few of the details. I don't know how or when Paul met Holly. I don't know if Holly sought out the young filmmaker, as he did with Tina, or if Paul went to him for help or funding. Maybe their association stemmed from something else entirely. At some point, though, Paul came close enough to the strange doctor to discover the curious black pendant we were later sent to retrieve from him. I didn't know it at the time, but the disturbing design on the necklace was in some way connected to that fucking play *The King in Yellow*. I've had a lot of opportunities to see how drugs and cults can destroy someone's personality, how they can utterly ruin lives. And yet I have never seen anything that can compare with that play and the cloud of associations that constantly emanates from it. Fundamentalists talk about the dangers of heavy metal music or movies or video games. But *The King in Yellow* is so outside of all things human and civilized that it sets up vibrations in your mind that invariably end in corruption. And it never brings pleasure with it like with some corrupting substances. It sometimes comes with a brief glint of awe, but never pleasure. Never freedom.

For the relatively brief period that the Yellow Sign possessed Paul, his output was glorious. Hack thought that Paul had unlocked some kind of door in his mind or even in his soul where he discovered his true connection with a vision that made him great. Paul's connection to the sordid world of the village punk scene became more and more tenuous. His films took on references and themes that often struck him as medieval if not far more disturbingly ancient. Figures began to appear in his movies, often masked and robed, that had a powerful presence. They stared straight into the viewer. The barrier between viewer and viewed melted during the run time of these short films, as the boundaries between Paul's fictional and obviously fantastic settings and the mundane locations of the film shoots also dissolved. Paul's films no longer had the effect of offering a brief moment of escape to their viewers. Now they fixed their audience by eliminating the frames of reference by which they navigated reality.

Hack explained to Tina that this is where Swayne became jealous of Paul, though I have my doubts about that. Up until this point, Swayne had been a loyal Musketeer. A brother in arms. He was reliable in his enthusiasms and contributions. But as Paul and his work became more powerful, Swayne pulled away, first alarmed and then later hurt. Hack figured that Swayne was jealous of what Paul and even he was doing. I think it is more likely that Swayne was afraid. Maybe he heard more about *The King in Yellow* at some point. Maybe Burroughs had told him that some drugs weren't worth it, that there were some loaded pistols that you should never touch, under any circumstances.

Hack's story was punctuated by increasingly rare visits from the diner's waitress, who obviously wanted them to move on. From the diner, he invited Tina to his place to show her the films he had been working on most recently. His apartment was a couple blocks away above a kosher deli and though smaller than the pad on the sixth floor or Lur's place, was considerably nicer. Not fancy or anything but Hack had some actual furniture, if used, and there was even food in the place. But mostly Tina was there for the editing station set up on a desk in Hack's bedroom. It was one of those older flashy red Bakelite things with a tiny screen. You put on a reel of film and a take-up reel and then turned the crank by hand, and your movie appeared on the screen. No projector; this was more intimate. Hack used it to make his movies, but it also had the advantage of bringing them closer together. I imagined Tina sitting in his desk chair, hunched forward staring into the small screen, while Hack leaned over her from behind, maybe placing his hand on her shoulder as she turned the crank. She started out fast, slowed down, found the right rhythm for the film. Hack squeezed her shoulder, told her to stop, rewind, he wanted to show that to her again. Maybe one more time. They laughed.

I don't know if Tina slept with him that day. She did later. He was a good looking guy, but there was always something about him that I thought of as forbidding. Maybe I just felt like he was Tina's. Maybe there was something else keeping me away, wary. This was early for them, but Tina could be unpredictable like that. She was attracted to someone, wanted them, took them. She dropped them just as easily. At the same time, she could be distant or friendly with someone else, like me, and then all of a sudden after months or years of knowing you, there was the lust, loud and salty. She could loathe you and never show it. She could manifest utter indifference. I'm not sure I ever figured out her "taste," if that was a thing she had. She didn't love or hate kinds of people. And, to tell the truth, I don't even know if she loved Hack. They had fun together. More than fun. He might have told you something else, but I didn't think that what they shared had anything to do with romance. They were two artists who discovered that they could create things together—films, events, orgasms—that they couldn't create on their own. For a while, I think they were fascinated by the possibilities.

Whatever else they might have done at Hack's place that day, what they did do was talk about Hack's new film. He had this grand plan to make a movie about Vietnam and Nixon and Kent State and all the greedy fat pigs wallowing in the shit sty that was America back then. There would be mass slaughter in gas lines, people gutted while they sprawled on the hoods of their cars waiting for fuel that never came. There would be suicide chambers that were finally the only thing to tempt lazy and stupid Americans out of their recliners. They would march happily to their extinction, singing about a terrible swift sword. That sword would be wielded by a buxom Lady Liberty in a bikini. Hack had shot lists written out on the insides of cereal boxes and storyboards modified from panels in the funny papers. He had a scenario all typed up and ready to go, and in a couple weeks he expected to have enough money to get the immersion tank he needed to be able to develop his own film, since there was no way he was going to be able to send this film away for processing normally. He had a corral of people lined up who agreed to be in it; most of them had even been sober when they agreed.

The one thing that he didn't have yet was a title. He had long lists of possible titles, but nothing was jumping out at him. Nothing captured what he had in mind, that sort of thing that he woke up from his most feverish nightmares feeling. A lot of his ideas had enough profanity in them, in word and idea, that they would have attracted attention, to be sure, but they wouldn't necessarily have conveyed his vision, and that's when Tina named his masterpiece for him: *The Imperial Dynasty of America.*

CHAPTER NINE

The thousands of questions I have been asked over the years about Tina's films have forced an unexpected education on me. I've picked up things from the people who ask me, but it also became clear that many of them expected me to know something about "independent cinema," since I had played a walk-on role in it. It's no secret that Robert Hackett's *The Imperial Dynasty of America* is one of the most important bridges between the No Wave film movement of the 1970s and the Cinema of Transgression of the early 1980s. It's a film that carries over the activist political consciousness and the affinity with conventional narrative cinema evident in the No Wave films while also dipping its toes into the shocking sex and violence of the films soon to come from artists like Nick Zedd, Lydia Lunch, Richard Kern, Kembra Pfahler and others. From its opening close-ups of some of our fake Imperial currency to its closing shots of a sunset over Bannerman Castle, every frame is a testament to Hack's vision as seen through Tina's camera. Aside from Beth and Scott B, there weren't a lot of male/female filmmaking teams that worked so closely on directing, writing, and shooting in the way that Hack and Tina did. It was far more common for a man to have the pen and the camera and for the woman to act as muse. It wasn't unusual for those women to break out and tell their own stories in their own voices, but the more or less equal teams were few and far between, and in every case they were not long-lasting.

By the end of December 1978, Tina and I had decided not to go back to school. We were doing precisely what we wanted to be doing in one of the most amazing places we'd ever been. Both of us found worlds and chosen families to join that filled our lives with meaning. I don't want to give the impression that somehow Tina and I had completely separated or that we rarely saw one another. That wouldn't be right. We saw each other nearly every day. We lived in the same room in Lur's apartment, after all. For the most part, we were unable to share clothes because of our difference in sizes, but we shared nearly everything else. By the second week in the city, both of us raided a thrift store for enough clothes to get by.

It wasn't until sometime around Valentine's Day that Tina took a bus back up to Red Stone and gathered as much of our stuff as she could put into a big suitcase to lug back with her. The school had been sending us official notices, but neither of us cared. We both failed out at the end of the fall semester. We could have returned in January on academic probation (something I did later), but we didn't want to. Neither of us had given a thought to returning, but it got to the point where we realized that we had all these things back at SUNY that might be helpful to us if we could get to them.

Our RA wasn't very forgiving about our sudden disappearance, and she wasn't willing to ship our stuff to us. In fact, we wondered whether she had thrown everything away. We never stopped to think what it looked like for Tina to disappear with me so soon after the screening with Donny's film and all of the rumors that flew after that. Tina volunteered to be the one to go back. We both figured there was no reason to spend the money on two tickets, even though we could have carried more things. Tina stuffed one large case, gave as much of the rest of it away as she could, and then threw away the remainder.

The bigger obstacle for both of us involved calling our parents to let them know where we were and what we were doing. I had it much easier than Tina. I knew that if I couched the whole thing as an adventure, a new experience, my parents would acquiesce without much trouble. I was in New York City, learning about urban gardening. Yes, my grades from the fall were a concern, but I said that this helped to focus me and to get my enthusiasm back. When I returned to Red Stone, I would be prepared to be a college student, and I was still learning in the meantime.

Tina's mother was in tears, I remember. Her father seemed strangely okay with it, but her mom viewed this as her ultimate failure. She sent her daughter off to a good music conservatory, and she had dropped out within weeks. I think it also hurt them that we were in the city, but Tina seemed adamant about not going home. She was careful not to tell her parents exactly where she was, saying that she wanted to be on her own for a little while.

Once we severed our school ties and contacted our families, it felt like we could truly get down to the business of living in New York. Tina promised to go out and look for a place where she might get a job and bring in more money, and once I had figured out the rhythm of my duties in the greenhouse, I said I would do the same. I never said it until one night during a knock-down drag-out argument, but I considered my apprenticeship with Lur and the steeply discounted rent that I had arranged for us as a significant part of my contribution to our living expenses. Tina had a harder time of it, when she actually did go looking for work.

I think that this is one of those parts of her life—and there were many—where she was made to feel like a minority. To me, Tina was always Tina, and she was unusual and weird, but I like to think that I never thought about her as fundamentally different in the way that some other people regarded her. I worried that Hack did a little bit of this, that he was one of those guys who liked the idea of a little Japanese girl in his bed, even better that she was only half-Japanese heritage. Tina was all-American; that's the truth of it that so few people ever got. Her family's story might have been a bit unusual from one point of view, but it wasn't different in kind. Her father's ancestors chose to emigrate to Peru in order to find work at the turn of the twentieth century. Later, members of her family were forcibly removed to Texas. After the war, her family remained in the U.S. and assimilated. I don't think Tina ever thought of herself as a Japanese-American, or a Japanese-Peruvian-American, or whatever. Her mother's family had a Norwegian-Irish background, but of course that's not something that most Americans ever read in her face. To others, her features were carved using the invisible tools of whiteness, and those features were different enough to make them judge her.

When it came to looking for a job, the places where Tina applied tended to see her as Asian, and she wasn't applying to jobs where a lot of Asian women worked. There were people interested in hiring her, but always for reasons that creeped her out and made her walk away or run in the opposite direction. At first, I was not very understanding about any of this. I thought she was being too picky. We still had money in February, but it wasn't going to last forever. Tina compromised in early April when she took a job in a shabby movie theater not far from the porn theaters on 42nd.

She knew that the manager thought she was attractive, and she suspected that the job offer was as much to have her around for him to ogle as it was for the possibility that she might also entice customers to come in and keep coming back. She suspected all of this, but the job also gave her free access to a steady supply of films she would never have the money or inclination to see otherwise. She figured she could handle herself both with her manager and with the patrons, who turned out not to care much about her anyway. That job put the two of us back on a more solid footing, too, since Tina was bringing in a small but steady paycheck. This is the job that helped to finance *The Imperial Dynasty of America* and led to my own hatred of popcorn, since Tina occasionally brought home trash bags full of the stuff at the end of her shift. I appreciated the gestures toward supporting our home, though, and it did go a long way toward helping the apartment smell better.

Hack shared with Tina all of his shot lists and scenarios and storyboards through the winter months, and by March they were working together intently on revising those materials for the shoot which they expected to begin as soon as the winter broke. Hack wanted New York at its dreariest but not so cold that they couldn't work for hours on end. Everyone still had the previous winter's blizzard freshly in mind, and Hack wasn't taking any chances on these kinds of logistical details, because he was going to be taking so many chances in other ways. He was a tremendously calculating filmmaker in that way. He was free-wheeling and even anarchic in his art, but there was a ruthless organizer under all of that. And yet, he had no desire to be any kind of leader. Hack was out for himself, and he maintained interest in other people for exactly how long he estimated that they remained useful to him for his purposes. This might sound judgmental, but I don't mean it that way. This was his hustle; it was how he had adapted to the special challenge of surviving in the city. You had to know the particular kind of animal you were dealing with when you got into a cage with him. If you misread the situation, or you projected your own values onto Hack, then you were likely to be hurt. But if you assumed that he was always acting in his own self-interest and never in yours or for the sake of some altruism, then you were probably fine. You could at least make informed decisions.

My decision was to mostly stay away from him, because I always felt that whatever it was that he had wasn't worth the possible

danger of getting too close to him. Tina was different, of course. I
think she did see him as a kind of opportunity, but not in a cyni-
cal way. He was a charismatic guy that was making the kinds of
movies that she saw herself wanting to make. He was someone who
could show her how to do that. She had been finding her own way
for months, and the feeling of discovering a fellow traveler was
overwhelming and intoxicating. Whatever it was they recognized
in one another, both of them probably mistook for a kind of love
or it stood in for lust. But it was that recognition that made them
lovers and collaborators, and it was the lack of anything else that
made the whole thing fall apart by the end of the summer. By then,
though, the film was in the can and the infamous premiere had
already happened.

Despite the hours that I was putting in with Lur in the greenhouse, I was still able to come along with Tina and Hack as the
IDA shoot got underway in late March. They started out with a lot
of moody establishing shots and inserts that both of them felt were
necessary to build the atmosphere. They involved shots of bridges
and vacant lots and neo-classical facades and homeless people and
mounted police and uniformed doormen and adult theater mar-
quees, and the famous footage of an enormous rat devouring the
remains of another rat. The two of them were getting into a groove,
and they wanted to be sure that the best actor they had—the city
itself—looked right. There were towering hollow-dark skyscrapers
looming in gray skies, and misty night streets under elevated train
tracks. They went in for as much ironwork as they could find, trying to denude the city of its plant life, even though there was no
greenery to speak of at that point in the year.

While we were out on these shoots, I was often the lookout again,
while Tina and Hack were shooting using both of their cameras.
Hack insisted that they keep the shots short. He was hoping for a
mosaic-like montage of imagery to assault the viewer with the ran-

dom juxtapositions that make up city life. He wanted to show the looming face of the city as the embodiment of a fascist America, and in that America no one got time to contemplate anything. Things were always moving, and there was never any rest and nowhere to hide. Sometimes I was standing by a door, smoking, while Tina and Hack were on the other side where they weren't supposed to be, on a roof, even once in a brothel. Another time I paced along a subway platform while they were inside the tunnel on the tracks. I was keeping an eye out for the rare transit cop, but also keeping an ear out for approaching trains. Hack said that he knew the schedule by heart, but he was a genuine risk taker when it came to other people, so I wasn't about to leave it to his judgment.

One night in mid-April, after we had been out for the better part of the day in alleys that smelled of wet and warming garbage, we were in Hack's apartment. I was looking through the planning material for the film that Hack and Tina kept in a loose folder. Hack and Tina were at a small bistro table, cleaning their cameras. They were rehashing the places we'd shot that day and thinking out loud about the images that they still wanted to get and the shots that would make the film, if only they could capture them. And that's when Tina said it.

"That alley would be perfect." A chill ran down my spine.

"What alley?" said Hack. Tina was looking at me.

"That night we met you; when we left we got a little bit lost in the neighborhood and then wound up in this weird alley. It has to be near our building."

I wanted her to stop talking. I realized that the reason I hadn't thought about the alley and that night—despite the title of the film we were making—was that I was desperate not to think about it. That experience had terrified me in ways that I was not fully awake to, but this conversation was waking me up for sure.

"How was it weird?" Hack had stopped cleaning his camera and was looking from Tina to me and back again. She had hooked him. He both trusted her artistically and knew that she normally didn't talk about things as "weird," so this alley had to be something.

"It was really old and cobbled, and it curved back and forth like a snake."

"What? Curved?"

I shrugged at Hack, trying to make it stop.

"And not just like one of the open spaces behind the buildings, you know? It was a street that ended in a court with an archway. We met—"

"It was the night we met Paul," I said. "I think maybe we were both..."

"Both what? High?" Hack knew that Tina was neither a square nor a stoner, and he thought he remembered that night pretty well.

"I don't think so."

"We had arrived in the city that day fresh off the bus. I think the whole thing was overwhelming, and we didn't have anything at that party, but there was all sorts of shit in the air, right? I mean, the contact alone..."

Both of them were looking at me now, but I think Tina was catching on that I was terrified.

"Whatever, it doesn't really matter. I've never found it again, and I've looked for it a couple times. Tried to retrace our steps and get lost in the same way. It's just not there."

"Well, what'd you bring it up for?" said Hack.

The crisis was averted then, but Tina had managed to plant a seed. In the weeks ahead, whenever we passed by an alleyway in the neighborhood, Hack asked about it and looked at us both for any indication that we recognized it. He didn't do it every time, but he was carefully cataloging, because he never asked about an alleyway twice. He had sensed something during our conversation. Even if we couldn't remember how to get to this place again, our memory of it and my fear of it were enough to make it real for him. He was getting a taste of the hidden weirdness of the city, but it all felt like it was on the mundane side of weird. It was strange to a lot of people like our parents and teachers and whoever, but he had an idea that what we were talking about took strangeness to an entirely different level. He wanted it for his film.

Even if I could have found it again, I wasn't going to give it to him. I didn't think that anyone needed to be in that street, meeting masked figures, hearing heavy footsteps. If I was the only one protecting him from that world, then so be it. I didn't think that Tina could lead him there any more than I could, though our conversation made me understand for the first time that she might.

We never revisited that topic between the three of us, and as April turned into May, we started shooting more scenes outdoors with the actors. Many of the scenes required them to wear elaborate and gaudy military uniforms from the nineteenth century. There was one guy that I always called Captain Crunch because of his gilt shoulder boards and tall hat, and there was a trio that were always together in their scenes so that Tina took to calling them John-Phillip-Susan, one word, even though none of them had those names. There were French military uniforms and marching band uniforms; I think there were even a couple of *Nutcracker* costumes in the mix. Most of these came from Hack's connection with a ratty theater troupe in Brooklyn who allowed him to raid their costume and prop collection, as long as he had everything back in place the same day. This is where Tina found the blue-tinted aviator sunglasses that became a trademark with her. She said it made it easier to tell what the world looked like in black and white. After she found them, it was rare to see her without them. She retreated behind those drooping blue lenses and never really came back.

Tina's sunglasses aside, we usually managed to have everything back on time, but there were a couple of times that Tina and Hack held on to Yorick's skull for a couple days at a stretch, and the stage manager noticed. Hack had been hoping to use the theater itself and some of its scenery flats in a few of the interior scenes between the square family at the heart of the *IDA* plot, but this series of irresponsible oversights eroded his good will, and the stage manager banned him from using the theater or any more of the costumes and props. Hack conceded the use of the theater, but he had enough of a fetish for continuity that he couldn't give up the use of the costumes, so we basically stole everything we needed and returned it the same night every time we did so.

We couldn't do that every day; someone was sure to notice. So, Hack and Tina took a good long look at the scenes they still wanted to shoot and planned out some marathon shooting days. Tina suggested that we use Lur's apartment for some of the scenes, but I put my foot down there. We had already brought ourselves into Lur's world, and not all of that was bad, but I knew that she wasn't interested in a bunch of kids invading her space and trampling over her supplies. It was one of the few battles I was able to win regarding the movie, but I think it also precipitated Tina moving out of our place and into Hack's.

The interior scenes happened mostly in a couple of rooms in the sixth-floor apartments; one of them the very room where we first found Paul filming with his trio of actors. This is where Hack first figured out that I was a better script girl (script supervisor) than I ever was a lookout. I had the eye for consistency and continuity. With a group of non-professional actors, many of whom were variously drunk or high, it helped to have someone who could stand in for the observant film viewer, and that was me. Hack was making sure that the insane shoot schedule was being followed, and Tina was making sure that the images were artfully framed and properly exposed. They weren't going for the Oscars, but they did want people to be able to see something on screen. The acting was universally melodramatic, as Hack wanted it to be. That was not only the acting style appropriate to the film; it was also the way to live your life in *The Imperial Dynasty of America.*

I think it was during these day-long endurance shoots that *The King in Yellow* came back into our lives. One of the actors, a guy named Simon, had it on him. He was playing a professor, a historian who helps to set the scene for the viewers near the beginning of the film and then comes back at the end, a bit like the stuffy guy in *The Rocky Horror Picture Show.* The slim black book poked out of one of his tweedy jacket pockets. I first took note of Simon because his pipe reeked and had a tendency to make the set unbearable. It smelled like those meaty little cigarillos that Horace smoked when he drove us to the barn party. Hack was friends with him, and Tina said she liked the way that the smoke photographed, so this was one of the arguments I routinely lost. I secretly tried to leave windows cracked open when I could.

When Simon wasn't in a shot, he usually lounged somewhere in the background, the play held open between the fingers of one hand, his other hand wrapped around the pipe he occasionally raised to his lips. I didn't think much of it beyond whether or not it was in the same pocket when he was in the same scene shot from a different angle. It was a prop, albeit one that he had brought himself. What made me look twice was the moment when Hack called him over for a shot, and when he tucked the book into his pocket, the light from the exposed naked lightbulb overhead caught the embossed leather cover in such a way that I could make out the Yellow Sign carved into it.

For a moment, I couldn't quite tell if my heartbeat had stopped or if it was fluttering so quickly that I couldn't count the beats anymore. I kept my eyes locked on the book as he walked across the room and allowed himself to be positioned and then ran through his lines, which might have been brief or as long as Homer reciting

The Odyssey for all I knew. I wasn't brought back to myself until I heard Tina asking me if everything had gone well. There was no way to conceal my distraction, but I went ahead and lied and just said that everything was fine. Hack didn't notice anything wrong and immediately dove into the next shot. Tina gave me a look and then asked the room if we needed coffee. No one took her up on the suggestion, and then suddenly the moment was gone.

From that point on, I found myself staying aware of Simon's position whenever I was in the room with him; it was like he was some kind of pit viper and no one else fully appreciated how dangerous he was. I did my best never to have my back to him and never to be alone in the same room with him. He acted perfectly normal, or as perfectly normal as you were likely to find on our set, and aside from his possession of *The King in Yellow*, I had no reason to hate him. But there were times during the shoot when I showed up to a location and he and Tina were already talking about something. More than once I overheard him talking about "black stars," "cloud waves," and "doomed Cassilda." They were talking about it so matter-of-factly. I remember I stayed up all night, pacing in my room, working up the courage to confront both of them. I felt that I needed to put a stop to it, but I didn't have the courage to face it. And then we wrapped.

It wasn't until weeks later, before Hack and Tina were done cutting the film, that we saw Simon's picture in the newspaper. He had become famous as the man who had disemboweled two strangers on the street in Alphabet City and then led police on a foot chase into a nearby apartment building, out onto the roof, where he leapt from the edge and fell eight stories onto a spiked wrought iron fence. The next day, a tabloid ran a photograph of the body before it had been pulled from the fence, with a dog lapping at the stream of blood that flowed into the gutter.

CHAPTER TEN

The premiere of *The Imperial Dynasty of America* came on a gorgeous day in late June of 1979. I hadn't seen much of Tina in weeks. Once she and Hack had everything shot, they spent two weeks hand-processing the film in the new lab that Hack had built in his apartment. When she did come home, she smelled of chemicals and cigarette smoke, and the look in her eye was both maniacal and inspiring. It was like she had seen some truth in that immersion tank, staring into its liquid depths, and it set her apart. Whatever it was that she saw there, it determined her course and lent her an air of confidence, but that confidence was a little bit disturbing.

I never got a chance to visit Hack's place during this period, but Tina told me about it. One room had the work table with the viewer and splicer where the actual cutting was done, and that room was spider-webbed with lengths of twine from which they hung strips of film. Hack moved around the room looking at lengths of film and choosing which would go next on the reel, while Tina sat at the splicer, using press tape to join the shots and then run them thorough the viewer slowly and then faster to make sure that the whole thing was coming together in the way that they wanted it. After a week or two, the strips of film began to migrate out of that room and into other parts of the apartment, as though they were taking over the living space.

An open doorway into the bedroom was given a modicum of privacy with a curtain of unselected shots that hung from the transom, curling this way and that at waist level. Snakes of Super 8 film filled waste baskets and boxes, spilling out here and there. It was only the best shots that were hung up for eventual use on the reels.

There were some cataclysmic arguments during those weeks. Hack was the one making the editorial selections, but once Tina had the shots spliced together, she offered her opinion on the resulting montage. Hack had ideas about cross-cutting that worked incredibly well in his head, or at least that was his claim, but Tina was convinced that they didn't work so well once they were actually on a screen. He argued the tiny viewer wasn't doing justice to his vision, but Tina tried to convince him that the problems would be that much worse when they were projected onto a screen. They screamed at each other, and sometimes Hack grabbed strands of celluloid and tried to tear them apart, but he never touched the hanging takes when he did this, and he never came near the actual reel they were constructing.

Tina sensed that he was blowing off steam and in some cases actually listening to what she had to say. He was frustrated that his vision wasn't completely adequate to the film that they had shot, and he was chafing under the reality of having a creative partner. Neither of them felt like they had the resources to cut multiple versions of the film, so they were fighting to agree on every cut. Sometimes it turned into a horse trading match. Hack got a cut that he wanted, but only in exchange for a shot placement that Tina felt adamant about.

This situation reached an impasse in late May, when they flew into a raging argument that took both of them into the hallway outside the apartment. Tina said that when she finally walked away from him and went outside to breathe something like fresh air, she worried that he wouldn't let her back in. She actually came back to our place that day and told me all about how things had been going. I could tell how important the project was to her, and I had heard enough about how their working relationship could be tempestuous at times, so I was hopeful and encouraging to her about giving him a day and then going back to it the next.

I tried to take her mind off of it by showing her what I was learning from Lur in the greenhouse. Over the weeks of spring, there was less and less need to follow a heating schedule for the water lilies, so it became more about looking after them and learning how to harvest the seed pods for the extract that Lur made from them. Lur had shown me how the drying and desiccating process worked, and then I learned how to grind the materials and make sure there were no impurities. She even taught me about how the extract was best used with certain alcohols, usually wine, since the plant was a particular kind of alkaloid that was not soluble in water. She had recipes for all sorts of different kinds of wines along with additives for different kinds of effects that you might want from the final mixture. It had certainly helped her confidence in me that I had a textbook knowledge of the lotus, so the learning curve for me wasn't very steep, and I caught on quickly to the knowledge that she was choosing to share.

I mixed Tina up a jar of wine with some of the lotus extract that I had been making and told her that it would help her to relax and get herself centered again before going back. She was pretty skeptical of the whole thing, but we were still friends, maybe even more so since she had spent some time away. We sat on the edge of the roof, looked out over the neighborhood, and she sipped while we caught up. By the time she was done telling me about how the editing had been going and what she saw as the possibilities for this film, she was drowsy and looking for a place to crash. We went back down to the apartment after I locked everything up, and I tucked her in on my mattress.

She slept for almost thirteen hours until around sunrise the next morning. I watched her for some of that night, when I was worried that maybe I had gotten the mixture wrong somehow, but I think it did its trick. She had been driving herself, and the drink gave her a nudge to let it all go for a while and reset her body and mind. My worry was that she was obviously having some intense nightmares while she was asleep. She tossed and turned, occasionally crying out, shouting names like Uhot and Cassilda, and other names I'd never heard before, though I've come to understand certain dark associations since then. I debated waking her from these visions, but in the end I decided that she was working through something necessary to her psychic health and that I should let her experience them in full. It was hard.

When she woke up, she said nothing about any nightmares, and I didn't pry beyond asking how she slept. She didn't look particularly refreshed, but she had clearly made some firm decisions in the night. We ate breakfast together and then she disappeared again out of the flow of my daily life.

I started seeing flyers around the neighborhood for the film screening and concert before Tina had a chance to invite me personally. There might have been a momentary pang of neglect, of feeling like I had been left out or left behind, but the fact that the flyer named Hack and Tina as co-creators of the film reassured me that some sort of reconciliation had taken place and their collaboration was salvaged. The flyers advertised the premiere of *The Imperial Dynasty of America* with special guest Lethal Chamber. The image was a photocopied enlargement of the back of one of the counterfeit bills from the package we'd received. The name of the film was, of course, taken from the bill itself, and the implication was that the columned building depicted in the center of the design was the Lethal Chamber that inspired the band name. There was something vaguely familiar about the group when I finally saw them perform at the premiere. I couldn't tell if I had seen them at some other club over the past few months, or if I had seen other flyers with their name, or something else. But it was a déjà vu moment I found it difficult to shake.

I asked Lur if she wanted to come with me to the premiere, but she huffed and walked away. She was a music fan, I knew—her radio ping-ponged wildly between Sinatra and Nina Simone, classical and nueva canción—but I never saw her go to the movies or take part in any of the more avant-garde stuff that was happening in the East Village at the time. She kept to herself, so I was going to go by myself. This was another reminder to me that I had not spent much time trying to make new friends while we had been in New York. It was me and Tina at the start, and then I began spending more and more time with Lur when Tina found Hack, but I hadn't gone out of my way to expand my circle of friends.

When Tina finally did come to the apartment one day in mid-June to hand deliver a flyer as a formal invitation, she also made it clear that she was going to need to be there in an official capacity, making sure the projection equipment was working properly. Hack was able to find a projector at a pawn shop that he could afford, but they were borrowing another one from an acquaintance of his. When I asked why they needed two, Tina smiled and made me promise that I would come. Of course, there was no way I was going to miss it.

The event took place in the basement of a disused building in Alphabet City. Later I found out that it was a place that Paul originally found. It had an access door that opened onto what used to be an alley but was now the edge of a vacant lot after the neighboring building burned to the ground a few years before. Paul had forced the boards that covered the door and then carefully replaced them in a way that allowed him to return when he liked. Since then, Paul had used the basement as a set in a couple of his film projects.

Others had of course found the way in or heard about it by word of mouth, and it had become something of an open secret in the neighborhood. Bands in particular found that it was a good place to play. Paul had figured out how to jury-rig the electrical panel to get power. ConEd inevitably figured this out and shut it down, but they never did anything that prevented someone from doing it again. For the one-off party, concert, or happening, it was perfect. You had to watch out for rats, and you might have to make a deal with squatters, but you could jam over a hundred people into the space and control access if you wanted to take money at the door.

When I arrived on the night of the premiere, there was already a crowd of people in the vacant lot and a line of people at the stairs down into the basement door. Swayne was there taking two dollars from each person who wanted to listen to Lethal Chamber or see the show that Tina and Hack had prepared, and he was backed by a corn-fed lineman from the Plains in mechanic's overalls and a combat helmet. The helmet had the letters IDA stenciled on the front. Swayne was in his full formal wear and silent film makeup and in command. I'm not even sure that he remembered me as I paid my two dollars and moved with the flow of humanity into the darkened space.

The basement was mostly an open area with steel poles holding the ground floor over our heads. It was a forest of metal trunks, rusty with ancient flaking paint. I overheard a group of guys talking about them later, and they thought the pillars were part of the original construction of the building when it was a fire station, support that was necessary to make sure the fire truck didn't come crashing down into the basement. A few women had gotten good seats already on a flight of stairs with a finely wrought iron banister that rose up to the ground floor, where a heavily padlocked cage door prevented access. They had chosen to stay well back from the band, knowing that the more frenetic and violent guys were going to be right up front.

Lethal Chamber was setting up in the corner of the basement farthest away from the stairs and the access door, and I could see that
on a table in front of the drum kit were the two projectors, each
one pointed at a different joining wall. I didn't think much about
that at the time, I think I assumed that the projectors were not
fully set up when I saw them, but they were the first thing that had
been set in place earlier that day, and then the band found spots
around them. The other telling detail about the coming show was
that the drummer's chair was not a normal stool but instead a mock
electric chair built out of discarded (or, as always, stolen) lumber
and painted brown and black. The seat between the arm was extra
wide, and the back was taller than you might expect—though I
had certainly never seen an actual electric chair at that point in my
life—lending the whole thing an exaggerated and unreal quality.
The angles were off, too, which made its corners seem sharp in a
way that increased the sense of danger it gave off.

Someone had spent some time painting the basement. You could
smell the paint, and I imagine that this was not a bad idea all
around. But the way that they had chosen to paint the basement,
and particularly the corner where the band was setting up had obvious nods to *The Cabinet of Dr. Caligari* and German expressionism
in general. Flanking the band, rhomboid shapes were painted on
the black wall in lighter grays. The sharp corners of the frames were
ready to leap out and slash at the crowd. Of course, in the harsh
light of the handful of naked bulbs hanging from the basement
ceiling, it looked incongruous, but once those were extinguished in
favor of the show lights, it took on its full effect.

It was almost a half hour after I found my way into the basement that the show got started. The crowd was getting a little bit
restless, since the only refreshments were the ones that people had
brought for themselves or their group. Hack and Tina had not fully

absorbed the lesson that the money in film exhibition is almost entirely to be found in the sale of concessions. They were there for the art that night, and so were a lot of the rest of us. Those that weren't were starting to make a ruckus when the members of Lethal Chamber gathered in the corner and took up their instruments. The drummer sat down in the electric chair that dwarfed his slender frame, and then the design became a little clearer to me: it was probably big to be exaggerated, but the chair's size also meant that he had a lot of room to drum. An arm chair normally was an extremely poor choice for a drummer, but it looked like this one was only trouble if he got gymnastic. Lethal Chamber was one of the more stylistically vicious exponents of the New York punk scene at the point, so gymnastics were not entirely out of the question.

The band took the stage and after only a couple glances at one another, they launched into their first set of two that they expected to play that night. They were angry and loud and likely more full of themselves than talent, but the assembled crowd reacted immediately, and bodies started moving around me. At first this was a lot of bouncing and flailing of arms, something for which the relatively generous basement ceiling offered plenty of room. By the second song, though, the bouncing had developed into accidentally and then deliberately slamming their bodies into one another. People were getting knocked into the steel pillars, launching themselves off of the same pillars or strangers standing next to them. Maybe the band infused the audience with their anger, or maybe everyone brought their own with them, like the drinks that most people openly carried into the place.

There was a vehemence, an anger, in the room that I hadn't felt at any other show that I had attended in the city, though the punk scene wasn't my thing, I'll admit. I saw at least two people stumble toward the entrance with bloodied faces before the end of the first set, and I was wondering whether this kind of chaos was what the band and Tina and Hack had been expecting. It didn't feel like her; I didn't know about him. I'd brought a small packet of lotus extract with me, but nothing to put it in. I thought that I would probably be able to find something if I wanted to take it.

More and more I was thinking I wanted to mellow out for the rest of the evening. When I arrived earlier, I had been excited to finally see what they had made, but as the set went on I began thinking more in terms of getting through the night, enduring it rather than enjoying it. It made me sad at first, but eventually I felt a growing determination not to let Tina down. She hadn't spent a lot of time with me or shown me all that much attention since I'd arrived, but I thought she would be hurt if I left. As long as I didn't get hurt, I knew I could hang in there and support her.

It wasn't all that difficult to find a drink, but it took a little searching to find someone who had brought something that was a good fit for the lotus powder. It took me most of two songs and a lot of dancing through sweaty dynamos of rage to find a couple of people who had backup beers. That wasn't what I was looking for, so I kept on going. Then I saw something more promising. One of the girls on the stairs was passing around one of those stupid leather pouches of wine. I grabbed an empty beer can off the floor, shook it out, made sure that there were no stray cigarette butts in it, and then made nice with the crowd in their box seats. They were uptown kids, not village punks, and I wondered which one of them had thought that this is where they should spend their evening. Most of them were deeply stoned, but the girl with the skin looked drunk. She was on the verge of being sloppy. I offered half of the powder I'd brought for some of their wine. She was reluctant, but the others in her group were keen to try whatever it was that I had in the small plastic film canister. I convinced her that it was fine.

It was a tricky operation in the darkness, with all of the screeching and pandemonium around us, but I got the cap off, poured in most of the powder, spilling only a little bit of it on my wrist, capped the pouch and shook it vigorously. As I did, smiles bloomed over their faces, though the drunk girl swayed and shook her head in doubt. I squirted enough into my beer can to fill it about halfway, and then I passed it back to her. She immediately held it over her head again, in that idiotic and anachronistic display, but the stream of blood-red lotus wine hit its mark and satisfied her. An overeager young man snatched the skin out of her hand, spilling wine over her shirt, complaining that she was hogging all of it. I turned back to the band and gulped down about half of the potion, tasting a swirling ghost of crappy beer among the more familiar flavors.

Lethal Chamber was in the last song of their first set when I sucked down the final dregs of my drink. The extract was already having its effect on me; I could feel the tension that I was carrying around with me slip out of my body and float through the scene, making loops around the pillars and rising to the ceiling above the heads of the audience. There was a crash and a final strum from the band, as the last chords of "Past the Fates" vibrated through the basement from the amps. The lead singer, guitarist, and bass-ist left the corner where they had been playing, but the drummer remained in his electric chair. He had been enlisted into the show that evening, and was game for whatever it was that Tina and Hack had dreamed up. Hack came up to him and handed him a cigarette and put a metal colander on his head. The drummer adjusted the colander and gripped his sticks. He nodded at Hack and Tina, who were standing by next to their projectors. It was clear that the pro-jectors needed to be started at exactly the same time.

The drummer gave the count, and then as his sticks came crash-ing down on the snares one more time, Tina and Hack brought their machines to life. The projectors were neither level nor point-ed perpendicularly to the walls, so the white leader images that they cast in those first moments were not at all rectangular. In fact, it quickly became obvious that the expressionist frames that had been painted on the walls had probably been painted that day, *after* the projectors were set up and tested. The film images fit their crazy skewed frames perfectly, but even those images were skewed. I could tell by the first few shots that all of the footage that they had used in the film, with the exception of some footage taken from other sources, had been filmed from odd angles that were made only more odd by the strange angle of presentation.

The unknown face from the counterfeit bills stretched along the basement walls, one on either side of the drummer, as he beat out a primal rhythm on his set. None of the other band members approached the stage area, and the films only had a drum solo accompaniment. His drumming started out tribal and then rippling drum rolls transformed the mood into a patriotic fervor, though no one in the room was likely to join in on that feeling in any genuine way, and so it came across as ironic.

Images flashed back and forth, filling the weird frames on the walls and stirring the audience into frenzies of recognition and awe. There were shots of buildings from the neighborhood and from other parts of the city, shots of homeless people in the parks, shots of police arresting prostitutes as a rousing march thundered from the drums. There were shots of gun camera footage from World War II and slow motion shots of napalm blossoming in the jungles of Vietnam. Some of these shots were drenched in a red tint that was timed to pulsate faster and faster, eventually reaching the alpha wave range similar to Hack's dream machine.

And every now and then, and then more frequently, there was a shot of Hack on the left wall and a shot of Tina on the right. In each shot, we got a bird's-eye close-up shot of one of them in bed, head on a pillow. They were each naked, at least above the waist, and looked like they were in the throes of some great passion, one that was building over the course of the film. You had the sense that each take, cut as it was between other shots in the film, was footage of each of their faces as somebody else (presumably the other) went down on them. It took me a while to see what it was that I thought I was seeing, but it's an impression that you can't shake if you've ever seen Warhol's *Blowjob*.

The images of this passion built in intensity along with the ever-heightening images of war and nationalism until they climaxed in an orgasm of mushroom clouds and gaping mouths. But in the moments immediately following their supposed bliss and the destruction of the world, each of them turned to the other projection and smiled these genuinely warm smiles of accomplishment. They didn't smile down at their lover, and not out at the audience who had been sharing this moment with them (fairly raucously, as it turned out), but at each other. As they looked into each other's eyes across the edges of their own frames and the dark gap in between the screens, their faces were intercut with the startling image of the marble grim reaper from Fritz Lang's *Metropolis*, separating from its alcove and swinging its scythe again and again across the screen. The angel of death reaped its bloody harvest as Tina and Hack lay smiling at one another over the head of the condemned drummer, whose sweat flew into the audience as he pounded out the climax on his drums.

It was only later, when many of the attendees got home, that they saw the drops of real blood on their clothes and faces and wondered whose it was.

CHAPTER ELEVEN

H ack and Tina were both hoping that something would happen after the screening of *The Imperial Dynasty of America*. They were hoping for some kind of launch, some kind of increase in their material or social standing that would encapsulate what they had accomplished. No one said "masterpiece" or anything like that, but they talked about it like it was a real and worthwhile opening gambit in some longer artistic game. For Tina, that turned out to be true, from a certain point of view. For Hack, well, for Hack it was the looming shadow of the end.

For almost a week after the screening in the basement, Tina did reap the rewards of having done something. She saw other people on the street or ran into them in bodegas and coffee houses and bars, and they wanted to talk to her about it. A lot of them hadn't even been there, but they had heard about it from friends who maybe had (or maybe they hadn't). The thing was taking on a life of its own with its own mythology and legends. Apparently, some people who had been at the premiere claimed that the film featured a robed and masked figure that seemed to be able to move from one screen to the other fluidly, as though the screens were merely two windows into an adjoining room. They wanted to know when they could see the film, when and where Tina and Hack hoped to screen it again. Tina nodded along with them and thanked them for their interest and said that they hoped to screen it again, but they weren't sure where and they weren't sure when. This was always a problem with Tina as a filmmaker. She needed someone else to think of the distribution and exhibition side of things. With her early films, she just made them. She created her films, but she never thought deliberately about what happened to her work after that initial process. With the first film of Donny, Holly bought it and it went out of her life. Now, with *Imperial Dynasty of America*, they showed it and it went out of her life. If she had been thinking more about a real career in movies, she would have been trying to turn all of this interest into more opportunities to make money. At least for now, all it was doing was adding to her and Hack's reputations and to the myth of the film.

I say myth, because as many people know, *The Imperial Dynasty of America* passed out of this world a few days after it was screened to those crowds in the basement venue. I remember the day that it happened, and also how the whole thing felt like it unfolded slowly. I was walking up the stairs in the building when I saw Swayne coming down. We had seen each other on and off, but we had no occasion to speak with one another when we did, so I hadn't gotten to know him any better. After that first encounter, I didn't feel any desire to know him any better anyway. I thought he had shown his true colors, and they were not colors with which I wanted to decorate my life. That was all. But as he passed by me on the stairs, he looked straight at me and said, "No fires on the roof. Bad news for your friends."

I kept climbing, not even acknowledging that he had said anything; it was exactly the kind of odd comment that the squatters who lived in the building made while stoned. You could spend the rest of your life trying to make sense out of them. I assumed that by "friends" he was referring to Tina and Hack, but as I climbed, I began to think that maybe he was talking about the lotuses or even Lur. And then I was wondering about what sort of fires there were on the roof and whether or not someone sober should get up there to see whether or not the whole building was in danger, despite Swayne's more specific warning.

I started to take the stairs two at a time and sprinted past our floor and up to the roof. I had been working with Lur long enough that I was allowed my own copy of the roof key so that I could tend to the plants without bothering her. I reached the roof with no plan other than to find out what was happening. The building didn't have fire extinguisher or anything like that I could have brought up with me, but I figured there was plenty of water in the greenhouse itself. I could figure something out if necessary.

When I burst onto the roof, my heart leapt to my throat. Tina was kneeling at the far corner of the roof, a small pile of material smoldering in front of her. From all those yards away, I could smell the burnt plastic odor of all that celluloid. It looked like Tina had carried the film cans of *Imperial Dynasty of America* up to the roof and then set them on fire and watched them burn (after opening them), sobbing over whatever terrible impulse had made her do it. She was rocking back and forth, inconsolable as I came up and knelt down next to her, gathering her into my arms and asking her what she had done. In retrospect, it was bad timing that I asked that question as Hack also emerged from the door to the roof. What I saw left me at a loss. What he saw enraged him. He was convinced that Tina had done this thing, and in her own confusion and pain, she was unable to understand that Hack was accusing her of having destroyed his work.

It took more than an hour to calm her down enough to learn that she had found the canisters much as I had, still burning, but only just. By the time she realized what they were and looked around for water or some kind of extinguisher, they were all gone. It had happened so fast. But it wasn't her. She swore that it wasn't her. She would never do such a thing, and I had no choice but to believe her, because I had no reason to think otherwise. She wasn't self-destructive like that.

But Hack reacted in the white hot crucible of the moment. Something inside him, or something sitting on his shoulder, whispered to his inmost soul that Tina had done this thing and he would never forgive her for it. His passion, which he had shared with her in the film and in bed and elsewhere was now focused like a cleansing ray of light entirely on her. He wanted to destroy her utterly, to consume her in the way that she had consumed his work. In this moment he also took full responsibility for the film. It was in no way Tina's film to dispose of as she saw fit; it was his, and she had no right to touch it.

Hack rushed at Tina, and I put myself in his way. That was a mistake. He wasn't a big man, but he had dozens of pounds on me. I was an obstacle, but one that he could easily push aside. The problem was that pushing me aside basically meant pushing me off the roof of the building. We stumbled over Tina's feet, and I grabbed onto him rather than trip. I think my scream snapped Hack and Tina out of their emotional spirals long enough for them to see what it was that they were doing. Tina staggered to her feet and grabbed onto Hack's arm, while Hack grabbed me roughly and pressed me against the ledge that surrounded the roof. He wanted to use his strength for something else, for something destructive, but instead he used it to keep me where I was, to press me into the brick. I had a bruise across my chest for over a week after that.

Tina ripped him away from me.

"Leave her alone, asshole."

"We had one fucking copy, Tina. How could you do this?" Hack was screaming, spittle webbing the corners of his mouth.

"I didn't do anything."

"Fuck you! Didn't do anything." Hack stomped over to the smoldering remains and kicked the warped steel film can across the roof. Sparks plumed up from the black mass that popped out of the can, and the smell of burning acetate was again sharp in the air. "*Dynasty* just spontaneously combusted?"

"I didn't do it, but maybe you did." Tina's voice was ragged from crying. Her words slurred. "You sure showed up here fast enough."

"Why would I..."

"Because you're a jealous little prick. That was my camera work; I'm the one getting the attention now. You just had to take it all away because you can't share."

Hack laughed at that, angrily, dismissively.

It got even uglier from there. I couldn't watch the whole thing, but I didn't want to leave either. I was worried that the words would fail, that their passion would flare up again, and someone would wind up hurt or dead. But it was too painful to watch, and even though it was playing out in full daylight in front of the entire city, it felt like a private moment.

I busied myself by staring at the smoldering remains of the best film that Tina had helped to make up to that point. I felt some loss, too. I hadn't fully realized how much I was looking forward to the next time I would be able to see it. And now I would never get that chance, *no one* would ever get that chance. There was only one copy of *Imperial Dynasty of America*, and it was a blackened and bubbling mass of melted acetate at that point.

As I looked at the burning mass in the steel film cans, I could see that on the asphalt surrounding them some obscure symbols had been drawn in black. I couldn't tell right then, but it looked like the symbols were scrawled using charcoal or maybe even the blackened soot from the film material itself, though that would surely have been painful. I looked over at Tina's hands; they were covered in a similar black soot, but that could have come from her trying to save something of the footage when she found them burning, if that's how it actually happened. I could tell that I had no idea what the truth was at this point. My friendship with Tina was such that I didn't have absolute faith in her innocence; I just knew that it didn't make any sense to me.

But then, I also knew that I didn't care, other than my mild or detached sense of disappointment that the film was gone. What I was more worried about was whether these two people I knew were going to try to physically hurt each other. The bells that were ringing in my head were too faint for me to answer. Those symbols on the ground were vaguely familiar to me; I had seen them before but the scene was too fluid for me to remember precisely where it was. I was too worried about what was going on. The memories came later, and those memories had me casting my mind back to that brief encounter on the stairs with Swayne, trying to remember if he, too, had the soot on his fingertips, and wondering why he might be so threatened by Tina's and Hack's film that he would resort to black magic.

The actual fire had gone out before the two of them stopped screaming and clawing at one another. Hack threw up his hands at one point, told Tina to go fuck herself, and then said he was going to get the cops. It was an absurd threat. The cops don't care; this barely rose to the level of reportable vandalism. He was looking for a way out of the moment, some way that he could leave the roof and not look like he was retreating. Before going, he gave the smoking cans a good kick, obscuring some of the black symbols on the ground and sending the cans skittering across the asphalt and caroming off of the brick roof ledge. He stormed back to the stair-well and disappeared into the darkness, slamming the door behind him as he went.

I returned to Tina and rubbed her back, while she stood there shaking. I couldn't tell anymore if she was angry or hurt or some-

thing else, or some combination of all of these. She needed someone, but I didn't know what to say that did not sound completely
stupid, so I opted to be there. I didn't fully understand what was
transpiring, and I could sense that Tina didn't know either. It was
a clear and hot day, but we might as well have been in thick fog on
a moonless night. The only thing that felt certain was that we were
surrounded by deadly cliffs on all sides. I wanted to get Tina off the
roof and back to the apartment. She hadn't been staying there for
a while, but Lur wouldn't mind if she came by for a visit, and now
was the time for that visit. I slowly steered her down off the roof,
promising her a chance to wash up and a cup of tea.

Lur was puttering around in the main room when we got down
to the second floor. She was arranging bags of potting soil and laying out wire forms for some new project. The lotuses didn't require
support of any kind, but these were obviously wire forms for some
plant with heavy blooms or creeping vines. I hadn't seen them in
the apartment before. She also had a couple of small boxes on a
table near the forms. They looked like Chinese take-out boxes, but
they didn't have the red designs you usually see on them. One of
the boxes was open; it was full of black soil and had fat reddish-
brown worms oozing inside. When we swept into the room, she
immediately stopped what she was doing and came over to us.

"Are you two okay? What happened?" Lur wasn't normally this
nurturing or attentive, but she must have sensed that there was
something different then. We had the whiff of magic about us
maybe. She was fluttering around, telling me to go put the kettle
on and arranging the bags and tarps a little more comfortably than
their usual positions allowed.

Tina was still crying, but more quietly now. She let herself be
led, but she wasn't responding much to the questions that I put to
her now and then. I wasn't interested in the answers themselves;
they were a way of getting her to open up to me. Lur's method was

more direct. She told me to stop pestering my friend and go put the kettle on, which I did.

When I came back, Tina was lying down on the floor with her back propped up against a small stack of bags. Lur was holding a damp rag to Tina's forehead with one hand while the other hand worked a small fan she produced out of nowhere. Just seeing that made me more relaxed, too. It was remarkable. Lur's presence was calming, but maybe only after you got to know her a little better.

When we heard the kettle whistling, Lur jumped up and put the fan into my hand. I took over while she fixed Tina's tea, and I now suspect also added something else to it. I thought this first as soon as Lur gave Tina the first sip, and I could see Tina's brows knit in the reaction to the occasional bitterness of the usual lotus powder concoction. But what Tina described later makes me think that there was something else in that tea.

Lur had Tina drink slowly as she soothed her more. She said that there was nothing more to worry about at the moment, but that she needed to be vigilant in the days and possibly weeks to come. "That man is dangerous, because he has a little bit of knowledge, which is precisely what makes men so dangerous. It's never what they know, but always the things that they don't yet know that give them teeth. The teeth of ignorance."

"But why would he destroy the film?" Tina said.

"To drive the two of you apart."

"That makes no sense. Why would he do that, when he could just break up with me, or tell me to get lost."

"But there would still be the film. He had to get rid of the thing that was holding you together, and all the better if each of you thinks the other did it."

My mind was reeling.

"Wait," I said. "Are you talking about Hack?"

"Swayne. Swayne did this. He worked a curse on the two of you."

"I saw him in the stairwell before I found you on the roof," I said. "He said that fires on the roof are bad for my friends."

Tina sipped at the tea, taking a long slurping draught and then laying back. She closed her eyes. She looked like she was trying to project herself out of her body, which was wracked with pain and fear. She was trying to get clear of all the shit so that she could try to see the truth.

"Curse," she whispered, and there was the barest hint of a smile on her lips.

"But now you know," said Lur. "The power is weak."

"Hack doesn't know." Tina's eyes were still closed, but her voice was clear and strong. "He thinks that I burned the film."

Tina pushed the cup into my hand and then sat up suddenly. "Finish the rest of that. We need to go find Hack right now."

Lur was already fiddling around in the kitchen, or I would have looked to her for some sign about whether I should have the tea, too. But without her around, I decided that Tina was getting ahold of herself, so I threw the rest of the tea down my throat in one gulp. There wasn't much left in the cup, but instantly I knew why Tina's face reacted the way it did on her first sip. I was used to the lotus powder mix by then, but this wasn't that. It was something wholly other, something *holy*. As the rapidly cooling tea slithered down my throat, viscous and alive, the world suddenly grew long and then collapsed, like that effect Hitchcock used in his films. There was no nausea in the pit of my stomach, though. There was a sense of the world fading out of focus and then quickly snapping back into frame, but not at all in the same way that it had been before. I could see and feel and taste and hear other things now. And around Tina there was this miasma that I hadn't previously been able to see. It was dense and murky and it carried with it an inexplicable foreboding of doom. Lur gave the tea to Tina because Tina needed to see, and Tina gave it to me because she needed my help. We moved toward the door only to be halted by a bark from Lur.

"Be careful of your friend. Remember, his ignorance makes him dangerous. When the two of you are together, this thing is stronger. You'd be better off if you stayed here."

Tina nodded and thanked Lur, but then headed out the door all the same. I knew that we were on our way to Hack's apartment, and I assumed that Tina planned to tell him about Swayne and the curse. I have no idea how she planned to convince him that it was real and that she seriously believed in it.

I was still reeling from the effects of the tea myself. Being on the street was not making it easier. I had been in the city long enough that I usually paid little attention to the mass of people flowing down the sidewalk. But now I could only see their skeletons, the knobby and angular frameworks that held up the forms shambling by me. Gaping, hollow eye sockets leered at me when I dared to look at them in bewildered awe. The giant insectoids that scuttled along the floors of the steep urban canyons were magnificent to look at. I had never seen bugs so huge—I laughed out loud when I realized I had not—or so colorful. Now and again, one of their iridescent carapaces opened, and translucent mullioned wings unfolded from beneath. A deep vibration commenced, and the insect was slowly pulled skyward, serenaded by the sharp bleating of the other creatures.

The caves that pocked the walls of these slate canyons were rimed with unbroken sheets of quartz, and out of more than one of them came rich aromas that I soon realized I was more apt to feel than smell. The velvety smoke that wafted from one cave jarred against the the prickly and metallic mist that spewed from another. My stomach churned at the same time that my skin crawled as though stroked by the withered hand of a serpent priest.

There was something fascinating about it, while at the same time I found myself hoping that the effect wore off sooner rather than later—and then I wondered if the effect was permanent. I didn't want to see these things for the rest of my life. I was very much afraid that if I spent too long in this new world, that I would come to believe in it and never be able to unsee what I could see. There was nothing I wanted more at that moment than to stop seeing it.

I knew that I hadn't forgotten the way to Hack's apartment, so I was caught off guard when Tina grabbed my wrist and yanked me into a subway stairwell for the 14th and Union Square station.

I was asking what the hell she thought she was doing when she pointed and said, "There he is."

Hack was pacing back and forth on the platform at the far end of the station. He hadn't seen us yet. He looked like he was talking to himself, which made perfect sense. He was still angry, and he was continuing the argument that I had managed to interrupt on the roof. No, that he had walked away from. The station wasn't full, but there were clumps of people waiting for the next train. Tina pulled me off of the stairs and into the station, moving straight toward Hack.

It was a hot day, like I said, and the station smelled of creosote and urine and sweat. For a moment, I thought that there might be some kind of smoke coming from somewhere, but I soon figured out that it was that miasma that I had seen around Tina, and that here was combining with Hack's as we got closer to him. No one else in the station had a cloud following them around like this, but I did notice that many of the people we passed by gave off these musical notes, almost like odd vibrations. The notes came from their skin or from something inside them. It wasn't loud, but it was a new layer to the mundane city sounds that I almost didn't notice anymore.

We were maybe thirty feet away from Hack when it happened. There was a flowing rush of air, like there was a train in the station already, though we had only started to faintly hear the approach of an express train. The wind moved swiftly across the tracks rather than along them, cutting across the platforms. Hack turned with the first hint of the wind and his eyes locked with Tina's. Immediately the rage welled up within him, and that dark miasma grew darker still, until I could barely see him in the center of it. He shouted something as the train grew louder, and a pale shape flashed in the corner of my eye.

I'm still not sure exactly what I saw. It looked like a tall thin man in a tattered pale robe rushed across the platform and tackled Hack onto the tracks as the express train exploded into the station. One moment Hack was yelling at Tina and the next moment he wasn't there anymore. My soul was pierced by the combined shriek of a witness and the brakes of the subway train. Tina stopped in her tracks and stared at the space where Hack used to be. People on the platform moved toward the car, some rushed and others approached more gingerly, but all of them were trying to see if they had just witnessed the horrific tragedy that they thought they had seen.

It all happened so fast; no one was sure. Instinctively, I wrapped my arms around Tina and held onto her. I could tell that her heart was racing, but she didn't start to cry again, like I was crying. She just stood there.

We stood there for a long time. Police came. Transit guys came. Paramedics came. Hack was down there, but he was alone, surrounded by himself. His body was in so many pieces that they weren't sure at first whether there were two or one, but I soon realized that we were the only ones that saw the figure in the robe, or maybe I was the only one who saw him. Everyone else around us said that the freak wind had blown Hack off his balance and sent him onto the tracks as the train was transiting the station. No one had seen a robed figure. I still don't know for sure if Tina saw him. By the time they got around to us, we told them who we were and that we knew the deceased, but that the whole thing happened before we had made it over to where he was, and that our view was obscured by the crowd. They asked us some more questions (was he despondent; did we think he jumped on his own; they saw that a lot) and then let us go. As far as I know, the paramedics never found Hack's left hand.

Tina and I had been growing apart for a while before this, but I date our true split from Hack's death. Whether because of that event or because of the tea or both, Tina saw something that day that she was never able to leave behind. From that point on, she was more fully in possession of herself as an artist and a filmmaker, but less fully in possession of herself as a person.

She became fascinated by subways and by sewer grates and all of the underground parts of the city that we so rarely see or even think about. Tina moved her few possessions back into the apartment, but she was rarely there. She haunted the underparts of the city, supposedly making a film that started her on her new career, her own artistic vision. When I asked her about it, she usually avoided the conversation any way that she could. She told me that it would be better if I didn't know much about what she was doing, that the effect would be better when I saw the film, or that she didn't want me to worry when she was out. But sometimes I caught her when her eyes were alight and her soul was on fire with whatever she was doing: cleaning her camera, looking at footage, or staring at new boxes of worms that Lur brought in each week. Then she would tell me about the truth of darkness, what lurks beneath the waters of Lake Hali, and the foaming moons that hang over dim Carcosa.

I wish I had listened to her.

I wish I had never heard.

CHAPTER TWELVE

O ur return to Red Stone came sooner than either of us thought it would. Tina had been dropping hints that she was building up to a new film project, one that was more ambitious and more important than *Imperial Dynasty of America*. She started to weave into those hints the possibility that we needed to return to Red Stone in order to complete it. She wasn't saying that we needed to go back to school, and this is what threw me off at first. At first, I heard it as a retreat; the city, the New Dreamers, had defeated her, and she wanted to turn back the clock. But it wasn't that at all. She did have a new film project, her masterpiece, and she actually had to return to the North Country to realize it. If I'm being honest, I was the one who wanted to go back to school. There was much about the city that I loved, and I was learning a lot that eventually was useful to me, but I had been serious about school when I arrived in Red Stone in the fall of '78, and I was still serious about it. I was hoping our interlude would draw to a close and I could get back to becoming an ethnobotanist. So when Tina finally came out and said she wanted us to go back, I was ready to jump at the chance.

We more or less fled the city in the dark of night, taking our few belongings with us. Aside from some second-hand clothes and a number of Tina's film cans, we didn't have much more with us than when we had arrived in December the year before. I wasn't sure if I believed in Swayne's ability to curse us, and that doubt was probably enough to protect me. But there was the question of Hack's fate, and the figure in the pale robes tackling him to his death and then disappearing into the subway tunnels and the rest of underground New York. No one on that platform, other than Tina, saw anyone but Hack leap or be blown into the path of the express.

Lur tried to reassure me that Swayne's curse was probably satisfied by that outcome, but I had no desire to wait around. Between that dream, our experience in what I now thought was Carcosa on that first night in the city, and the several deaths we had been present for, I was ready to run away back to the boring safety of the North Country.

The city hadn't been all bad, of course, and I knew that there was a lot about it that I was going to miss, and I presumed the same about Tina. That's why I wasn't all that surprised when she told me on the bus ride to Red Stone that she had recently heard about a scene a couple hours away from school at the northern end of Lake Champlain. It was supposed to be unlike anything we'd seen during our one semester at school; it was even supposed to be interesting to someone who'd spent time in a bigger city. I was fairly tired of the intrigues that come with scenes, but I wasn't ready to hang up my party hat yet. I was just looking for a party that wasn't going to get anybody killed.

Lake Champlain was a couple hours by car from our sleepy campus, and the bus didn't take us all the way there. We could take it to Plattsburgh and then hitch, or we could try to arrange some kind of car out of Red Stone. Neither of us were keen on spending that much, even for the flexibility, so we went with the bus and the hitching plan. I asked Tina about this scene, but she didn't tell me much. All I could get out of her was that the crowd was eclectic and

I should dress for the outdoors. It was late August, so I was think-ing this was going to be a private camp, something right up on the border that drew people from all over. Labor Day revelers.

It was only a week or so after we had returned. We found a girl who had a rented house all to herself until her roommate showed up closer to the start of the semester and who didn't mind earning a little extra with a short sublet, as long as we were out on time. We told her we needed a few days to find a place of our own. As I recalled, those days rapidly evaporated while we searched for something we could afford. One evening when all the SUNY Red Stone students were throwing bashes because they had moved back to campus from wherever they were for the summer, and their par-ents had pulled away in the station wagons and sedans, Tina and I jumped on the late bus to Plattsburgh.

"Maybe we want to take the earlier bus?" The North Country was much more boring than the city, but I still wasn't interested in being on our own in the middle of nowhere in the middle of the night. "How do you know you can even find this place in the dark?"

"Relax. No one's going to be there in the middle of the day, and I'm not going to just wait around for hours like a dweeb. You'd never show up first to a party either."

"That's fair." Tina knew me well enough. I liked to watch people, but if you showed up too early, there was no way to do that without being creepy. "Where are we going?"

"The ass end of the universe."

"We go to school in Red Stone. Wanna try again?"

"We're going back in time, then." Fine. She didn't want to ruin the surprise. I could be patient, but I was still leery from our time in the city. I trusted Tina to be Tina, but nothing more than that.

The bus ride was uneventful. Tina spent most of it inspecting her movie camera and making sure the glass was polished and that she had a count of the film cartridges she was bringing with her. It was a hot day, uncomfortably so for hauling around a big bag, so I offered to be her camera assistant and take half the cartridges. She gladly accepted, and we stowed away about half a dozen Kodak boxes in my now bulging shoulder bag.

I could see during this operation that Tina also had a stamped steel film can with her, a 200-footer with fake wood grain. I asked her if Dr. Holly was going to be there (despite what he said about never leaving the gatehouse). She said that she wouldn't be surprised but that she wasn't expecting it. She said that she knew that there were film enthusiasts there, people she was hopeful about meeting, and she didn't want to show up empty-handed and then introduce herself as a filmmaker. She said that she had heard they had a way to screen it if they wanted to see it.

We disembarked in Plattsburgh and immediately got out on the road and started walking and hitching toward Rouses Point and the bridge to Vermont. The bridge was a little over thirty miles away from where we were, so we absolutely needed that ride. We couldn't make it on foot that night. But this was back when you could pretty reliably count on people to pick you up, especially if you were two young college students. There were some added rules to hitching while female, but the biggest one (never do it alone) we already had fixed. The others were no windowless vans and never be outnumbered in a car (except possibly by younger family members, hitchhiker's call).

It was a glorious feeling to be off the bus and stretching our legs, but that glory didn't last long. It was still late summer in northern New York State, so I warmed up pretty quickly. I was wiping away the sweat from my face—Tina was occasionally turning and walking backwards with her thumb out when she heard something approaching—when I saw Tina's expression go a bit sideways.

It was a bronze-colored sedan, and I didn't even realize until it had stopped beside us and peals of basso laughter tumbled out the passenger window that it was driven by Horace, the same man who had driven us to the barn party almost a year ago. I gasped, but I tried to turn it into a pensive inhalation instead, trying to be cool. In the low August sun, the smells were asphalt, gasoline, and his meaty cigarillos.

"You two are lucky I stopped for dinner. I wouldn't be on this road otherwise."

"We're not going back to Red Stone," I said. I'm not sure why.

"Did Eva tell you I was coming?" Tina's voice was even, matter-of-fact, but I thought there was an apprehensive edge, too.

"Woman, nobody tells me nothing. You getting in?"

Tina looked at me and nodded toward the back seat while she reached for the passenger door. I watched her slide into the front and close the door before I got in back. The car flowed away from the berm like a bronze wave. I thought back to the giant buzzing insectoids from our city visions, but this was utterly different. I was more afraid in this guy's car than I ever was of those iridescent monstrosities. I couldn't tell then whether I was afraid of him. I don't think that I was. I was more afraid of what sorts of things happened when we were around him. He seemed cool: quiet and aloof. In fact, this was the most I had heard him speak, ever.

"Where are you from?" I asked. Tina whirled in her seat and glared at me, but if she insisted on getting me into stuff like this, I felt she owed me. "Are you from around here?"

"Yeah," he said, letting a cloud of smoke caress his face before it slithered out the window. Even at speed with all the windows down, the oppressive heat of the day made it seem like there was little air movement in the car. "Sure."

"Are you Akwesasne Mohawk?"

"C.C."

"What? It's not insulting."

"I'm not Haudenosaunee," he interrupted. I got the sense that he was annoyed by the tone of our exchange. "My people are from long before."

"Wait, what?"

"Haudenosaunee are young. A lot of older peoples have lived here."

My disbelief must have shown on my face, because Tina was making a face of her own at me.

"Are we going to a tribal meeting?"

"No," said Tina. "Not really. Someplace else."

That place turned out to be Fort Montgomery. Just a couple hundred yards north of the New York end of the bridge sits a low-slung American folly. Fort Montgomery was built to protect against incursions into Lake Champlain from the Canadian territories. Later on I learned that this was the second site for the fort, the first having accidentally been built north of the Canadian border. This first 'Fort Blunder' was torn down and some of the material used to begin the existing fort farther south along the shore. It is a gray mass of stones in the irregular pentagon style of early nineteenth-century military architecture, but it had been partially demolished to provide base materials for the bridge from New York to Vermont that stretches nearby. Almost completely overrun by trees and other foliage, in late summer the fort was at peak green, effectively hiding activities inside from prying eyes, especially after sunset.

We were well past the pink and yellows of the evening sky when our driver turned his sedan off the road before we reached the bridge, and we bounced along a rutted dirt path into a tree-dotted field west of the fort. I noticed he killed the headlights when we turned off the road into the darker realms. I was filled with a momentary thrill of fear as we plunged headlong into darkness. I knew that there were trees and large bushes all around us, but the car sailed on without hitting anything. To distract myself, I looked out the back window, where our driver's occasional tapping of the brakes bathed the thin cloud of dust behind us in an eerie red. I could more easily make out the lights of Rouses Point and the marina on the other side of the two-lane highway, but there was nothing to see in that direction that helped me understand more about where we were going or why.

We came to stop smoothly amid a jumble of cars and trucks and even a handful of bicycles, all of which were left haphazardly under trees and in between large shrubs.

The three of us got out of the car. Tina and I stretched, but Horace strode off to the east toward the fort. Tina took my hand gently and pulled me after him.

We moved to the narrow port in the long western wall of the fortifications. Two small torches flanked the opening, and smaller lanterns lined either side of an actual drawbridge that extended over the swampy moat that ran on this side of the building (the northern, eastern, and southern faces rising up directly from the larger waterway). I could make out the dim figure of a large man standing inside the doorway on the far side of the drawbridge, probably making sure that everyone had their invitations.

As we approached, I wondered if Tina had invitations for both of us to show this man, or if we were actually crashing this party. My curiosity changed to anxiety when I heard a low but persistent drumming coming from within the fortifications.

"Are we expected?" I asked.

"I have a pass. We'll be fine. Just stick with me at first."

Our driver traversed the drawbridge before us. The man pulled a folded paper from his jacket pocket and unfolded it for the bouncer, who nodded at the paper without ever looking at him directly.

Tina pulled a similar paper out of her back pocket. When she opened it to flash at the hulking guy in the doorway, I only got a glimpse, but I knew it was the same symbol from the cover of *The*

King in Yellow. Once again, the hulk nodded at the pass and we entered the cool stone gloom of the fort. Just inside the entrance, three people in robes were busy handing out more robes. They seemed to be sizing up each arrival, because the same figure held out two robes to Tina and me. We took them without a word and slipped them over our heads before continuing.

We went straight through the initial gallery into the open parade field beyond, though the field was certainly less open than it was when the fort was occupied. Vines crept up the exposed inner defenses onto the tops of the protective walls, and trees grew up within the parade field itself. There were several small fire pits already roaring to provide a modicum of light out there. The fire pits had odd metal vented chimneys that shined orange light across the field without also throwing it up into the trees, where more people were able to see it from outside the fort. This meant that it was difficult to make out too many details about those gathered around for whatever scene this turned out to be. I'll admit that all of this was fascinating, but it also did little to calm my anxiety about what kind of scene it was.

I actually started to get the sense that we weren't there for a scene. It wasn't a scene like a coffee house or a bar or whatever, but it wasn't a happening either. That is, it felt a lot more like the preface to a ritual, and we had been invited to attend by the cult, for who else has the authority to invite a stranger to something so secretive and intimate? And it certainly wasn't a tribal ritual, because what tribe could account for the wide diversity of attendees. No, this struck me fully as a cult. As soon as I made that determination, I started to look out for the leader, because there is always a leader, always fascinating, always dangerous.

My conviction that we had been invited to a cult ritual made our immediate situation easier, while it also ramped up the dread. In a cult, no one expects you to engage in small talk or get to know one another. Everyone presumes you belong and that you know the steps. In that way, secret societies are often excellent places for people with introverted personalities to feel like they belong. At the same time, since I didn't have any real knowledge of this group or its workings, I was left with the gnawing fear that perhaps we had been invited along to be part of the ritual in a more objective way. I had no reason to believe that this was a satanic cult that performed ritual human sacrifice. But things were strange enough and had been strange enough for me for quite some time now, that I didn't feel entirely safe.

It wasn't long before Tina whispered to me that she spotted someone she was there to meet. I assumed that this was the person she thought might be interested in the film reel she brought with her, so as Tina turned and walked into one of the gaping galleries within the walls of the fort I followed several steps behind as quietly as I could. When Tina left the parade field, she vanished from view, and I had to continue straight into the darkness with her. Once my eyes adjusted, I could see that there were two silhouettes near one of the narrow windows facing northeast.

One of the silhouettes was obviously Tina, but all I could tell about the other taller figure is that it looked a lot like a woman. They spoke to one another too quietly for me to hear what they were saying, but the tones, gestures, and stances were very familiar to me. It was the familiar dance of the drug deal. The taller woman was buying, and Tina was her potential new supplier. And in a situation like this, the buyer is justified in wanting some assurances about the quality of the product. To that end, she had brought a long a small 8mm movie viewer and editor that she had rigged with a battery (as Tina told me later). Once they had mounted the reel on the viewer, threaded it through the gates, and fastened the leader to the take-up reel, the taller woman flipped the switch for the viewer, and the five-inch screen came alive with light. As Tina steadily cranked the handle on the viewer to advance the film, the woman leaned down to the view screen, and I recognized her as Eva, the woman from the barn party almost a year before.

I didn't know what to do with my dread. I felt like her presence was confirmation that we were much further down an inescapable spiral than I thought we were. The city had been crazy enough for me, but here we were back where we started but on some totally insane side path leading us into actual cults. On top of that, I didn't know exactly what was on that reel of film running through that viewer. I assume they were shots from Tina's underground expeditions, but I didn't have the right angle on the tiny viewer to be able to make it out.

Whatever it was, though, Eva was duly impressed and handed over a thick packet not so different from the one we got in that weird alley in the East Village. Tina stuffed the packet into her bag. When she had done that, the woman also handed her what looked like a business card. Call me and we'll talk more, she must have said. I edged back toward the parade field once the exchange had taken place, and when I left the gallery I immediately cut to the right and moved through some trees hoping to avoid Tina seeing me. When I came out of that small stand of trees, the entire scene had changed.

Now the assemblage stood around three of the shrouded fire pits. The vents on the chimneys had been turned toward the center of their grouping, which now illuminated a single robed and hooded figure standing next to a small depression in the ground. The cowl on this hood drooped low and loose, so I could make out nothing of its face. I had not even seen the small depression in the grass before, but now I could make out that it was maybe ten feet across, circular, and its sides gradually sloped down about two feet. In the bottom of the depression was a circular slab. The slab looked like stone, and though the firelight made it hard to tell, it seemed like the stone was similar to the red sandstone common to the area.

I walked slowly around the group of strangers gathered in a circle around the fire pits and that lone robed figure. As I reached the farthest point from the gallery where I had witnessed Tina's exchange with the woman, I saw Tina coming around from the south side of the parade field. She caught my glance, and her eyes went wide with what looked like exhilaration. I had no idea if it was about the packet of money or the strange thing that was unfolding before us.

At any rate, we were both surprised by a pair of men emerging from another nearby gallery. The men carried an empty stretcher between them, although given its careful design, polished wood and intricately woven canvas bed, I guess it was more of a litter than a stretcher. The pair cut a path between Tina and me and then through the assembled group and into the center of the ring. We looked after them with utter fascination mixed with a growing apprehension.

The men set the litter down in front of the central robed figure and then they moved silently to merge with the rest of the crowd. No one said anything. There were apparently no greetings, no speeches, no sermons, and no masses black or otherwise. Just a waiting. It was impossible to tell under these circumstances whether or not the figure in the robe was the leader or whether it was the entity being worshipped.

In the flickering light from the chimneys, I could see that something was carved on the surface of the stone disc at the bottom of the depression. Since I was now closer, it was easier to make out. The stone itself looked like a millstone. It rose several inches above the earth, but there was no way to tell how deep it went. It did indeed look like a red sandstone millstone, one with deep furrows in its concave face that spiraled away from (or toward) a small dark hole at its center. Although it was a simple design, it struck me at first as a profoundly beautiful representation of life. It was a flower opening onto the world.

As I watched, the masked figure near the stone raised its arms wide. I think the figure said something, too, but I couldn't make it out. At that moment, I felt my blood pressure drop so quickly that my vision blurred, all sounds seemed warped and slow, and I must have swayed on my feet, though I didn't fall down somehow. I fought to remain conscious, trying to shake my head and clear the cobwebs. I was afraid, even though I wasn't thinking well enough yet to be able to focus my fear.

As quickly as the swoon came, it lifted. I was still looking at the stone and the masked figure, but I needed to blink my eyes clear anyway. There was someone else there now, a woman, naked and curled atop the stone. Her skin and long dark hair were shiny and slick, and the reddish-purple blotches that covered her body made her appear more than a little like a fully grown newborn.

"She is come!" This came from the masked figure. His voice slammed into my head, rooting me to the spot and also threatening to destroy me and my understanding of the world. "Welcome!"

"Welcome," the crowd intoned in unison.

The body on the stone shuddered and began to move. I thought at first that she must have been shivering in fear (it certainly couldn't have been because she was cold that night), but in a moment as she gained her knees and rose to her feet, I recognized the throbbing of her shoulders as laughter. The fluid that covered her skin made it hard to tell, but I could swear she was crying and laughing as she took great gulps of air into her lungs. She turned her back to the masked figure and raised her hands like his, her fingers jutting into the night, as she erupted into a primal scream of joy and triumph. There was no fear or malice in it, but it was still terrible in its ferocious and unfettered power.

Confronted with the unknown, my body rebelled and I retched. Tina grabbed my wrist as my other hand flew to my mouth to clamp it shut. She pulled me away into the darkness of yet another ivy-shaded gallery, where I could empty my stomach out of sight if not entirely out of earshot. I might have appreciated some chanting then, but there was no way to deny my body. Tina held my hair and rubbed my back until I was spent, and then she disappeared.

I remained where I was in darkness, bent over and making sure there was nothing left that wanted out of me. When I spit out the last of that awful bile, I turned and brushed back my hair with my fingers and looked for Tina. I could make her out at the cascade of ivy that covered most of the gallery entrance. She was filming from cover. It might have been the dizziness of having vomited, but I was suddenly overcome with a profound dread. Tina should not film this. No one should ever film this. And the last thing you want is for any of these people to see you filming, most especially the masked figure and the woman in front of him. I still had no idea what all of this was about, but all my instincts told me that what Tina was doing with blatantly suicidal, not to mention that there was very little chance that she was going to be able to capture any properly exposed footage under those conditions. She might have learned some new techniques while she was filming in the sewers and subways of New York City, but her camera had limits and she didn't have her light bar with her, nor did she dare use it.

I didn't know it at the time, but this was the very first footage Tina filmed for *Dragon's Teeth*.

CHAPTER THIRTEEN

Horace drove us all the way back to Red Stone. Though I was worried about what Tina had done and what we had seen, neither of them seemed the least fazed. It was dawn when we rolled into town, and I was so exhausted my vision was buzzing.

Though we had returned to Red Stone from the city, we had not returned to school. I was more interested than Tina in resuming my studies, but I had disappointed my parents enough that they were not interested in helping out with tuition. I needed to make some money if I wanted to get back into classes at Red Stone. I didn't have a lot of money of my own, but as long as I was with Tina, that wasn't a problem. I never got a good look at the packet that Tina got at the fort, but whatever was in it paid for our apartment in town and our groceries and a battered maroon Chevy Corvair that she bought straight out of some guy's garage in the village. It didn't feel right to ask Tina to pay for my degree, too.

She also bought absurd amounts of Super 8 film. Tina took me to the drug store not long after the night at the fort so that I could help her carry all of the store's film. I guess it wasn't quite all of it; Tina had no use for the film that came with a magnetic strip for synchronized sound recording. She wanted as much film as she could get her hands on. When we stripped a store of its useful film,

Tina drove us to the next store and then to the next town and its stores. We had scores of film cartridges in their small boxes that we kept in a larger box in the car's trunk. More than one of the men behind the photo counters at these drug stores suggested that Tina order what she wanted straight from Rochester, but Tina wanted the boxes now, right away. Whenever one of them got upset by what Tina was doing, she offered to put down an order for ten more cartridges right there. Only one clerk took her up on that offer.

The two of us were weird in that town. Red Stone has never been affluent, though certainly there were times in the past when more of its inhabitants were doing better than they were in '79 or than they are right now. So, the clerks weren't used to a couple of college coeds showing up and buying all of anything that they carried. You might buy the last one of some item in their inventory, or try to buy it only to discover that they are out of it, but if you buy all of a fully stocked item, then suddenly you're strange.

Within a week, there was somewhere in the vicinity of one hundred film cartridges in the apartment. Packages started to arrive at the post office for Tina, too. She took delivery of a new viewer/editor along with a supply of leader, press tape, and glue. Then came a special film case that I think she had custom made. It was a standard case for carrying and organizing up to a dozen 8mm film cans of either five- or seven-inch size, but it was covered in a shiny dark green reptilian skin, stretched over the wooden box. I remember the day Tina picked the case up from the post office. She opened it and beamed. It was the happiest I had seen her in some time. If she had been a painter, it would have been as though she had found the perfect frame for the painting she had not yet finished, but she knew that this was the right home for her masterpiece. She had found the vessel into which she was going to pour this important work for safe keeping.

It was clear from all this preparation that Tina had a project in mind, but she never told me anything about it. I asked about it early on, but her answers were vague or nonsensical, and I gradually stopped asking. I was still curious about what she was planning to shoot, but I thought I would probably find out more by keeping my eyes and ears open than trying to get her to explain it to me. I was worried that she was going to get us into trouble again, and I wanted to be prepared for it. But then I knew that there was no way she was going to lay it all out for me. And at least she was buying things. This was a far cry from shoplifting a couple film cartridges the past year before we went down to the city, and to tell the truth I felt better about all the money Tina was lavishing on some of the same stores from which we'd previously stolen merchandise.

At first, we spent days in the Adirondacks getting a ton of establishing shots. We hiked for hours through forests, along streams, and up the piled hills that pass for mountains there to find the vistas she had in mind. Then she shot a few seconds of film, panning across or tilting down from the horizon to the ground beneath us. She rarely used a tripod for these shots. Instead, she shook out her arms and her whole body and then breathed deeply, trying to release whatever tension she had. I thought that she had the look of someone who was trying to commune with her surroundings, like she was opening herself up to a presence that I could not detect. It was her gestures that suggested the idea to me; she was expectant. You could see it in her entire being. She shook out her limbs and then stared out across the horizon until she heard or felt some signal that she had been waiting for the whole time. When that signal came, she raised the camera to her eye, confidently dialed in the focus ring, and pressed the button to unwind the spring motor. Her movements always appeared so fluid and smooth when she did this, and I can attest that the resulting footage had a pleasing authenticity about it; you knew you weren't looking at tripod shots or crane shots, but it also wasn't the jarring movement of a combat photographer. Her frame felt organic.

Infamously, this was not always the way the audience feels about the figures in her frames. Tina's reputation is as an underground horror film director, and every horror film director worth her reputation needs her monsters. Tina Mori certainly had her demons, as we all do in one form or another, but she also had her monsters. I was never able to discover when she made contact with the group of people from the fort and how she ever convinced them that they ought to be in her film. Whoever the robed people were, they were not particularly camera-shy. I never saw beneath their heavy woolen cowls, so I can't be absolutely sure how many of them there were, but I was present at one shoot where there were seven of them in a clearing in the woods. I never saw any more than that in one place, except for our visit to Fort Montgomery.

That there were seven on that day of the shoot made some sense, given Tina's predilections at the time. When we were still in the city and Tina was still living with Hack, Tina used to haunt the strange and somewhat offbeat movie theaters. She didn't go see the new stuff in the movie palaces. She went to European art films and retrospectives, Cinema 16 and the Cinematheque. Up until she arrived at college, Tina had a vanilla film education, and she was doing what she could to improve upon it. She listened to the suggestions that friends and acquaintances made regarding the films that she should see, and then she sought them out when she could. She was told that she should see Ozu and Kurosawa, but she found herself much more interested in Seijun Suzuki's thrillers, though she wished he could have done something other than gangster films. When we returned to Red Stone, we didn't go back to college, but Tina did attend every screening of the Cinema Art program run by the college. The films were not quite as edgy as the ones she was able to see in the city, but they were often films she hadn't seen before anyway, and she appreciated the chance to learn something new. She was inordinately fascinated with the idea that Kurosawa had filmed *Seven Samurai* and then Hollywood cadged it to release *The Magnificent Seven*. She wondered aloud to me once whether she, too, was the American version of the Japanese original, and what that might mean for her. What it meant during this shoot was that she was riffing on the idea of seven warriors.

I've had many years to think about my take on *Dragon's Teeth*, and I have ideas, but I don't think that I have locked it down with some kind of indisputable meaning. What I can tell you is that Tina was reeling from the kinds of betrayals and wounds that were reminiscent of those dealt by the sowers of discord. There may not have been seven such people in our circle during our year in the city, but then again maybe there were, and we didn't see the whole picture. Maybe Paul and Hack were the two warriors who killed one another before the remaining survivors are convinced to join Jason and the Argonauts for the rest of their quest. And certainly there's very little about Tina's film that is about people falling into conflict with one another. There is much more on screen about people leaving behind the relative safety of society and traveling into the wilderness where they meet up with members of some other mysterious in-group. It is this in-group, one of the other meanings of the title *Dragon's Teeth*, that presents the real danger to the victims on the film.

There is also the fact that Barron Circle, hidden in the northern foothills of the Adirondack Mountains, is a formation of seven shards of red sandstone jutting up as much as eight feet amongst the pine and birch. Seven stones. Seven teeth. Seven cowboys. Seven samurai. Seven robed figures. What is there between all of these things? I know a lot of people have spilled a lot of ink over it, but I don't think there's a decoder ring for this one. Tina didn't leave any breadcrumbs for us. What we see is what we get.

And getting that footage must have been harrowing. Even though in the Greek myth, the dragon's teeth are cast on the ground where they grow into fully armed warriors, in the film, Tina has a handful of red sandstone splinters tossed into a lake. It must have been harrowing, because when I finally saw the film, it was obvious that I had not been there for the entire shoot. I saw scores, maybe hundreds, of familiar shots, but many of the most disturbing ones I never saw filmed, even when I could identify the shooting location and remember our hours and days there.

I could spend some time here telling you about the mundane things that happen on a two-person guerrilla film crew in the backwoods with a mostly anonymous cast (anonymous to me, anyway), but I'll bet that's not why you're reading. People talk about blood, sweat, and tears all the time. I can tell you about mosquitos, black flies, ticks. I can tell you about unexpected storms, off-season hunters, and bears more surprised to see us in their living room than we were to encounter them in the wilderness. And I can tell you about waiting hours for the right shot and not getting it, about coming back the next day, and the next. If you have never experienced it, let me tell you that there is something unique about being led by a person with an unwavering vision. As long as you have faith in them and in their vision, your capacity to weather danger, discomfort, and even failure seems limitless. Instead of giving you all of those details from the shoot, I'll answer some of the questions that I get time and again when people find out I was there.

Were there orgies among the cast and crew?

Absolutely not. The one "sex scene" at the beginning of *Dragon's Teeth* was the result of a moment of opportunistic voyeurism. One of several days we spent shooting at and around Barron Circle, Tina and I heard shouts and laughing. Tina didn't want anyone straying into her shots, so we snuck up to get a look at who was there. In another clearing a few hundred yards away from the stone circle, two couples had set up a pair of tents. They had a radio, an unlit fire pit, a case of beer between them, and apparently no sense of shame. Tina gestured for me to stay put and be quiet while she moved to several concealed spots in a wide arc, filling a cartridge with shots of their frolicking. Later she cut this together with other footage to make it look like the protagonist of *Dragon's Teeth* was the lame "fifth wheel" among these partiers, who snuck off by herself to read and ignore her rutting friends. Aside from her, none of the people in the scene could rightly be called cast or crew.

Was Tina a Satanist?

Not hardly. Tina had very little interest in religion, organized or otherwise, that I could tell. She never went to church, she kept no shrines or sacred scriptures. And I never got the impression that she was against anyone else believing in anything. It wasn't for her; that was all.

Did Tina run out of film and then conduct a ritual in the woods, summoning a demon who could bring her more?

No. We ran out of gas once (bum fuel gauge). Tampons another time. Food all the time. Never film.

Is it real?

I don't know. What do you mean by real? I think I know what you mean. Is the castle there? Is Carcosa a real place? Can I get there? If you've seen even a part of the film, you know how real its effect is, and how tempting it is to think of Tina as a documentarian. But I don't know how to answer that question honestly. Knowing Tina has altered my relationship to what I think of as real. I'm no longer certain how to communicate that understanding clearly.

I helped Tina shoot in the woods off and on for about two months. As I said, we didn't spend all of our time together. We were both young, of course, but Tina was full of a kind of energy I couldn't fathom. I needed to rest from our wilderness film odyssey, and sometimes I needed a bed and a shower and a meal I cooked myself. Tina was very accommodating, and later I realized it was because she didn't want me around for some of the shooting. Or maybe the people she was working with on those shots didn't want me around. Either way, she took the car and sometimes was gone all day or all night. She always came back and rarely said anything unless I asked, and then she usually gave the briefest of answers. It had gone well, or it was exhausting.

By the time the leaves were changing, Tina had what she needed and she transitioned into her role as editor. She sent off dozens of cartridges for processing, but she also kept back a handful that required hand-processing. A drawing of a nude model might be considered art, but voyeuristic footage of college students fucking in the woods was never coming back from a commercial process-ing center. I don't know who she found to do it for her, but every-one who has seen the films knows she succeeded. As the reels came back, sometimes in batches and sometimes singly, Tina ran them through her new viewer/splicer. Her bedroom was criss-crossed with twine from which she hung long strips of film according to some system of her own. She stayed in her room for weeks, com-ing out to eat and to use the toilet or shower. We talked less and less. She looked haggard, haunted. Even though the weather was cooling early, as it usually does in Red Stone, I usually saw her covered in a sheen of sweat, her hair plastered to her face. She went through white cotton gloves and editing press tape like Kleenex.

Tina didn't like anyone to watch her edit. She told me more than once that it distracted her. But living together, I caught her at it on a couple of occasions and was able to see her in action before she noticed me and told me to go away or closed her door. Though she was open to spontaneous opportunities when she was shooting, Tina was disciplined and business-like on location. She knew what she wanted to capture, and she respected her camera enough to negotiate her vision through its capabilities and limitations. But sitting at her desk in front of her editing machine, she was a musician again. She was an artist. Others have used these analogies, and I cannot disagree. Tina approached her film the way that Kerouac approached his typewriter, the way that jazz greats talk about blowing, the way that Burroughs approached cut-ups.

Cut. Blow. Flow.

Cut. Blow. Flow.

Dragon's Teeth had no script, no scenario. We weren't working from any pages, no blueprint that was written down. It was all inside her. At the very least, the shot list was retrospective, so there was no way that Tina was shooting for continuity. She could have shot coverage if she wanted to, because she was very astute about the films that she watched and what she learned from them. But continuity wasn't her goal. She wanted to leave her audience with a particular experience of the world she was opening up to them. She wanted to convey that experience as it had been conveyed to her, but since the audience couldn't be there, she needed to refract it through the lens of not only her camera but also of her perspective and experience. She needed people to think that what they were seeing was part of the world in a way that they had never understood, or in a way that they had long put away as fantastical and childish. She was a revelator, and she was happy to think that many people who saw the film would experience those revelations as the uncanny. This was a world that should not have been real, and yet here it was. The celluloid did not lie, did it?

Of course, most people thought it did lie, but they were happy to credit Tina with a potent lie. She was a master horror filmmaker in their eyes, though they hoped she was going to make her next film a bit more legible, a bit more polished, a bit more sexy. Some people viewed the revelation for what it was and they became lifelong devotees of Tina's work and legend, and others simply saw the nascent work of someone who might well become a mainstream director of some note, though few people had many misconceptions about the likelihood that a woman of color would break into the horror film boys' club in the 1980s and 1990s. In the end, though, it wasn't Tina that broke into that club; it was her work. When well-known horror directors saw *Dragon's Teeth*, they were starkly split. One camp hailed it as a masterpiece that verged on being unwatchable it was so disturbing. The other group said nothing but quietly set out behind the scenes to do whatever they possibly could to destroy the film and Tina's reputation. There was something so deeply and fundamentally offensive to their humanity or to their sanity in that film that they simply had to do everything their power to wipe it from existence.

But in the end this kind of crusade can never succeed in the way that the crusaders hope. Certainly, Tina never went on to reach millions of people through a career in mainstream Hollywood horror films, but it's also probably true that forcing her and her films underground made her immortal in ways that mainstream releases never could have. Tina and her work became forbidden. Though she appeared too late on the scene for her work to suffer the same kind of obscenity trials that the previous generations of artists had to endure, nevertheless her films were subject to a sustained effort at informal suppression that has been arguably quite effective. It is not easy to find *Dragon's Teeth* in any but fragmentary condition. What portions of it exist out in the world as part of bootleg compilation VHS tapes are tantalizing but not at all totalizing. There are constant rumors among an elite community of collectors that there is a complete transfer, or someone knows where the original set of Super 8 reels is located. But none of these ever pan out. No one can even agree on whether or not Tina Mori is among the world of the living. Surely this level of misinformation makes it virtually impossible to say anything authoritative about anything other than the memories people have of seeing the film screen. That's all that remains.

CHAPTER FOURTEEN

Tina was convinced, based on her experience screening and viewing films, that she wanted the premiere of *Dragon's Teeth* to be a happening, an expanded cinema event. The idea of a happening wasn't new; maybe it had peaked a few years earlier. Warhol and all that. Artists were looking for a way to shake things up and do it all differently, and they came up with the idea of extending painting into the three-dimensional exhibition space. It wasn't the flat plane of the canvas in a room with a bunch of eyeballs. The art was happening around you, and often it was happening in time, not just space. You could make a pretty good argument that it doesn't matter what time of the day, month, or year you visit a work like the Mona Lisa. You might be different at any given moment, but the painting won't. You can grow with it, but it's not going to grow with you. But the happening is something that you can miss; it's something that you'll never be able to experience in quite the same way if you aren't there for it at the right moment. To all of the many cultural anxieties one might display connected to art, we can now add the fear of missing out.

However, the happening turned out to be one of those ideas that Tina had that she did not share with anyone else. If there was planning to do in preparation for this happening, she was not going to bring me into it. I resented this at the time. Even though we had had our tensions and our arguments, and even though I was aware that we had grown distant, it still hurt that I couldn't be her partner in this thing. I wanted to help her achieve her big goal, and I felt like I had done relatively little on the shoot itself. It was all her; this was her work of art, through and through. In the years to come, I frequently looked back on this time, and how I thought about it waxed and waned. Most of the time it felt like a loss, like an ache. It was a missed opportunity to be close to Tina one more time before she disappeared from my life, even though I didn't know that what was coming was going to look like a disappearance.

But more recently, I have come to think of it differently. In fact, writing this book has helped me to think of it differently. I think Tina didn't want me to help her plan the happening because she wanted to be able to give it to me instead of share it with me. I think she didn't want me to be her magician's assistant on stage with her, even though we'd had such fun doing that together. I think just this once she wanted me to be in the audience; she wanted me to see the magic without knowing how it was done. She wanted me to experience the wonder. It's quite a gift. It comes from a place of love, which might sound counterintuitive but actually makes a lot of sense when you're talking about a nightmare like this one.

I know a lot of people have speculated that Tina was reluctant to go public with the film, that the happening in Red Stone was a trial run, a kind of sneak preview in order to test a cut on an audience prior to a more elaborate or at least better-attended release in New York City. But I don't think all of that makes sense. I think Tina did it precisely how she wanted to do it. Sure, it made sense that Tina wanted to show her masterpiece in the city where she had experienced most of her significant artistic successes so far and where there were so many more people who were able to appreciate what she was doing, but Tina didn't want to impress those people. That wasn't on her list of things to do that fall. She actually didn't care if people loved this film or hated it. She wanted to fire this arrow into the heart of the future, and she felt a kind of joyful camaraderie with those people who happened to be there when that arrow leapt from the bowstring.

It did feel a little bit like coming full circle when I found out that she was going to premiere *Dragon's Teeth* in the same barn where we first watched Maya Deren's films on 16mm. It was a good space for what she wanted. It didn't have the sterility of an actual auditorium or movie theater, which she could have rented if she wanted to. No, her challenge in some ways was the challenge of a lot of underground filmmaking at that time. How do you show your film to a lot of people, when your film was engineered to be shown in a living room? Tina had the resources to shoot and develop dozens of cartridges of film, but she didn't quite have the money to blow that footage up to 16mm and certainly not to 35mm. She wasn't going to be able to show it in a traditional exhibition venue, so she needed something more creative, and that's exactly what the barn offered. She would be able to fit a crowd into that space, and they would get a good show, and then they could go tell other people. That must have been what she wanted. Nothing else makes much sense.

Tina Mori premiered *Dragon's Teeth* to a packed barn on the evening of December 21, 1979, her nineteenth birthday. I had seen the photocopied flyers posted around town in the windows of the more bohemian hangouts and stapled to telephone poles. A movie premiere and masquerade ball: Costumes Required. She was inviting anyone who had an interest in transformative cinema to come and see her work. Transformative cinema. I read a book last year about transcendental cinema. Someone should write the book on Tina's idea of transformative cinema. She wasn't looking to see beyond the here and now of the world in which she lived. Tina's goal was to utterly change the world around her, and she was convinced that she could do it through her little Russian Super 8 camera.

Of course, whenever we talk about wanting to change the world, we're usually only talking about one or two small parts of the world. We don't like this or that kind of commercial product, or we don't like a particular kind of education, or we want people to drive on the left instead of the right. We fail to understand when we set out to change these things that the world is a system, that every time we set out to change the world we are committing ourselves to transforming the entire system, because there is no other alternative. Most such enterprises fail, because they do not fully appreciate the scale of change necessary, and in the end the revolutionaries are not at all interested in the kind of change they think they want to see. They are nerve endings walking around raw and exposed, and they suddenly resonate with some stimuli around them and they believe in that moment that they feel pain or discomfort. They don't like pain and they don't like discomfort, so they set out to eliminate either the effects or the causes. It's like what they actually don't want is to be in the world that they are in. They want to be in a different world, but they don't appreciate the scope of their desire. They want to get rid of the tiny little thorn that is causing them so much trouble. That's what activists try to do. They think the world is or can be a fundamentally good or fair place, and they think that if they could only show people that things are not fair or good everywhere, the natural goodness in humanity would recognize injustice and then rise up and materially transform the world around them into something beautiful and just.

It's tempting, isn't it?

Tina Mori wanted to show us the grave, worms and all. I think she felt that honestly confronting that reality would also have a transformative effect on her audience. But it wasn't enough to film the reality of death for her audience. To convince them that they didn't already know the score, Tina had to give them some concrete hint that the world does not work the way they think it does. She had to do more than fill the screen with iteration after iteration of fatal actualities, like those perversely popular videotapes rented by awkward boys with twitchy eyes. That was not enough. In fact, that would take people in the other direction. Guardians of morality worry that children become desensitized to violence and sex through video games and pornography and all the lesser *aurora borealis* of popular culture, as though a heightened sensitivity means that we will have less violence and less aberrant sexuality, whatever that is. Greater sensitivity only renders those things less bearable. The great twin poles of the debate are usually sentimentality and cynicism. But Tina was onto a third: therapeutic dread. What if you could imagine that the world didn't work the way you knew that it did? What if that idea filled you with a nameless foreboding that heightened every receptor in your poor human frame? What if dread of the unknown is the only thing that has any chance of preparing you for a world different than the one you know right now? Do you still want to change the world?

Tina did. She saw something in New York, she walked in Carcosa, and then she saw more when we returned to Red Stone. I have no idea what it was exactly. Even thinking back on what I did see at the fort, I have no way of reworking that into some kind of framework that will make sense given new information. All I know is that when Tina saw these things and more besides, she made a film that looks to the uninitiated like a monster movie without the monsters. It is a black and white film in which every single frame gestures shudderingly to what is beyond the edges of the frame. How does she film nothing and yet compel you to know?

Once we arrived at the barn on the night of the screening, I could tell that it wasn't going to be a live music and film screening like we had with Lethal Chamber and *Imperial Dynasty of America*.

Most of the people in the barn were dressed up for a masquerade. Some had snazzy formal costuming and intricate masks covering their faces, while others had makeshift costumes, perhaps left over from Halloween weeks before. If I knew many of the people there, which wasn't likely anyway, then there wasn't much chance I was going to be able to recognize them. There was music playing from a turntable over a PA system, but it was an odd selection of chants and madrigals. This was less party and more theater. About twenty minutes after the flyer had indicated the film would screen, Tina moved in front of the screen that had been stretched tight against the barn wall.

"I have something to show all of you. I've been working on it for a while now, and it's finally ready." She looked back at the blank screen, as though she heard something or sensed that something was watching her. When she didn't find it, she turned back to the crowd.

"Don't blink."

Tina stepped away, and the several lamps hanging in the barn went out, one after another. It only vaguely occurred to me that I didn't know who was helping her with the lights and the projector and putting on the whole event. At the time, I pushed those questions away, because *Dragon's Teeth* was finally right in front of me, and I didn't want to miss any of it.

In a plot that obliquely recalls a classical Hollywood movie structure but in the style of Deren's most powerful works, *Dragon's Teeth* presents its audience with the story of a young woman's journey away from the familiar world and into a new dreadful one. The opening shot is of Barron Circle, serene and empty. The seven shards of sandstone jut toward the sky. The camera pans slowly and then begins to move through the forest, cutting cleverly until we pan in on the group of young lovers we found that day. The camera doesn't linger long on them before it moves again, cutting to a young woman trudging through the trees away from the group. She looks back over her shoulder, betrayal etched on her face. She turns away in pain. The young woman finds a fallen tree and stretches out on it to read a tattered book. We see the book's cover: *The King in Yellow*.

The film includes inserts here of animals and insects. The animals all react in a way that appears to show them moving toward where the woman is reading. The insects teem across the screen in the same direction. The young woman glances away from the play. Her face is already tense, apprehensive. She sits up and looks around. We see a couple of urgent whip pans, but then she focuses her gaze in one direction. She slides off the fallen tree trunk and begins to move in that direction. We follow her, over the shoulder, now scanning the trees, now seeing a close-up of her face, curious and eager.

She emerges from behind a tree, her expression turning to one of confusion. In front of her is Barron Circle. In between each massive stone is a robed figure, face hidden from view. All but one of them face into the circle. The other faces her and beckons her forward. She is compelled. She advances.

The beckoning figure steps aside and welcomes the young woman into the circle. She walks gingerly to the center. When she gets there, she turns and looks at the other figures who seem to stare at her, though she cannot see their eyes. Something about them fills her with shame. She looks down and away, and slowly begins to undress. Tina's camera does not linger on her nudity. Instead, the camera holds the young woman in a close-up as she grows more and more comfortable the fewer clothes she has on. When she is finished, she stands straight and stares ahead. The robed figures raise their arms wide so that their fingers almost seem to touch the stones to either side of them. When they lower their arms and turn away from the Circle, the young woman is gone.

She emerges from the edge of the woods on the shores of a smooth lake, her slim form a distant pale sliver against the trees. There is virtually no beach here, just a sloping apron of sand and stones. She stares out across the water. She looks down and then reaches for a handful of stones. When she stands back up, we see in close-up the seven sandstone shards she holds. Languidly, she tosses them away from her into the waters of the lake.

In a stunning over-the-shoulder shot, we see a low island backed by mist some distance across the water, and on that island is an immense fortress with towers and battlements and pennants silhouetted against the mist. The young woman can't believe what she sees, and neither can we. She looks away from the camera and then toward it before we get the reverse shot. Farther along the shore, perhaps near where the camera had been that captured her arrival at the lake, there is a robed figure standing next to a gleaming wooden canoe. Without changing her expression, the woman turns and walks toward the figure.

The audience sees shots of the figure paddling away from the shore with the woman seated in the front of the canoe, and then a shot of the canoe approaching a jetty with the tree line far across the water in the background. They have covered the distance in a blink. The woman reaches for the wooden piling eagerly and climbs ashore. A shot from the furthest lake-ward end of the jetty follows her as she walks to the entrance of the fortress. She enters and disappears.

When the audience sees the young woman again, she has on a beautiful pale gown and a domino mask. There is a masquerade in progress in the main hall. Dancers swirl around a glittering mosaic floor. A shot from the lofted balcony reveals the mosaic to be a curious mixture of nautical and astronomical imagery. There are moons and ringed planets and eels and crabs and what look like winged cuttlefish. A series of seven immense tapestries around the hall cover the spaces between entryways, each one of them depicting a fantastic serpent or dragon or worm in a different environment, their long bodies stretching from doorway to doorway. The tapestries are all clearly the work of the same artist or team of artists, and in their thematic motifs are not unlike the Lady and the Unicorn collection of medieval tapestries.

The young woman is approached by a series of masked suitors, all of whom hold out a hand to her as they dance and bow and twirl out of frame. She smiles at each one in turn, but dances with none of them. She allows the festivities to continue without becoming a part of them. It is not clear whether she refuses to participate or if she is simply waiting for the right opportunity. However, the dancers suddenly stop what they are doing. The woman looks around her in confusion. Everyone else looks down at the ground as they take off their masks. They almost appear to be in mourning, and the strange weight of the moment compels the woman to remove her domino mask. The crowd parts, directly down the center of the main hall. At the far end of the room, a regal stranger in pale costume, still masked, stands alone in between the parted sea of dancers. The stranger faces the woman and she stares back. From opposite side of the room, they advance steadily toward one another.

Tina's camera captures the two figures in profile, facing each other as they step into frame on a two-shot. They are within arm's reach, and the woman does in fact reach up, her finger tips almost grazing the terrifying mask of the stranger. Her hand trembles, but she gestures at her own face and those of the crowd around her. She seems to say, "You should unmask." But the stranger stares back impassively and then slowly shakes its head. In close-up, the young woman considers this refusal and then her eyes go wide in shock blossoming seamlessly into terror.

"No mask?" say her lips. "No mask!"

It was while the film was unspooling in the barn that it took place. The happening. I wasn't prepared for it, so I think I got the effect that Tina was going for. I assumed that it wasn't a sit-down film screening, but I didn't know exactly what it was going to be. It started as a smell, a fragrance of lake shores and open hearths, of damp cobblestones and something more strange. They were smells that disoriented me, because none of them made any sense. I remember that when I glanced around, nothing appeared to have changed, but in the periphery of my vision, the timber framing and exposed boards of the barn siding looked more like the interior of an Old World tavern. I couldn't put my finger on precisely what was conveying this impression to me, but I was suddenly convinced that I was inside one of the buildings I had seen that night in the alleyway in Manhattan, or Carcosa, or wherever we had been. I thought it might even be possible for me to get up and go to a short wooden door with a rounded top that I knew to be behind me and off to one side. I had not seen it, but I *knew* it was there. If I went through this door, I might see Tina and me stumbling away from a pair of loud footsteps, or I might even find myself in Dr. Holly's house again. I shuddered at the possibility that if I opened Dr. Holly's back door, I might be confronted with myself and my friend. And then who would that make me?

I wanted something to hold onto again, something that grounded me in a reality that made some sense, because this deviation was making me nauseous. I tried to concentrate on the film again, but I was unable to find the edges of the frame. There was the young woman and the masked stranger, and the courtiers around them, but where was the frame? The more I looked for it, the more I was left with the creeping impression that I was in the castle, too. As I glanced furtively around the space, I registered that the young woman's dress was white or just off, while the masked stranger's attire was a stark and repulsive yellow. Before I had the impression that the courtiers were afraid of the stranger, and certainly there was fear in their averted gazes, but there was something of disgust, too. But now when I looked at the stranger, there was a tinge of familiarity. Maybe it was only the mask, but I thought that there were similarities of height and movement, too, a certain way of holding the head, a particular hand gesture.

Dr. Jean L. Holly.

When the name occurred to me, it was like I had said it out loud. The stranger's head snapped in my direction, locking me with its gaze. I was frozen to the spot, and in that moment wanted only to flee. Instead, all I was able to do was cry. Tears streamed down my face, and my body convulsed with deep wracking sobs. What I felt was a species of utter despair in the presence of the stranger. It was a combined blooming of horror and lust, a craving and a refusal, each so categorical that I felt my soul tearing apart.

It was an artifact of the film that brought me back to myself and distracted me from complete disintegration. The film jittered in the gate, throwing the entire image of the masquerade around me into a shuddering mass. Then the film snapped. The screen went white. Dozens of people around me gasped at once, as though their rapture had been interrupted. Now the masked people around me were wearing mundane (even stupid) costumes, and Tina was right where I had last seen her, near the back of the crowd. Even with her blue sunglasses on, I could tell she was in tears. She darted to the projector, stopped it, and rethreaded the film. In a few moments, *Dragon's Teeth* began again, but the moment was irrevocably lost.

On screen, the young woman was fleeing from the castle. None of the revelers pursued her as she raced from the main hall, out of the castle, and down the jetty. By the time she hit the wooden planks, her gown flying behind her, the woman's feet were bare flashes of white on the screen. The camera, once again positioned in low-angle at the end of the pier, captures the woman's mad flight from the ball. Two strides after the top of the frame obscures her face, she leaps over the camera, presumably into the churning lake.

The screen goes black.

A small shimmering iris appears in the center of the screen, filled with the spiral millstone from the fort. As the iris opens, I confirmed that this is the footage Tina shot at our night at Fort Montgomery. The footage is muddy but discernible. Inserts of robed figures positioned around the stone give the impression of an intense sense of expectancy surrounding it. The lead figure, again leading my thoughts to Dr. Holly, raises his hands wide and high.

And suddenly, there she is. It is not the young woman. It is without a doubt the woman I saw that night in the fort. She is older than the young woman, perhaps in her thirties. She unfurls her body from its fetal position on the stone and slowly rises and blossoms like a flower in a time-lapse film. She is filled with a strength and an experience that cannot be contained on film or on the page. She has transcended and returned.

She danced in Carcosa.

And then she came back.

CHAPTER FIFTEEN

Tina and her imagination had shown everyone something that they never asked to see, and now they weren't sure what they were going to do. When new sights reveal themselves, most people chose to look away. For almost a year after the premiere, there was a simmering lawlessness in and around Red Stone. It was as though the town had been awakened from a nightmare by a knocking, and they were damned if they were going to get out of bed and rush downstairs to see who or what was pounding on their door. They pulled their covers more tightly around them, shut their eyes, and let the nightmares roam free.

I'm not interested in blaming them. I was one of them. I had seen too much, as well, and I could feel myself wavering between fleeing into what I perversely hoped could be a lifetime of normalcy and finding my own mirror-like lake in which to drown myself for the greater glory of *The King in Yellow*. I still have nights where I lie awake turning over in my mind the awareness that the extent of my mediocrity at the time was evident by the level of my fear. I wasn't exhilarated by what I had seen and experienced; I was shaken to the core. I wanted to deny it, to turn away like everyone else.

Tina, of course, kept me from turning away completely. Not that she prevented me directly. It's not her fault; it's that I cared for her, cared what happened to her and whether or not she was okay. Turning away from what I had seen and what I thought it might mean also meant turning away from Tina. In a supreme fit of squareness, I worried that she was spending too much time with the wrong crowd.

I was a bit surprised when she grabbed me the night after the screening and said she needed me to go with her. I asked where we were going, and she said that she needed to go see Holly again, and she didn't want to do it alone. But I wondered why not? Was she afraid of Holly? We had been through a lot since the last time we had gone to the gatehouse to see him, and frankly there was a lot about that intervening year that one could reasonably consider terrifying. After seeing *Dragon's Teeth*, I was surprised to find that Tina was scared to visit with Holly.

Throughout all of this, it was actually Tina's unflappable demeanor that helped to keep me grounded and sane. I think I always figured that if she was going to make it through all of this unscathed, then it was probably smarter to stick as close to her as possible. In hindsight, I think that was enormously misguided. I could have been next on fate's agenda at any point during that year. There was nothing special about me, nothing that made me particularly different from Donny or Paul or Hack. I agreed to go, and Tina was visibly relieved by that. She breathed easier and squeezed my hand in hers.

We couldn't go until after dark. I had no idea if this was an affectation on the part of Dr. Holly, or even Tina, but I didn't like it. The guy was doing well enough without trying to be extra creepy. But Tina needed to see him, and he insisted he was only available after ten o'clock. We walked the same river path that we had over a year before. It was a clear winter night with a fullish moon that made the river and its surroundings glow under a charcoal night sky. We could see the stones of the cemetery thrust up through the unmarred late-December snow before we turned away from the river and toward the gatehouse.

Even then, in the days of honest winter, Holly still had the hand-painted sign that read NIGHTCRAWLERS leaning up against the side of the house near the veranda. This time, I wondered whether it was an advertisement at all, or whether it was a warning to those who already knew better. If you knew he didn't mean worms, then did you need the sign? Maybe. People are weird and quite often stupid.

We made our way around the house to the back door near the kitchen. Tina knocked, far less timidly than I would have.

"You didn't need to come," Tina said to me after she knocked. I stared at her, dumbfounded.

"Are you serious?"

"I just mean that it didn't need to be you."

"Who else was going to come with you?" She shrugged and gave me one of those smiles that were all too rare at that point. I'm sure I didn't want anyone else to come with her on this adventure.

We both heard the door being unlocked and fell silent. I thought I heard retreating footsteps as Tina turned to me again with a question in her glance. I nodded my encouragement, and Tina opened the door and led us inside. Things were precisely as I remembered them from before. The same darkness and shabby disarray, but nothing that would alarm someone who already expected this un-lived-in domain.

We found our way to the sitting room, and there again was Dr. Holly, sitting in his enormous leather wingback chair, robed and masked as before. I was hoping that he would have on a new robe and mask, or I was hoping that he would have on a combination that I might have recognized from the *Dragon's Teeth* screening. Ever since I found out that Tina wanted it to be a masquerade, I suspected that some of that had to do with her desire to have Holly attend the screening in public like everyone else. But when that night came, I couldn't tell if any of the people there were Holly. Despite my suspicions, I didn't know for a fact that the King in the film was Holly. There were many who I could tell were not Holly, but that left a frustratingly large pool of people who were roughly the right height and build. I didn't get to talk to all of them, but wearing a full mask sometimes has the effect of obscuring a voice.

Holly was arranged and dressed as he was a year ago when we came to his house. He inclined his head toward us as we entered the room, and his hand slowly arced in front of him as he gestured for us to sit.

"Welcome, Ms. Mori," he said deliberately and then nodded at me. "Ms. Waite. Please make yourselves comfortable." We took our seats in front of him, and if I remembered correctly, we took the opposite seats from the last time we had been there. Tina set the film case down in between her feet. Holly's mask didn't move, but I could tell that he was staring at the case and not at us.

"How much?" said Tina.

"How much what?"

"How much for *Dragon's Teeth*?" Holly's hands slid along his upper arms as though he were going to cross them and sulk, but he rubbed them up and down slowly, like he was warming himself.

"Though I would be honored to purchase *Dragon's Teeth* from you, I am quite certain that you will not sell it to me." I looked at Tina. She was surprised, but only that Holly said it, not what he said.

"Why not?" I asked.

"Ms. Waite, she will not sell it to anyone. The film is quite simply not for sale. It is too...dear." Tina smiled. She loved that her work impressed this creep. Sure, he had money, but he also had approval, and the latter was much more precious to her than the former.

"Well," I said. "What are we doing here?"

"Yes," said Holly. "I could well ask what you are doing here. I asked to speak with Ms. Mori. It seems that whenever I do this, I am also asking to speak with you. It is frustrating."

I shrugged. "Not my call, pal."

"Answer the question," Tina said.

"The film you've made is singular in many respects, but none more so than the most obvious one. I would like to ensure that it can be properly preserved by having it copied to a better storage format. As a separate matter, I am also keen to finance your next project."

"I don't have a next project."

"Let's not fence, Ms. Mori. You will always have a next project. That is beyond question. The immediate uncertainty is where you will find the resources to pursue that project."

Tina didn't respond for a moment.

"This is the only copy of *Dragon's Teeth*."

"Yes," said Holly. "That is my point exactly."

"I mean, I don't think I can hand it over to you. What if I never get it back?"

"I would be perfectly happy to arrange for you to be present during the transfer. You could bring the film to the lab, attend the transfer yourself, and then deliver the copy to me personally. In fact, I insist."

"And you can store the copy," I asked.

"I have access to the proper facilities, yes."

"Where would you have this done?"

"A lab in Montreal. They do excellent work."

"I'll have to think about it," Tina said.

"There's little to think about, Ms. Mori. You have already risked the only existing print during the screening at your barn event. How many times have you shown an 8mm film with no mishaps? What is the life expectancy of this film? I should like to secure its posterity and lift it from the realm of ephemera."

Tina nodded. "I'll think about it."

"Remember what happened on the roof in the city," he said. There was more than a hint of desperation in his voice.

Tina stood, and I stood a moment later, surprised by her reticence.

Holly spread his hands wide. "I will be here."

Tina lifted the green-skinned film case and strode out of the room, and I followed close behind, since I had no interest in being left behind alone with Holly. I'm not sure what I expected, but it wasn't to be leaving the house quite so soon, so I was somewhat surprised to find myself out in the cold again, moving through the snowy forest along the river.

"What's up, Tina? Are you going to let him copy it?"

"Didn't you hear it?"

"The offer? Yeah, I heard."

"No, didn't you hear the sounds coming from underneath the house?"

"No."

Tina stopped and listened intently. She spun around and looked behind us, and then spun around again.

"Wha—"

"Shh." Tina held up a finger.

Now I thought I could hear it. Now I thought I could hear everything. My heart. Her heart. The wringing of Holly's hands like a melodramatic villain. The scratching against the cellar door beneath the gatehouse. The scraping of sandstone and marble coming from the cemetery. The burble of voices trying to cry out from beneath the surface of the river flowing by. I thought I could hear all of it.

"Let's get out of here."

And we did. We moved as fast as we could down the forest path and back to our apartment above the music store downtown. I was reassured by the people we ran into on the street as we crossed the bridges and ran into town. Their laughter and the clouds of vapor escaping their mouths as they jammed their hands in winter coats beat down the nameless terror that had risen in me since I saw the gatehouse again tonight and its NIGHTCRAWLERS sign.

I often complained about how cold our apartment got, especially because not a single window sash sat firmly in its frame. But as we tumbled into the apartment, it felt warm and welcoming like never before. Tina collapsed onto the battered love seat in the main room, while I moved into the kitchen and put on a kettle for tea. She sat there and stared at the green case filled with the steel canisters of her genius. It looked as though she was staring at her doppelgänger, like a moment from "William Wilson" or something like that. There was a fascination and a terrible recognition mixed up in the glance I saw on her face while I waited for the kettle to scream.

We spent the rest of the night talking it over, sharing what we noticed from our meeting with Holly and also from the premiere, trying to compare notes on people we had noticed at the screening and wondering if Holly had been there. Tina was inclined to think that he had been, while I was more convinced that he had sent some kind of spy along to see what Tina had produced. Tina couldn't imagine that he would give up what might be his only opportunity to see the film and know whether or not it was worth it, whether or not she was still worth it.

We talked, too, about whether or not she should take Holly's offer. I poured the tea and helped her through her thinking while it steeped. There were lots of reasons to take his help, and also lots of reasons (though not all rational) not to trust him. I talked through all of them with Tina, but in the end I felt like I couldn't go so far as to make a suggestion. This felt too important. She needed to live with whatever decision she made.

The argument that was strongest to her was not one that I expected her to make. Tina was concerned that perhaps preserving the film was precisely the wrong choice to make. She never came right out and said it, but I sensed that she was possibly even a little scared of the film she had made. It was bigger than anything she had conceived of before, richer and more complex and ultimately more powerful than she had imagined possible. You hear people talk about how artists' works are like their children, and this usually with reference to gestation or the love of a parent for a child, or even in the sense that a good artist must be ready and willing to kill her darlings. But I think Tina meant it in the way that when we give birth to children, we are giving birth to another human being in all of her full and terrible potential. This film was alive for Tina. It was full of glorious and terrible possibilities. And it was fragile. Some part of her probably wanted to destroy it, to hide it away from the light where it could do so much damage. But part of her wanted this child of hers to set out into the world and conquer it, to transform it, remake it in its own image. She wasn't sure what this meant for the film, or for her, or for the world, and that uncertainty was what was holding her back.

We talked like this for a couple of hours, well into the night. The tea was doing its work on me, drawing the stress and sourness from the day out of my muscles and leaving me calm, content, and more than a little sleepy. Eventually, I fell asleep right there on the sofa. I woke up in the morning wrapped in a knitted afghan and curled into a ball on the too-short couch. I was cozy but creaky as I wandered into the kitchen, afghan still around my shoulders, to replace the tea with coffee.

It was probably half an hour before I realized that Tina was gone, and it took me longer than that to realize that she was *gone*. Tina was gone. The film was gone. Her clothes were gone. No note. Nothing. She had vanished.

Even now it's hard to talk about that morning. It's a wound. Tina was torn out of my life by the root, and one of the most difficult things is that I don't know who did it. Did Tina leave on her own? Was she taken? Was she lured out and then taken away? Did I do or say something to drive her away? I've tortured myself with these questions for years now. And others, like Tina's family and the police and journalists have tortured me with their questions, too. But since we share these same questions, I always do my best to answer them. That's what this book is about, of course. I want to answer these questions, even though I know that what I have to say won't satisfy anyone about what happened to her.

And I know that there are those who believe that Tina is still out there, that she has gone on to have a lucrative career as a filmmaker who releases her films under a pseudonym, that we've all seen her work, that she's a millionaire who's having the last laugh. And I know that some people want to believe that she got out when she realized that she couldn't have a career, that if she had any talent at all (and these people are emphatic that she did not) she would never be able to make any money off of it, because her art is too strange, too perverse to appeal to an audience that would reward her for it. Some think she dropped out of having dropped out. That she's living a normal life somewhere as someone's wife and someone's mother, because she couldn't hack it as an artist. And then there are those who think she's dead. Overdosed. Mutilated. Slowly decomposing in the trunk of a car that is itself rusting at the bottom of the St. Lawrence River, having been driven out onto the ice during the winter but fallen through before reaching the other side.

More understandable but no less maddening are those people who claim to have copies of *Dragon's Teeth*, or even *Imperial Dynasty of America*. They have clips on battered VHS tapes, or they have stills blown up from frames of Super 8 film. Most of the time, these are images from some other project by some other artist, sometimes by the very person who claims to have found the real deal, wanting in some way to make themselves part of the real deal. But I can't deny that some of these people have managed to find clips of the actual film. I have no explanation for this. Did Tina actually take the film to Montreal to be copied? Were these clips made when the film was originally developed? I mean, there are whole sequences of that film that might have been of interest to a lab technician with a certain set of predilections. Maybe there were fragmentary copies of the film before Tina even finished her rough cut of the film. I don't know what to say about any of that, and there are many other people who have said many other things. There is no need for me to add my voice to the chorus. This memoir is my voice. It is all I have to say about Destina Junko Mori and the birth of her dark art in the shadowed forests of the North Country. Maybe Tina will read it. Maybe she no longer can. Regardless, I will keep my memories of her and hold them close, because I have nothing else of hers to hold.

[A hand-written sticky note affixed to the first page of the 'Long Lake Letter.' –BRH]

Dear Billie,

Thank you for sharing *Final Grrrl* with me. Your timing was perfect. It feels like you've joined us on this path. I'm sending this along to you, because it's just as much for you as it is for me. I could try to explain, but I think Tina says it best:

Will you come?

C.C.

THE LONG LAKE LETTER

February 4, 1996

See See,

I'll bet this letter reached you and gave you a shock. Where has she been? What has she been doing? How is she alive and we haven't talked in all this time? Or maybe not. Maybe that is me being stupid and narcissistic. Why would you ever want to hear from me again? Haven't I caused you enough trouble? But is it possible that I also caused you heartache? If it is, then I hope there is some corner of your heart that still welcomes me, still calls me native and resident. Is there? I want there to be such a place, because it would match the space that I keep clean and dusted for you.

I have thought about you every day that we have been apart. I have thought about you there, wrapped in that blanket, or I have thought about you at my side on so many film shoots, or at those memorable premieres and happenings. I have thought about that first moment I ever laid eyes on you when you were a stranger to me, beautiful and stoned. I know you are far more complex, but that one image of you losing your grasp on the moment in favor of the transcendental is how I think of you. It's a warm memory, unspoiled by what came after. I'll admit that often when I think of you, I am cut to the quick by a sense of guilt, of things left unsaid, debts left unpaid. I don't mean material debts. I know that you have done all right in the meantime. I mean the psychic or spiritual debts we owe each other after we come out of the darkness together. It's not always easy to know who you owe these debts, and most often it seems nearly impossible to repay them.

I'm including some photos and a book for you. These are snapshots I have taken and picked up along the way. I think one or two of them might even be from our time together. I know that when I left, I tore a hole in your day-to-day. I erased myself from the chalkboard of your life. This is me trying to make up for that. Maybe those memories can still bring you some warmth or some kind of smile—I hope they don't bring you any kind of pain—they belong on your shelves, not mine.

I have also included for you my copy of *The King in Yellow*. In the past, you have shied away from its truth, but if you are truly to hear what I have to tell you, then you will need the key. *The K.i.Y.*

I'm sitting here in my tiny wood-wrapped room at the Starling Motor Lodge. I can tell you, because I won't be here by the time you get this letter. My work is taking me to the City of Light and then beyond, but I wanted to write to you before I go. I have so many questions about you and your life, but this isn't a conversation in the way that I want it to be.

I've read your book.

At first, I read it filled with anger. I took it as an insult that you would ruin so casually what had passed between us, airing our secrets in front of anyone who wanted to read. I was on fire. It made it difficult to work and almost impossible to think. Even though I often wanted to hurl the book across the room, and okay, maybe I even did a couple of times, I kept at it. I owed it to you. You had my attention, and I was going to make sure that I heard you in full before I gave you a piece of my mind.

But then a weird thing happened. I started to understand more about where you were coming from. I fell asleep and dreamed of you, but then I dreamed *as you*. I recalled all those events, of course, or at least the ones in which I was involved, so I had my memories, and it was the gap between my memories and yours that was angering me so much. I thought you were fabricating it, and I couldn't understand why you wanted to do that. But then as I went on I realized that you were being honest and true to your experience, and the chance to relive those days from your perspective became the particular pleasure of that week. For me, the premiere of *Dragon's Teeth* was an abject failure. I was so close only to see the future ripped away. But for you, it seemed like a triumph. A masterpiece.

I'm writing to you because I want to thank you for everything you did all those years ago, but also to thank you for your memories and the book that you wrote so that it could eventually find its way into my hands. I want to think of it as a resurrected letter. You know about dead letters, right? The letters that are sent to addresses that don't exist, at least not in this world, or to people who no longer exist at those addresses. Those dead letters are sent to some obscure postal facility in the Plains or something (odd that a place so productive should be the place we send dead letters), where they remain. There is no afterlife for them. I thought of your memoir this way, as a letter you sent to me, but I was no longer of the world. There was no way for it to find me directly, so you threw it into the ocean or burned it and sent those ashes and sparks up into the air to find their way across the country by riding on the jet stream. You've been all over the world since last we saw each other, just like you had been all over the world when we first met. I'm glad you were in one place long enough for us to meet. I don't think I would give up that time and our friendship for anything, even if I could get to my new life faster.

You have seen so much of the world, but I have seen so far beyond it. The push and pull of our friendship, our love, our sisterhood, has been this common ability to see more than there is right in front of us, our ability to rip off the shackles of popular belief. Your interest in school was always about observation, and that's the part that might have frustrated me when I started reading your memoir, but really, what drives you is your desire to experience, and to experience absolutely everything that you can fit into this life.

If there is a reason for me to be frustrated with your view, or for me to disagree with your project, it is that you are too content to receive the world as it is. You were correct at the end of your memoir; I am dedicated to transforming the world, while you were always content to take the world as it came at you and to suck the juice out of it with glee. I'll bet there is a lot of juice there for you. I think any well-educated person knows that there is more out there than they could possibly experience or buy or see or fuck. There's always more. The only thing that will ever be in short supply for humanity is time.

If time was running out, then I wanted to discover my goal and do it. People come up with all sorts of goals they want to achieve in life, right? The one most people expected of me is that I wanted to make more movies, go to Hollywood and be famous or make a lot of money, or something like that. The kind of thing that people usually want. It's not that I didn't want those things because everyone else wanted them. I'm not a contrarian. I just didn't want them. I only want money to the extent that I need it to get stuff done. Totally instrumental. I don't want fame. Not only have I never had an interest in it; I have seen what it does to some people, and I have no interest in that.

Of course, I did want to make more films. I still do, but my reasons for that have nothing to do with career or respect or anything like that. I want to make films, because it's the way that I strive for the beyond. It's the way that I have of changing the world, and I think the world is definitely in need of change. You will see when I have completed the next film. You will see what everyone else will see, but you will have a different perspective. I have planned for it. I didn't want you to experience it like everyone else. But then, maybe the years have changed us, or they have changed you? I worry about this. Not because it would change my plans. Nothing will. I worry because I don't want you to suffer, and I think that many people will suffer.

Change is never easy, especially when it's the kind of change that people try hard to bring about. It is difficult for them, of course, but you always hope that your effort and pain and sweat and even blood will someday be appreciated. Maybe it will. I'm not worried about those people. I am concerned with the Tattered King and our crossing to the dim shores of echo-haunted Carcosa. This is the change that I have sought for years and years. This is the change that I seek in my films. I know that others can see that change, too, when they watch my films, and that is why I have not tried to make my work more widely available. They are not yet perfected. The films that have come already have been excellent experiments. They have taken me farther along the path, but they are not the means by which we can deliver this world into the next.

This is how your book transformed me. I have often thought of our early adventures in the city, of the night that we met Paul and stole the Yellow Sign from him. He had been touched by the King, by the Living God. When we took the Sign from him, he had no idea what to do or how to live. I think if I had lost what he lost after having seen what he had seen, I would have gone mad, too. But I was guided by some feeling. Did you feel it, too?

I couldn't entirely tell from the book. I've been that way sometimes. I have been guided, but I have not wanted anyone else to know that I am being guided. Then people want to know about your motivations, but motivations must be cultivated more closely than that. Not everyone is worthy of the guidance. We must be careful, which is why I am writing to you here and now. Soon, I will be surrounded by people who will help me achieve my goals, but they don't want me to be sharing all of this with you. They actually take their secret cultivation very seriously.

You would like them in some ways, C.C. They're your people. Although, now that I think of it, you didn't like them. I'm talking about Horace, who drove us to the barn party our first autumn at Red Stone and then to the fort, and also about Eva, the woman we met. Horace and Eva and their cohort.

I told you when we first went to the barn party that I had met Horace in the city before I came up to college. That's basically true. I've known him almost my entire life. I haven't known Eva in the same way, but she has been part of the same circles for as long as I have known Horace. They were all part of my dad's friends when he was younger. The art and jazz and coffee house crowds. I suppose the drug crowd, too, but they don't go in for the regular stuff. You never asked me why I showed up to Red Stone a week late for classes. When I left home, I realized that I was free. I could go wherever I wanted. I realized I had *always* been free. So, I went to Horace and Eva's. I hung out with them for a few days. We talked about my future. We talked about *the* future. I used to be curious about Horace's cigarettes, but not anymore. No need to be curious, that is. People smoke to pass the time, right? That's it for him, too. It's just that his time is different than most people's time. Horace and Eva and I are almost done waiting. Soon, we will start out on our last film shoot, our last adventure.

It goes without saying that I would appreciate it if you didn't say anything about this to anyone for a while. You'll know how long. It will become clear to you and to everyone else. After that, it won't matter. I know that you will be true to me, but I think Horace and Eva won't quite understand in the same way. They can be secretive, and they don't want anyone messing things up at the last moment. They have been in search of these things for much longer than we have, but they have been waiting for us. Or maybe it's just that they're waiting for me. They talk about me like that, but I think it's mostly to make me feel special. I don't need that, or if I did at one point, I don't need any more of it.

The truth is that they have been grooming me for this my entire life. I don't know all of it, but it was something that they began before I was born. They knew my father. They knew him before he had ever met my mother. They might have even been the people who introduced my parents to one another. Have you ever thought such a thing, almost like in *Rosemary's Baby* (did you ever see that)? That you would one day be working for the people who brought your parents together so that they could fuck and then give birth to you so that those people could continue with their plans? I mean, it's medieval, right? Was it an arranged marriage? Not in the way that most people mean it, but certainly in the way the words mean when you put them next to each other.

That's something that has become more and more fascinating to me. The way that words mean when you put them next to each other. There is verbal grammar. There is film grammar. They are similar, though verbal grammar is far more subject to conventional forms of syntax than film grammar is. Film grammar is more flexible than the word kind. Than the kind words. You can do damn near whatever you want with moving images. It gets trickier when you start adding in sound. Will the soundscape act as a kind of bridge between the shots? Do you want that kind of bridge, or are you more interested in your audience having to leap from the cliff of one image to the cusp of the next. That leap, in all its terrifying glory, is usually where the power and the magic live. That's the place where the transformation happens. You don't want to do anything to soften that. The surrealists knew it. Deren knew it. Burroughs knows it, too.

Juxtapose. Cut up. Exquisite corpses. These are all part of the secret that is opening right now. I think this is what Horace and Eva did with my parents. They put these two people together, and they waited for the flash and the leap that sparked between them. I am that spark. There was something that they knew about the two of them, like they knew something would come of that juxtaposition. I am not certain what. Do we ever know what we are? I don't. And I don't have time to devote to it. I think there is nothing to find within myself, and I think that is probably what truly angered me when I started to read your book. It is so much about me, as though there was any value in finding out about me. I do not think of myself as special, and I think if Horace and Eva do, it is only incidental. I am a servant, who has the honor of ushering in a singular transformation. I am no more special than the trumpeter who lifts her instrument to the sky so that all the people may know that a king is born this day. Everyone hears the sound; no one thinks of the musician. I don't say this out of self-pity. It's an honest view of my place in the larger scheme.

When we were shooting *The Imperial Dynasty of America*, there was that young man who played the professor, and he had with him a rare and dreaded copy of the nearly forgotten play *The King in Yellow*. I knew about it enough to make references to it in some early films, but I didn't really know much about it. I actually think you knew more about its reputation than I did, and I see from your book that you worried that it might affect me in some dangerous way. I did read it then, and I think it did worm its way into my soul. But I didn't fully realize what was happening. I didn't become obsessed, though maybe I didn't have to become obsessed. Maybe it works in entirely different ways along paths stranger than mere human obsession. If I had tried to find my own copy and pored over it every night for months on end, perhaps I would have gone mad and your concerns would have been well-founded. But I was so wrapped up in the film, and truthfully also so wrapped up in Hack at the time, that I had little room for another obsession. They were my world. But the power of the play cannot be denied or diminished, no matter how rare the work has become. It waits. It dreams.

There will come a new day when *The King in Yellow* fills theaters with howls of laughter loud enough to split the fabric of reality and rework our essential ideas of time and space and adoration. We all have a part to play in it, and you have already played yours. Thank you. You reminded me, and now I will embark on my last film. Theater isn't what it used to be, but film has perhaps never been bigger. *The King in Yellow* will be bigger than any space battle. I have little doubt that when the movie hits theaters around the world, there will be people who have some interest in the original, and there will be a resurgence of interest in the play. I am glad for that artist, just as I am glad to do my part. We are all playing our roles.

You thought *The Imperial Dynasty of America* was an avant-garde anti-government film. I can see how others might think that, but you spent more time around Holly and Carcosa and all the rest and should have known that it was more prophecy than propaganda. The transformations of art and of society are nothing in comparison to the profound changes all of us will expect to undergo. Some have crossed over early, following those who've gone before as best they can. Of course, this is not the sort of thing that you can prepare most people for, not adequately anyway. It's only the people who can see it coming and are interested in what they see on the horizon who can be prepared for what is to come. If you meet someone who has been touched by the Living God, you should reach out to them. Help them. Most people will react to the change of regime with terror and all of the psychic pain that normally come with an apocalypse. It is, in fact, the end of much of what they hold dear. But what comes after is of such infinitely exquisite power and grace, that no one will honestly say that they prefer the old way. How could they? I know that some people will say that I am crazy. I know it. Swayne was one of these. When he looked at me or my films, he could only see oblivion. It took years for my celluloid straight razor to find its way to him, not because he was hiding but because I was busy.

There is much that you don't know, of course. How could you have known? I did not tell you, and no one else was going to bring you into the fold. I guess Lur could have told you some things, if she had wanted to. I still find her a mystery, and I have certainly met and gotten to know many people more mysterious than her. I never had a sense of what her game was, though I satisfied myself that she was not opposed to what we were doing. Not you and I, certainly. No, not us. Me and the others. We've had a project this whole time, and very soon that project will be complete and all of us will be able to rest in the knowledge that we serve the great Tattered King!

I have spent the past month in the Adirondacks making sure that everything is set for the transformation. There are dozens of people who are assisting in this project, larger than any film shoot that I have ever been on or even heard of. Do you remember those days we spent at Barron's Circle? Of course, I know you do. You wrote about it all as clearly in your book. That is where I have been spending a lot of my time.

When we made *Dragon's Teeth*, did you know that there was a dragon, lying under your feet, sleeping away the millennia, restlessly tossing and turning every few centuries, and unconsciously munching on whatever sustenance its attendants provide for it? This dragon has been served for thousands of years by those who live nearby. There were attendants long before there were Native American tribes in the area. These attendants were not always human. Before what we know of as history, there were others here, who came and fed the dragon. After the Europeans came, there have been a steady stream of attendants, and they have generally done a good job of keeping their work a secret. For a long time, we thought that secrecy was important to our work. But not long ago, there were those who helped the attendants to see that secrecy was keeping things the way they always have been. There was no reason that the status quo was the way that things should always be. Why do we think that those who came before somehow knew the right way to do things? They knew the secret, but having that privileged knowledge was not enough to make sure that they knew the best thing for everyone.

But I don't want to give you the wrong impression. They are not custodians or guardians or caretakers, not really. There is no one who believes that he or she has the ability or the wisdom to make decisions on behalf of the worm. The dragon exists in a plane well beyond ours, and our distractions of body and mind are too vast to presume that we could make decisions that will either please or displease the dragon. We are aware that the Tattered King, the man in the Pallid Mask, has an interest in the dragon and its continued existence and slumber in its current abode. There is every possibility that on any given day, the dragon could awake and take flight through the starry night and the fathomless shadows to find its way to a new home, perhaps in Lake Hali beneath the foam-shrouded moon of Carcosa. We cannot assume that the dragon will always and forever sleep beneath the piney loam of the Adirondack Park. All we know is that the *King in Yellow* desires that we feed the worm, and so we do so, to the utmost of our ability, in his honor.

You have met the attendants, of course, but I'm sure you didn't know it at the time. The robed people in *Dragon's Teeth*; they are the keepers of the dragon. They are the ones who have the advantage of seeing the glory of the process. We humans have a certain relationship to our own process, which is many times more profane than what occurs with the worm. We are lowly animals, but we do have a shadow of that divine process. For us, we find those plants and sometimes animals in our environment that we find pleasing to eat, or when we are most desperate, we simply eat what we can find. But those meals eventually find their way through our bodies, through our stomachs and intestines until we expel them, or what is left of them. We like to say that our feces is made up of the things for which we have no use, as well as some of the toxins that are left behind by the process of breaking down our food for our bodily use. We take in objects from our environment, and then we transform them and produce them again out of our bodies. The dragon does something similar to this, but the product is very different than the one familiar to us.

When the dragon eats, it takes the food into itself and ruminates over it for a long, long time. While it does this, it is of course digesting, but not in the sense that we understand. At least not scientifically, or biologically. The dragon has taken the food into itself, and within the dragon that food will be transformed. I can tell you that the food, if it is conscious when it enters the worm, is aware of this process of transformation, and that process is not without sensation. The dragon will commence to make the food into something else, taking what it needs for itself along the way, and when it has extracted those necessary components, it will then begin the final process of eliminating the food from its self. Consumption. Elimination. It is all very familiar. Very natural.

I have borne witness. The process is long and painful, and there is little left of our old selves after the transformation. Once you have passed beyond the *Dragon's Teeth*, as I have, and then set out upon the length of the worm in all its terrible sufficiency, what it requires of you must be given. It will not be refused. You cannot refuse your elements any more than our own poor breakfast can refuse our stomach acids. In some celestial workshop, they have been made for one another, and refusal is impossible. When you pass beyond the *Dragon's Teeth*, you spend a long time thinking about what you have left behind. It is perhaps not quite the same as having your entire life pass before your eyes. No, it was nothing like that for me anyway. My life didn't pass before my eyes. Instead, it was as though whole chunks of my life, vast icebergs of hours and days of my experience, were caving and falling away from me as though I were watching myself disintegrate. An ice cube under a heat lamp. It was like watching soil erosion in a flood. Now I see my doubts about money and career fall away in a huge mass that leaves a concave scar on my being. Now the natural arch of my sexuality cracks and topples into the bay of my not being. And if I had been directing or choosing, this process was not transforming me into something that I could have expected or chosen. I would not have known to get rid of some portions of my life and discard others. My ideas of improvement and self-doubt are tied to my human sense of success and failure and hope and doubt. The dragon knows otherwise. It senses what is necessary for itself and takes it, and what you are left with is a new you. I have seen people who have had so much taken from them, that there is nothing else for them to do in this realm. Perhaps they wait to be useful and fulfilled in the next realm, or perhaps they are already fulfilled. What was absolutely clear is that they were no longer a functioning person when they had completed the process and the worm eliminated them from the Circle of Life.

I should tell you about the Circle. Though we have generally moved beyond our attention to the rules of secrecy, the location of the Circle of Life is perhaps the last secret that the attendants wish to keep. They believe that it may actually constitute a point of vulnerability for the dragon, but I don't think so. That makes no sense to me at all. The Circle is what looks like a great red sandstone millstone, a reddish-orange grist wheel with a spiral pattern etched deeply into its surface. However, having been up close and personal with it, I can say that the makings and whatnot on the surface of the Circle are simply natural contours on its surface. This stone has never been carved, like those that make up Barron Circle. Despite the speculations of learned archaeologists and anthropologists, these sites were not erected by man; they have only been attended by man. The maw and the sphincter. The In and the Out doors. These thresholds, dozens of miles apart when you find them on a map, mark the beginning and the end of the worm, though as with so many things in this world as in others, the line between these two places isn't straight.

Will you travel between them, C.C.? I think you will. Though you have not been bending and stretching on behalf of the attendants you have certainly been drawn within their reach. They know of you, and in the process, that is as good as being named. Maybe you don't want to be named. Maybe you would prefer if the attendants never knew your name, that I didn't tell them. But of course, I didn't tell them. I actually did everything I could never to mention your name. It was you and your book that brought your name to their attention. Once you set those pages out in front of the world for everyone to see, then Dr. Holly and Horace and Eva all wanted to know more about the wonderful girl that they remembered from Red Stone. The one who tagged along on my adventures at the end of the mortal world. They remembered you. They said that they had even wondered about you. They thought you would make a good companion for the transformation, but they respected my desire not to name you. Though few of them still moved among normal people in the ways that you might expect, they had some vague sense that perhaps we fell out of friendship, or that we fell out of love with each other. We didn't, though, did we? I don't think that I ever fell out of love with you, and as the time for the transformation draws near, I can't imagine seeing the new pale dawn on the dim shore of Carcosa without you.

Will you come, C.C.?

The dragon longs for you.

Will you come?

                                                                    Tina

ACKNOWLEDGMENTS

No matter how cliché it seems, a book like this is never written alone. I owe debts to many people, all of whom have been extremely generous with their time and support. Some of these folks are sources who have answered my questions—or made good-faith attempts to do so—no matter how absurd or detailed or disturbing they were. Most of them are people who have simply granted me permission.

Miriam Jacobs, this book truly began in your daughter's bedroom. Thank you for letting me share Billie's work with the rest of the world. I hope I've done right by you both. Many thanks to Fred Colgrove and Bob Blake at Bloody Iris Press, as well, who made reprinting C.C. Waite's *Memento Mori* so painless.

The volunteers at the Red Stone Historical Society and the professionals at the SUNY Red Stone University Archives provided invaluable assistance with my questions about the veracity of C.C. Waite's written recollections.

I also express my gratitude to the faceless functionaries of the Library of Congress and the Sorbonne, even though they never returned my inquiries about *The King in Yellow*.

For assistance with the INTERPOL Yellow Notices on Tina, C.C., and Billie, I am particularly grateful to Special Agent Dana Pearce of the Federal Bureau of Investigation and Bern Gustafson with INTERPOL Washington. I'll let you know if I find anything in Paris.

And, of course, my most profound thanks go to Tina Mori, C.C. Waite, and Billie Jacobs. You showed me the way, and I followed.

When newscaster Abby Waite is diagnosed with a potentially terminal illness, she decides to do the logical thing... break her twin sister Martha out of prison and hit the road. Their destination is the Waite family cabin in Minnesota where Abby plans a family reunion of sorts. But when you come from a family where your grandfather frequently took control of your body during your youth, where your mother tried to inhabit your mind and suck your youthful energies out of you, and where so many dark secrets–and bodies, even–are buried, such a family meeting promises to be nothing short of complicated...

Trade Paperback, 268 pp, $16.99

ISBN-13: 978-1-939905-46-8

http://www.wordhorde.com

"*A Spectral Hue* paints dark, hallucinogenic colors deep inside your mind."
—John Palisano, Bram Stoker Award-Winning author of *Ghost Heart*

Graduate student Xavier Wentworth has been drawn to Shimmer, having experienced something akin to an epiphany when viewing a tapestry as a child. Xavier will find that others, too, have been drawn to Shimmer, called by something more than art, something in the marsh itself, a mysterious, spectral hue.

From Lambda Literary Award-nominated author Craig Laurance Gidney (*Sea, Swallow Me & Other Stories*, *Skin Deep Magic*) comes *A Spectral Hue*, a novel of art, obsession, and the ghosts that haunt us all.

Format: Trade Paperback, 228 pp, $16.99

ISBN-13: 978-1-939905-50-5

http://www.wordhorde.com

"When I took *Tales from a Talking Board* out of the box, my power went out."

—Anonymous Internet commenter

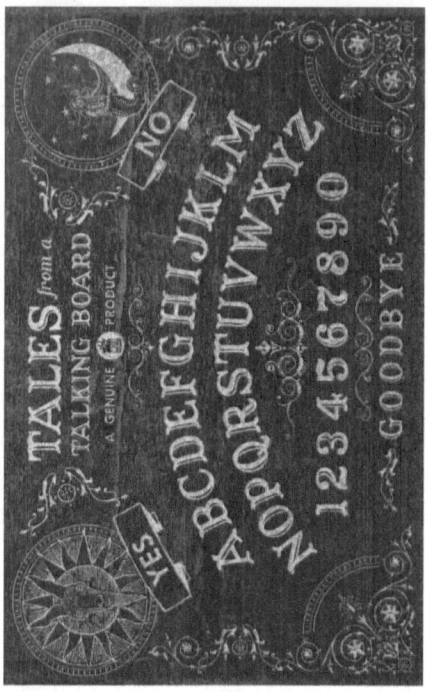

Can we speak with the spirits of the dead? Is it possible to know the future? Are our dreams harbingers of things to come? Do auspicious omens and cautionary portents affect our lives?

Edited by Ross E. Lockhart, *Tales from a Talking Board* examines these questions—and more—with tales of auguries, divination, and fortune telling, through devices like Ouija boards, tarot cards, and stranger things.

So dim the lights, place your hands upon the planchette, and ask the spirits to guide you as we present fourteen stories of the strange and supernatural by Matthew M. Bartlett, Nadia Bulkin, Nathan Carson, Kristi DeMeester, Orrin Grey, Scott R Jones, David James Keaton, Anya Martin, J. M. McDermott, S.P. Miskowski, Amber-Rose Reed, Tiffany Scandal, David Templeton, and Wendy N. Wagner.

Format: Trade Paperback, 228 pp, $15.99

ISBN-13: 978-1-939905-35-2

http://www.wordhorde.com

"...these stories and characters are sewn together to create one hell of an exquisite monster."

—*This Is Horror*

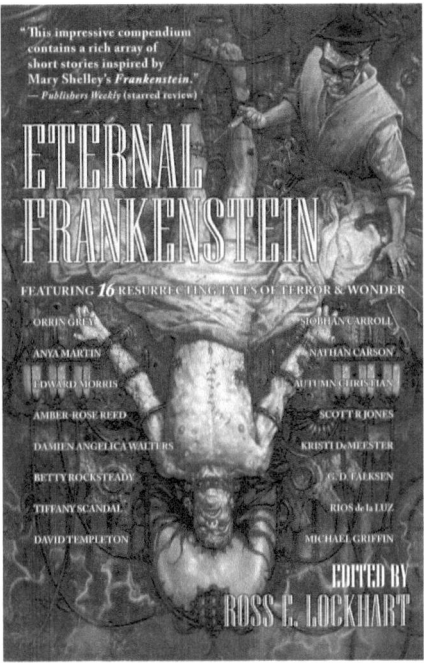

Two hundred years ago, a young woman staying in a chalet in Switzerland, after an evening of ghost stories shared with friends and lovers, had a frightening dream. That dream became the seed that inspired Mary Shelley to write *Frankenstein; or, The Modern Prometheus*, a tale of galvanism, philosophy, and the reanimated dead. Today, Frankenstein has become a modern myth without rival, influencing countless works of fiction, music, and film. We all know *Frankenstein*. But how much do we really know about Frankenstein?

Word Horde is proud to publish *Eternal Frankenstein*, an anthology edited by Ross E. Lockhart, paying tribute to Mary Shelley, her Monster, and their entwined legacy.

Featuring sixteen resurrecting tales of terror and wonder by Siobhan Carroll, Nathan Carson, Autumn Christian, Rios de la Luz, Kristi DeMeester, G. D. Falksen, Orrin Grey, Michael Griffin, Scott R. Jones, Anya Martin, Edward Morris, Amber-Rose Reed, Betty Rocksteady, Tiffany Scandal, David Templeton, and Damien Angelica Walters.

Format: Trade Paperback, 322 pp, $15.99

ISBN-13: 978-1-939905-37-6

http://www.wordhorde.com

ABOUT THE AUTHOR

Brian Hauser is a writer and filmmaker from Carter-era rust belt suburbia. He lives in northern New York with his partner and two cats. This is his first novel.